They filtered in, one by
Evan waited until the end. I
the wall, a mask on his face
pulse. Esther punched at the controls and turned the sub
back to the Dome. She and Char shared a glance, tight
lines framing their eyes. Ana sat with her knees up to
her chest, biting her thumbnail, a frown settling on her
brow.

Evan stooped and padded over to Khalid, laying a
hand on his shoulder, relief flooding him as the other
man's eyes fluttered open. He tightened his grip for a
second then straightened as much as the cramped roof
would allow. Avoiding Ana, he sank into a seat on the
other side of the sub.

He stared at his hands the whole journey back to
the Dome. Heavy wet fabric clung to his body, and he
shivered despite the heating in the sub turning the
enclosed space into a sauna.

The uplifting sense of camaraderie from the last
few days bled away, leaving chilled suspicion behind.
White marks lined his hands from where his grip cut off
the blood. He eased up a little, and as the blood seeped
back he thought of shifting kelp, watching eyes, and a
half-remembered sensation of arms lifting him out of
the water.

Something had been out there, and no one would
talk about it.

Praise for Clementine Fraser

2019 Winner of the Dark Paranormal category
On the Far Side Contest,
Futuristic, Fantasy, & Paranormal
RWA

Siren's Call

by

Clementine Fraser

Siren's Call

Cover Art by *Abigail Owen*

The Wild Rose Press, Inc.
PO Box 708
Adams Basin, NY 14410-0708
Visit us at www.thewildrosepress.com

Publishing History
First Fantasy Rose Edition, 2021
Trade Paperback ISBN 978-1-5092-3361-8
Digital ISBN 978-1-5092-3362-5

Published in the United States of America

Dedication

To my sons. You are my everything.
Thank you for always believing in me.

Chapter One

Silver lanced through dark water, and Sariana curled her tail, twisting to scan the seabed. Ever since the humans trampled their machines through the ocean, little pieces of metal and rubbish floated everywhere. The glint escaped her gaze, and she shook back her hair, her lips pressing together.

No time for searching for trash now; she had more important things to look for. Or one. *Baruthial.*

She swam on over the dappled seabed, the warmth of the shallows failing to calm her. Seven tides since she'd seen her brother. He'd been fidgety and anxious, his tail flicking and spiny fins on his arms twitching up and down. Of course, he'd said he wasn't. Said everything was going as planned. But she knew Baru better than she knew herself. The little brother who clung to her tail and copied everything she did had turned into a merman determined to prove himself. Worry coursed through her, and she let it fester into rage. Anger was easier to bear. So like Baru to keep them all waiting. Perhaps he had picked up bad habits from the humans with whom he worked. Working or spying, she'd never been sure which.

Sariana darted down toward a waving forest on the sea floor. Blood streamed through dying kelp like ribbons, tainting the sunbeams dancing through the deep water. She reared back, her hair twisting into a

1

floating halo. Her tail twitched, and a dark pattern shivered down her scales, rippling with the ice in her veins. *No.* Surely she'd know if Baruthial had died. The blood must belong to something—someone—else.

She pressed her lips together and arrowed forward through the water, fins lying flat against her hips. Crimson streaks curled around her, and she shuddered as she parted the swaying fronds.

A mangled body floated, limbs caught in the brown kelp. Sharp gashes cut along the ridged torso. Muscular legs twisted unnaturally. Sariana's gills fluttered open and closed in a racing rhythm, and she forced her gaze toward the face. Relief flooded her chest. Not Baru.

Edging closer, her tail brushing against the kelp, she peered at the body. Shadows played over the skin, and she frowned. Dark scales edged out from bloated skin in a haphazard pattern, lumpy and misshapen. Nothing like the delicate lacing of colors up her own torso. The markings weren't of any local mer; she would swear to it.

If this was a mer in a half-human form, where was his amulet? Gritting her teeth, she reached past the weeds knotted around the corpse and lifted matted hair from the side of his head. Clotted blood fell into the water.

No gills. No fins. *Human.*

She snatched her hand back to her side. *Impossible.* Baru's earnest face flashed into her mind, his passionate plea to the council that the humans meant no harm, that what they did at the base would change things for merfolk and humankind forever.

The man's lips pulled back in a silent scream. *His* life had certainly changed.

2

Fear coiled in her gut, the chill of the deeps cutting through her shock. If they would do this to their own people, what might they have done to Baru? She whirled around, tail whipping through the weed, leaving the dead man to the scavengers of the sea. She swam toward the human base, toward her brother.

A second shadow ducked and dived on the seabed below her, mimicking her movements. She tightened her tail and rolled, rising to meet the incomer. Her sister's lilac hair waved behind her like one of the human's flags, and her pearlescent tail caught the light as she angled toward Sariana.

"These are banned waters."

Amatheia's voice hummed in her mind, full of older sister scolding and fear. She skittered back, her tail swishing in annoyance.

"Did your mate send you after me?"

Amatheia jerked back and shook her head. *"After the council vote, I looked for you. I feared you'd do something foolish, and I was right."*

Anger flared in her veins. *"Searching for Baruthial is not foolish."*

Her sister reached out to her, and she twisted away. Amatheia's hand dropped.

"What do you believe you can do that the Council cannot?"

"Baruthial told me—" Sariana shut her sister from her mind. If he'd wanted Amatheia to know about the secret entrances into the Dome, he would have told her. *"You can follow me, but you can't stop me. What would you do? Turn me over to the Council?"*

Amatheia's fins shook, and a shadow fell over her face. *"No. Of course not."*

3

A little pang struck at her heart, but she pushed it aside, sweeping the water with her tail and swimming onward. *"Then follow or leave."*

Her sister's discomfort shrouded her mind, and she shivered, gliding faster through the currents. The water became heavier nearer the human base, sliding over her scales, oily and slick. She dove lower, scanning the ridges and scars the construction left on the shells and rocks of the ocean floor.

The Dome rose from the seabed. A parasite, a blight on the natural world. Feeding on *her* world. Heavy and squat, stiff glass pushed back the soft touch of the water. Humans threw down their mark on the world with such little care. Oil, plastic, dead and dying fish. Content to wallow in refuse.

Coral crumbled at the foot of the monstrous foundations. Her fingers tightened, her nails scraping against her tail. Perhaps if they'd taken longer to build it, they might have noticed what they were destroying. She curled her lip and darted closer, the mangled body in the weeds flashing into her mind. No. Humans didn't care what devastation they left in their wake.

Amatheia gripped her shoulder, yanking her backward through silt-filled water. *"No. I don't know what you're planning, but I cannot allow you to go further."*

She pulled away from her sister's hands, sharp spiny fins flicking up on the side of her arm as anger coiled through her. *"Leave me be. You might be content to let Baru rot in that tomb, but I am not."*

Amatheia pushed forward, her tail thrashing and her teeth bared. *"How dare you! It was I who told the Council to begin the search, I who warned them—"* She pulled back, the rapid flutter of her gills slowing as she calmed herself. *"Sariana, I know you fear for Baruthial. We all do. But this was his choice. His idea."*

Sariana looked away from her sister's stony expression, hiding the anger burning behind her eyes. Her gaze narrowed at the looming glass in front of them. It may have been Baru's idea to connect with the humans, to work with them, but the Council had given permission for him to engage in the humans' research. The air stilled in her lungs. The body in the weeds... What kind of experiments were they doing? Her gaze slid back to Amatheia.

"The research was not to find a solution to the warming of the waters, was it, sister?"

Amatheia's lids twitched, and her tail jittered.

"The experiments are a compromise, a promise to help both sides find a better way. A stronger way."

Dread flickered through her, changing the color of her scales to a dull gray. *"I don't understand."*

"They want our strengths; we want theirs. The experiments were to find a way to merge them."

Scales on a human body, twisted and damaged. Fear curled tendrils of ice through her stomach. She lunged toward her sister.

"What did you have him do? Why did you not tell me?"

Amatheia drew back, grasping the amulets at her neck. *"You forget yourself, sister. I am a key keeper; some secrets are not for everyone to hear."*

The great doors of the Dome slid up, and a wave rippled through the water. One of the human vessels shot out, bubbles streaming from the motors. Sariana darted toward the vessel, but her sister tugged her back.

"This is not the place to fight them. Wait for the others to come. The Council has sent Myrndir and his warriors."

She shrugged off the tight grip but stayed in place, gaze fixed on the yellow machine with its flashing lights and noise pushing against the currents.

A hatch opened, and a body tumbled out of the turning vessel to drift down to the seabed. This time she slid out of Amatheia's snatching hand and raced toward it, her tail pounding at the water and her arms cutting through the shadows as if she could get there in time, as if she could change what her heart knew to be true.

The body rolled over, and her brother's face, contorted in a frozen rictus of pain, stared up at her with lifeless eyes. It was as if the water around her turned to sand. She struggled to draw oxygen through her gills, fought to move her tail, to swim closer to his body. A scream tore through her mind, and she realized it was her own.

He lay discarded on the bottom of the sea. Broken. Dead. Another victim in the humans' endless wars. Sariana turned to face the Dome, the webbing between her fingers rippling with light as she curled her hands into fists.

They threw him out like the rest of their trash, as if he were nothing.

Fury raced through her, cold and deadly. They believed the mer were animals. But humans destroyed what they didn't understand. Didn't care for their own. Killed without thought. *They* were the real animals.

She allowed her sister to draw her away. Amatheia's hand shook on her arm as she urged her with frantic sounds to come to safety, to leave his body for the Council to retrieve. But Sariana's gaze raked the Dome until she saw the entrance Baru had shown her.

She would return and bring hell with her.

Chapter Two

10 months later

Evan leaned into the wind sweeping over the broad prow, replaying all the times he'd faced death. Morning sun reflected off the ocean in golden rays, and the occasional salty spray touched his face. His hand closed on the cool metal railing, slick with water. Foolish to think this trip would provide an escape. The vast expanse of water and open sky forced him to think, coaxed out memories whether he wanted them or not.

The tang of salt and diesel filled the air, so different from the musk of endless sand. Yet the sea and the desert were similar in so many ways—empty, ever-shifting, and somehow changeless. Deceptively calm on the surface but roiling and dangerous underneath. Orange sunrise on the water turned rippling waves to memories of crimson, like the blood on the sand. Minus the screams. His gaze slid down to the deck.

"If you're getting up this early, you should be the one making breakfast."

He raised his head. Daniel Kim, his old college roommate, strolled toward him with a thermos and a steaming plate laden with food.

"I would, if you didn't mind charred toast and water."

"Still don't know how to cook?" Dan's crooked grin spread. "No wonder you can't get a girl."

Evan grasped the offered dish and swore as his fingers burned. "Who says I can't get a girl?"

"Have you checked your batting average lately?"

An answering grin tugged at his cheeks, and he shrugged. "Hey, anything better than zero is a win."

"Keep telling yourself that, bro." Dan leaned against the railing next to him, scanning the horizon.

Bacon crunched between his teeth, a bit overdone but a million times better than what they got on deployment.

"You have a great crew on board," he said, "which is lucky because I'm a worse engineer than I am a cook."

Dan laughed, the breeze gaining in strength and ruffling his straight black hair. "Trust me, we'll need you at some point."

"You're in trouble if you're relying on my cooking."

"Who said anything about the kitchen? There are plenty of decks to be scrubbed."

Evan screwed up his face. "And planks to walk? Send me to swim with the fishes if I say no?"

His friend's smile wavered, and Evan narrowed his eyes at the tense lines crowding Dan's forehead. When Dan invited him sailing, he decided to go mostly because being home had turned into a never-ending cycle of disappointment and isolation. Once Grace broke things off, he'd drifted, rudderless. He wanted a purpose, to make a difference. *Strive for redemption.*

Two weeks at sea, and doubt started eating at his mind. He'd been left to fish on his own while Dan and his crewmates scoured findings from equipment way too complicated to be on a fishing boat.

"Funny thing. For a fishing trip, you've done very little fishing."

Dan shot him a glance, eyes dark despite the sunshine. "What are you saying?"

He huffed out a breath. "My sister figured you thought I could do with company. Give me something better to do than mope about Grace. That true?"

His ex-girlfriend's memory was a knife to his gut. Sure there'd been happier days, but now all he could remember was the disgust and fear in her face when he stumbled through the living room drunk, drowning the flashbacks and memories the only way he knew how. It might have been a year, and therapy might have stopped him from self-medicating, but the shame and anger surged as strongly.

Dan grimaced, and Evan stared down at his plate, pushing the bacon around with his fork. *Way to bring down the mood, Hunter.*

"Kelly is a smart woman. Break-ups suck, man. When my marriage ended, I moped for way too long. You needed to get out of your head." Dan crossed his arms, glancing at him sidelong. "But there's another reason. Something weird is definitely going on in these waters. Not quite Bermuda Triangle stuff, but weird."

Evan quirked a brow and shovelled in another forkful of eggs. "So why don't we see it on the news?"

"Sorry, couldn't hear you round the food."

"Har-de-har."

"You know better than that, dude. Lots of things never make it on the news. Doesn't mean they aren't real."

"So ships go missing? Happens all the time."

"Not only ships." Dan's smile faded, and he rubbed his lips as if deciding how much to share.

Evan swallowed the last bite and shoved the plate to one side. "Does this have anything to do with the seabed scanning you guys have been doing?"

Dark eyes glinted as Dan cut a glance at him, then away. "You noticed."

"You did a shitty job trying to hide it."

His friend laughed, and Evan grinned, shoving Dan's shoulder.

"Hey, man. You wouldn't have invited me on this crazy trip if you didn't trust me. Spill it." He leaned back and raised his brows at Dan expectantly as terns swooped over the water, wheeling in the air currents.

With a sigh, his friend stared back to the ocean. "We've been tracking this area for some time via satellite. The contours of the sea bed don't match up with older records." Dan scanned the white-capped waves cresting around them.

Was that fear on his face? "There have been more wrecks. More extreme weather events. It's not—let's say it isn't what we expected. To be honest, we don't really know what we're expecting. I invited you along because you've always been a good man in a bad situation."

A curl of tension wound through Evan's gut. "Who's *we*?"

Dan opened his mouth but shut it just as fast, jerking his head as a shrill cry rang through the still air.

Glancing up at the bird, Evan's hands clenched tight. Dark storm clouds broke the endless blue sky, filling the horizon with a roiling wave of black. Silence dragged his head around to Dan's stony face and shadowy eyes fixed on the gathering gloom.

"Dan?"

"Shit."

Dan raced toward the bridge, bellowing for his crew mates. The boat rocked underfoot as a sudden swell gained in height, and Evan fell against the railing. Pain sparked in his cheek, and he tasted blood.

The first mate rounded the corner of the bridge, white-knuckling the railing. He yelled something, but the wind snatched his words. The ship pitched again. Evan stood and pushed his feet into the deck, struggling to balance. Rain spattered down, the whole sky now a roiling darkness of wind and water. He reached the bridge as Dan wrenched the door open.

Waves thundered across the bow of the ship, knocking Evan's feet out from under him, pushing him across the deck. He'd thought he would welcome death, but as the ship reared against the grabbing tendrils of the ocean, the drive to live pushed him into action.

His fingers snatched at ladder rungs on the side of the bridge, muscles straining as the sea fought to take him. Salt stung a cut on his cheek, and he blinked water from his eyes. He dragged himself against the current, closer to the bridge flooding with surf.

The first mate's still body floated past in the pounding waves. Evan stared at the red streaks of blood trailing from the crewman's head and drew back his reaching hand. Another one lost, another person he hadn't saved. Cold bile churned in his stomach as memories of crimson-stained sand flashed behind his eyes. No. This wasn't his mission. Not his burden. Not this time. He blinked and turned to peer into the bridge, searching for Dan.

Metal groaned and shrieked as the boat shuddered. The darkening sky drew his gaze like a magnet. A giant wave sucked in all light, beautiful and deadly. The world turned to water as the wave crashed over them. Tumbling, smashing into iron railings, lungs screaming for air...

He sank.

Dark water churned, grabbing at his clothes and pulling him down through a minefield of whirling debris. Jagged pieces of wood and steel crowded the ocean. His lungs burned, and he clawed his way toward the dim light taunting him on the surface.

A large object slammed into the water, blocking the light, pushing through the detritus to pin him underneath. Hands scrabbling for a grip, desperate to pull himself out from under the warped vent, the last air escaped his lungs.

But I haven't finished living yet. I don't know if I ever started.

His fingers loosened their death grip on the steel sheet. As his eyes closed, a shadow fluttered through the inky depths trailing a pale glow behind it.

He sank into black quiet.

Chapter Three

Air filled Evan's straining lungs, and a firm pressure on his mouth eased. Paroxysms wracked his body, his fingers digging into the silky skin of someone's arms. He turned his head to the side, choking up salty liquid and bile, jerking back as his chin dipped into the water. Each heaving mouthful of breath stung the lining of his throat. His gaze shifted, streaming eyes trying to focus on the person holding him half out of the water.

Silvery curls shot with purple shone through the dark. He blinked. Seaweed stuck out of her hair. No, that was an ear or fin. He squeezed his lids shut, pressing a palm into his eyes. A sharp smile met his gaze when he withdrew his hand. The fin still poked out.

A splash to his left drew his attention to where a green tail of silken scales broke the still surface of the water. A braided net of multihued shells covered her shoulders and chest, the pale skin almost translucent.

"Better now?"

Her voice hummed through his ears, scratchy yet melodic. He pulled back against her arms and stared, his mind whirling. With a keening sound between a cry and a whistle, she turned him to where a dim light showed the roof of a cavern. Massive sandstone steps rose from the water to a long path heading to an archway. Land.

"Think you can make it on your own?"

The strong arms keeping him afloat dropped away, and he floundered before brushing wet hair and blood from his forehead and swimming with faltering strokes toward the platform. His fingers touched hard rock, and relief flooded through him. He summoned the last of his strength and dragged himself up the stairs to lie, chest heaving, on the flagstones.

Reflections played on the rocky ceiling from the light dancing on the water, a green glow skipping over dips and stalactites. The air tasted stale and thin; but he relished each breath.

I'm still under the ocean. Shivers ran over his skin. He pressed his palms flat on the chilled sandstone, trying to anchor himself. The last thing he remembered was blacking out, pinned under the wreck. Blood in the water.

Splashes echoed, bouncing from the walls of the cavern. He craned his head, wincing at the pain shooting down from his temple and encountered green eyes in a pale face. Bare sloping shoulders poked above the water, and small ridged fins poked through her hair. His mind went numb. She couldn't possibly be real.

"This is a trick, right? Or I'm hallucinating again." Dread curled in his gut. Right now, he didn't know which was worse, but it wouldn't be the first time he was lost in the dark and imagining things.

She smiled broadly, her mouth full of too many teeth. "I have no need to trick you." Her voice scratched out, as if rarely used.

His pulse pushed against his throat, and he thought of all those cheesy movies about pretty dainty mermaids. None of them had teeth like this. Trembling limbs resisted his efforts to sit, and he gave up. He let out a ragged breath.

"You can't be real. Because things like you don't exist."

A luminous shimmer of phosphorescence bled out from her hair into the water as she shook herself.

"Humans. You're all alike. Rude. I'm not a thing. I'm what your people call a mermaid."

Holy crow. This can't be happening. He drew his legs to his chest and leaned his arms on his knees, gazing at her blurry figure, trying to accept what his eyes told him.

The mermaid pulled on the steps and rolled herself out of the water. Her tail stretched longer than human legs would. Mottled and scaled, decorated with shining silver patterns, it waved back and forth, throwing droplets of water to the floor below.

He clasped his hands together, knuckles turning white. An actual fucking *mermaid.* Chilled stone sat hard beneath him. His wet clothes clung to his shivering frame. All real, all happening. Air congealed in his lungs, and he fought the spinning sensation in his mind.

The creature shifted her tail and leaned on one hand. "I am Amatheia. Do you have a name also?"

"Evan." He stretched out his hand instinctively, pulling back when she peered at him, her head cocking to one side in quick little movements.

"What brought you to the deeps, Evan?"

Dan. A rush of ice flooded through him, and he scrambled to his feet. He ignored the dizziness twisting nausea through his gut and scanned the cavern, as if by some miracle Dan would be sitting waiting for him at the other end of the pathway.

He spun back to the mermaid. "Where are the others? My friend?"

A shadow passed over her eyes, and she dipped her head, shining hair hiding her expression. "They are not here. You're the only one I found alive."

Blood trails in the water. Floating bodies. His hands curled into fists, and he focused on breathing in, out. Shouts echoed in his memories, explosions, screams. The names of all the people lost to him scrolled in his head like an honour roll, mixed with images of Grace pulling away from him, contempt in her face. One by one he filed them into the box in his mind, closed the lid. He forced his thoughts back to now, to a cave under the sea and missing friends.

"Did you look? Can you take me back to search?"

She brushed back her hair, her eyes dark pools of sympathy in a pearl-like face. "We always look."

His head throbbed. He wiped at wetness on his temple, blood smearing on his fingers. "*We*? There are more of you?"

"Some things I cannot tell you, Evan. I will not take you back. You are here, and here you must stay."

He lunged toward her but pulled back before he touched her, his muscles tightening with the effort to stay calm. "I'm not staying here to rot under the sea!"

Amatheia shrugged, the shells chattering. "Here, lost in the depths, you might find your soul."

Evan flinched and stared at her. His lip twisted, and he kicked at the water on the stone stair. Too much darkness in his head, trying to push through the blocks he placed around it.

"I've already got one, thanks. It's doing fine."

Her fins shook in a strange kind of laugh, and her sharp teeth gleamed in the green light. "Are you sure about that?"

He glared at her. "Rotting alone in a dark cavern won't help either way." Sinking back to the ground he gazed into her alien eyes. "You rescued me, but if you leave me here, I'll die. Why not let me drown?"

Webbed fingers stole up to the silver amulet hanging from her neck. "I'm not supposed to be here. We're not supposed to save anyone anymore."

Tension swept through him. "Why not?"

Her face twisted, and a strange shiver rippled over her arms as dozens of tiny fins raised and lowered. "Humans do us much harm. Many in the enclave wish you gone. My mate will be angry I have saved you."

He rubbed at the frown between his brows. "But we don't even know you exist."

Silence stretched for a moment, and he stared at the mermaid.

"Do we?"

With her tail coiled on the flagstones and her hair curling down around her neck, she looked every inch a character from a story book. Except for the eyes. Those eyes held much more intelligence and a lot more bitterness than he ever expected a fairy tale creature to possess.

Ripples lapped against the steps, and Amatheia turned to the water. Her shoulders tensed, and he stared over her head at the surface. A ridge of water bubbled and churned, and his heart leapt.

A familiar funnel broke from the surface, streams of water cascading off the rising submarine. Evan scrambled up, his thoughts roiling. A US sub. He'd bet anything. But no markings stood out on the dark metal sides, only a lighter shade where something had been scratched off and painted over.

Amatheia turned back to him, a fierce light in her eyes and her jaw rigid. "I apologize, Evan."

She swept her tail and knocked his feet out from under him. He fell hard, his head banging against stone. Pain arced through him. The world blurred.

Shouts cut through the ringing in his head. The clank of a metal ramp hitting rock. The thud of running feet.

Brisk hands felt his pulse, touched his face. He tried to focus, to see who leaned over him.

"Head injury." The man's voice came through a muffled hum. "We need to get him to The Dome."

His eyes drifted closed, and the green light gave way to darkness.

Chapter Four

Fluorescent light bore into Evan's head, and he squeezed his eyes shut again. His fingers crept up to pat gingerly at the rough edges of a dressing on his temple. Allowing his lids to lift halfway, he squinted at the room. White and compact. Shining benches lined the walls, steel cabinets above them. A sickbay. Vague memories blurred in his head—Dan's frightened face, streamers of blood, some crazy fish woman, water cascading off a metal hull. His eyes flashed fully open.

A sub. What the hell business did a sub have in these waters? With no markings? Pain lanced through his head, and he breathed out slowly. His heart pounded against his ribs, and he curled a lip. Getting up would be a sensible idea. Better to battle the discomfort than lie vulnerable in bed in a place he didn't know. Naked.

Crap.

He scanned the room, a frown lowering on his brow. Shifting under the thin scratchy blanket, his feet knocked against a pile of fabric, knocking it to the floor. He stared down at the fatigues. His fingers clenched in the blanket. This didn't mean anything. His clothes would've been soaked; a vessel like this wouldn't keep a store of civilian stuff.

The trousers sat on his waist like they'd never left. He hated the sense of comfort and home covering his skin. He pulled on the t-shirt and found his hand going automatically to pull out the dog-tags which used to always hang around his neck. Not anymore. There weren't any in his boots either. He resisted the urge to tuck in the t-shirt.

The bare sickbay held no further clues to where he was or who had rescued him. His gaze slid to the door. Time to go exploring.

The handle turned under his fingers. Unlocked. A burst of relief flooded him. He stepped out of the room, his boots clanging on the floor.

Odd no one else lingered around. Maybe, they didn't view him as a threat. His head throbbed, and he collapsed against the door frame for a second. Blinking away the fuzziness, he scanned the corridor and tried to orient himself. Deserts and mountains were more his experience than submarines. But some things always stayed the same.

He headed left, hoping to find the galley. Someone would be there for sure, and showing up there would be way less confrontational than turning up on the bridge. His fingers grazed the walls, iron bumps and rivets jarring in their familiarity.

Someone hustled around the corner and collided into him. He stumbled on unsteady legs. The man pulled back and eyed him, scanning over the bandage and settling on his face. Shorter than Evan by a few inches, but likely still over six foot.

The man smiled, dark stubble on his face and his black hair curling over his forehead. Another confirmation this was no regular navy outfit.

"So you're the survivor. Talk about lucky. How'd you end up in that old cavern?"

Evan stared as his mind replayed fuzzy images of a

woman with a tail. The man clapped his forehead.

"Sorry, forgot my manners. My name's Khalid."

He shook the proffered hand. "Evan."

"Marine, right?"

For a second he stiffened, before he realized Khalid pointed at the Devil Dog tattoo on his arm. "Yeah, you?"

"Army. You'll still hear some of the crew call me an air breather, but I'm used to this underwater thing now."

Evan gestured at the corridor. "And what exactly is this underwater thing?"

Khalid smiled widely. "I think you need the boss for those questions." He shifted back and waved at Evan. "Come on, I'll take you. This place is confusing otherwise."

With no other options, Evan went with him. He wanted to trust Khalid, the other man's open and warm expression invited trust. But this didn't seem to be a navy vessel, and as far as he knew, they floated lost under the ocean far from friendly eyes. He followed, but his back sparked with tension, and his wary gaze roved over everything.

The engine hum ran a soothing counterpoint to his pounding head. A reminder they weren't sinking to the sea bed.

Unlike Dan. Grief punched air out of his lungs, but he gritted his teeth. Since he ended up washed into a cavern alive, it could be Dan also landed somewhere safe. Questions pushed at the tip of his tongue, and he cast a glance at Khalid. Best to wait until he spoke to whoever ran this op.

Blood in the water. Shining tails. Arms holding him

up. His jaw tightened. He better ask to see a medic too.

They passed through a small galley where engineers lounged, hands warming tin cups of bitter-smelling coffee. His stomach rumbled, and Khalid raised his brows with a smile.

"I'll get you some food once you've talked to the boss."

A woman screwed her nose up as she sipped, her long black ponytail falling over her shoulder. "I wouldn't rush, food's better at the Dome. So's the coffee."

The dome? People sure had weird names for their bases.

"Esther is our coffee connoisseur," Khalid said with a grin, and Esther held out her hand for a fist bump as they passed.

"Damn straight I am."

She flashed him a friendly smile, but her gaze assessed him coolly, flicking over the tattoo on his arm. "So you're the survivor. Welcome aboard, marine."

He stiffened but forced a smile. "Evan. Not on active service anymore."

She turned back to her coffee, murmuring into her cup, "Time will tell."

The hustle and noise became louder as they reached the bridge in the nose of the submarine. Khalid punched in a number to a security pad, and the door slid open. Evan ducked his head under the steel mantle. Beeps and murmurs filled the small space. Technicians in headsets hunched over consoles of colored lights, setting off memories, like a tripwire. The captain approached. Like the others, this man wore no tags, his uniform the same shirt and pants everyone wore. But leadership sat in every carved line of his face and the set of his shoulders.

A coil of unease sat in Evan's gut. Everything screamed military but wasn't. *What kind of covert op have I stumbled into?*

"You're awake. How're you feeling?"

"I'm well thank you, sir." *Except for the hallucinations about mermaids.* "Might be a good idea to get a check-up if you have a medic to spare though."

"Of course, the medic at the Dome will check you out thoroughly."

His brow crinkled at this second mention. "At the where?"

"The Dome." The captain eyed him. "We're almost there. Better if you see it. Easier than explaining, I've found."

He gestured, and a technician pushed a button on the console. Metal shutters rose over massive plexiglass windows, and the ocean opened up in front of them. Headlights spread out in a giant beam, dancing over green kelp and small schools of fish.

A shimmering dome loomed in the middle of the ocean. Lights flickered around the base and shone from giant panes of glass. People moved inside, tiny compared to the rising heights of the sides of the structure. He sucked in a breath. *Shit.*

He'd seen covert bases before, but this was something out of a movie set. His pulse thundered against the bump on his temple, and he struggled to keep himself from cursing. He tore away from the unreality and met the satisfied gaze of the captain.

"What is this place?"

"Home."

Chapter Five

Massive metal doors slid open, and the submarine glided inside the Dome. Evan couldn't tear his gaze from the window. The dim green of the depths gave way to bright beams of light bouncing from the concrete dock. Water and bubbles of wake streamed over the glass as the engine hummed, and the vessel rose. The glare of lights stabbed into his eyes, and he rubbed at his temple. *Better see the medic asap.*

A few people hustled on the dock but not as many as he expected. Not as if he knew what to expect in a giant dome under the sea. His fingers traced the bandage over his brow. This wasn't another hallucination. This bit, the smell of recycled air, the metal under his feet. All too real.

The captain turned, clasping his hands together. "Let's take you onshore, show you around."

He followed the older man down the passageway, the measured rush of the crew all the more unsettling for its unexpected familiarity. The captain gestured for Evan to walk next to him.

"The Dome hits everyone a bit differently, but you get used to it after a while."

The airlock opened, and the gangway clanged. Khalid and another man stood at the door, saluting as they walked past.

The air in the docking bay hit Evan's nose with a

sharp mix of saltwater tang and diesel. His mind whirled back to thunderous waves tearing apart the ship, to Dan's white-eyed gaze. *Can't think of that now.*

He strode down the gantry, boots ringing on the iron and the chain railing cold beneath his fingers. A rising shield of plexiglass held back the ocean on one side of the cavernous room. For a moment, the walls shifted, collapsing in on him, enclosing him in a coffin of water and steel. He blinked away the claustrophobia, counting his breaths until his pulse slowed. Concrete and steel hemmed them in on the other side, green light waving in snakelike reflections over the surface.

Shouts echoed as the crew secured the submarine at the berth. The captain turned from signing in with a ground crew and grinned at him.

"Don't waste all your awe on this. Much more impressive things lie ahead."

Sliding doors hissed open at a swipe from a security card, revealing a long corridor beyond. *Not that impressive.*

"Tell me, Evan—it *is* Evan?"

"Yes sir, Evan Hunter."

"What were you doing in our waters?"

The question set off sparks in his head, warning signals racing.

A woman in uniform, her black hair in curly knots on the top of her head, raced around the corner. Evan jumped to the side to avoid a collision. He waved away her apologies and smiled tightly back at her, relishing the chance to think. Dan had been about to tell him what he'd been hunting for before the waves stopped him. Only thing clear about the whole mess was the secrecy around it.

The captain smiled. "Always rushing somewhere, hey Char?"

"You got it, Captain."

Their exchange pulled Evan's mind back to the present.

Warm brown eyes crinkled, and Char quirked a brow at Evan and saluted the captain as she moved away. Her pounding footsteps retreated into the distance. And he still didn't know how to answer the captain's question.

"I was on a friend's boat. A massive storm hit us, and somehow I ended up in a cavern." He rubbed at his bicep, the faint memory of strong fingers holding him. "I don't know how."

The other man's face didn't lose its genial air, but his eyes flashed hawk-fierce. "No idea at all?"

Evan pointed at the bandage on his temple, and the lines around the captain's eyes relaxed.

"Yes, we best get your head seen to."

Questions battled at the back of Evan's mind, but he kept his mouth closed.

****

The door of the small barracks room snicked shut behind his escort. Evan fought against the sudden sense of a jail door clanging. He glared at the handle, refusing to check if the door would open again. His fingers played over the small card the quartermaster gave him, full of instructions on how to set a new PIN on the lock pad.

The medic had been brisk and reassuring. Evan swirled the pain meds they'd given him in the small plastic cup. Hopefully, they didn't numb his senses further. The concussion check came back clean, but he didn't dare mention the blurred images of a half woman, half fish swimming through his head. Best to wait to see his own shrink. Not a doctor under the sea. His hand clenched.

Under the sea. Unbelievable.

A heavy weight sat in his stomach, and he huffed out a breath, thinking of how the captain's gaze had slid away when he asked about passage out of the dome and contacting his family. He still didn't even know the captain's name. Dread curled through his blood. He tried not to think of his sister. Kelly was strong. She'd cope.

She'll think I'm dead.

He glanced around his new quarters, desperate for something else to think about. Two squat cupboards perched at the foot of the narrow bed. One of the doors opened with a tinny squeak, prickling over his teeth. Nothing sat inside other than a ubiquitous Gideon's Bible and a generic uniform. He looked glumly at the olive drab and wondered where his clothes ended up.

The mattress bent a fraction under his weight when he sat down. He swallowed a sigh and wished they would come for him now. The walls were too close, too sterile, and too familiar. He didn't want to feel comforted by his surroundings. He wanted to leave.

"Home sweet home."

He grunted and flicked the PIN card between his fingers. Setting a code was too much like accepting a place here before he even understood the situation. Leaving the door without one might be foolish. He rolled his eyes skyward. Not like he had anything to steal. The longer they left him in here to stare at the floor; the longer this room was the only space in this submerged snow globe where he felt like he belonged. The same way if you stayed in a bivouaced tent for long enough it became your own space.

He stared at the door. Dan's face, grim and lined as he stared up at the towering wave, floated in his mind. His eyes burned, but he blinked away the threatening grief. He needed to find out what happened if the sub searched for other survivors. He needed to get out of here. A hot ache spread through his chest. And he needed to tell Dan's wife her husband was gone.

Why did I wash up in a cavern? Why didn't Dan?

A fuzzy memory of an impossible creature tugged at him, and he shook the thoughts from his head. Waves of guilt washed through him. Not overwhelming, not yet. His hands curled into fists, and he focused on breathing in and out. The bare walls of the narrow room closed in, and he stared at the table, tracking the grooves in the steel.

Screeching metal and the tug of water pulling him under the surface played in a loop behind his eyes. Blood trails drifting through the ocean pulled out darker memories of blood staining the desert. He shuddered and leaned over, his head resting on his shaking hands. Stale air redolent with the scent of some kind of pine cleaner caught in his throat.

Screw this. He pushed off the bed and stalked to the door. It opened as he reached for the handle. The guy from the sub—Khalid—grinned at him.

"Not set your code yet, bro? Want to do it before I take you to the commander?"

Evan uncurled his fingers and reached into his pocket. Khalid glanced the other way while he followed the instructions. His sister's birthday and the time of day he signed up.

Tucking the card back into his pocket he met the other man's gaze, open and friendly, like in the sub. But he'd been waiting for him. Kinda creepy. "Done."

"Right, this way."

They walked back toward the larger rooms he had passed on the way in. The weight of the water above pushed down on him. His chest tightened. Too many unanswered questions, too much death trailing behind him.

"What's the likelihood I can leave soon?"

Khalid glanced at him then down the long corridor. "Don't know if they pointed it out yet, but the mess hall is down this way."

Adrenaline coursed through him. He scanned his surroundings, tabulating possible exits, danger points.

"Avoiding the subject?"

The other man's shoulders lifted. "I'm not authorized to speculate."

Tension throbbed at the base of his neck. "Fair call. This commander, what's he like?"

"Used to be a high-up, but not sure exactly. He's all right."

He stepped aside as a young man in a khaki uniform strode past. "I don't get this place. Is everyone ex-military? Is this a private enterprise or what?"

Khalid sucked at his teeth. "Tell you what, the boss is the best person to ask."

Evan stopped dead, and the other man spun on his heel to face him.

"What?" Khalid's arms crossed over his chest.

"I got a feeling. And not a great one. At least tell me why you're here."

The other man leaned on the wall, averting his gaze. "You know when you get back home from a tour, and at first it's all good, but after a while you feel out of place?"

He knew. Every veteran knew. Endless banal conversations, applying for jobs but no one needed your skills, the constant knee-jerk 'thank-you-for-your-service' but nobody wanting to hear about it. Yeah. He knew.

"This seemed a decent alternative. A way to serve but not, if you track me." Khalid clasped his shoulder. "Trust me, the commander will explain better than I can. This place may be kinda strange, but there's a lot of folks like me who want a second chance to do the right thing."

The words echoed in his mind. He'd missed the mark in so many areas of his life, left too many people damaged in his wake. A second chance might be exactly what he needed.

As they strode on down the hall, he kept his face blank, hiding the turmoil inside. Too many dead civilians, too many dead brothers, too much loneliness in his life... The thought of another chance to get it right sure pulled at him, but he doubted anything they did down here would matter.

And people like me don't get second chances.

Chapter Six

Dim light pooled in the corners of the sparse room. The woman known as the Siren stroked a finger down the arm of the black chair behind her desk, pride sparking in her veins. Occasionally, it hit her all over again that she held sway over this whole operation, her code name gifted to the project.

Leather gave under her legs as she sat down, cool against the skin of her thighs as her gray pencil skirt hitched. Above her head, the Dome's roof curved in a gradual slope, close enough to touch if she stood on the desk. Dark water against the glass sang to her of secrets and hidden places.

She turned from the enticing darkness and switched on the monitor next to her desk. Blue and white light flickered to life, glowing over her pale skin. On the screen, a mermaid lay strapped down on a bench, human legs thrashing. Straps held her head immobilised, and gloved hands administered a dose into the side of her neck, right under where her gills would show. The mermaid's limbs slowed then jerked, muscles shuddering.

The attending physician darted a glance over to the corner where a uniformed figure gestured once. A quick slice of a scalpel, and the amulet around the mermaid's neck fell to the floor. A moment of stillness and the Siren stopped breathing, her fingers clenching the edge of the desk. Maybe this time the procedure would work.

Green stuttered up the edges of the mermaid's arms. Fins broke through her skin, her legs fusing and scales rippling until a large tail flapped with increasing urgency over the bench. Gills breathed in air, sucking in too much. The dying mermaid convulsed, and the Siren leaned forward and snapped the switch off with a trembling hand.

Failure. Again. Well, they had plenty more mer to work with. There would be more chances to replicate the experiment. She ignored the churning in her stomach and typed an email, sending instructions off to Doctor Jones.

Her nails clicked out an impatient pattern on the desk until a quiet *ping* sounded, and she stabbed the keys, downloading the experiment report. There must be something the scientists overlooked. The procedure had worked on one; it should work on more. She frowned. If only the findings hadn't been destroyed when the mer fought back. With a flick of her fingers, she turned off the computer.

A lock of blonde hair fell over her forehead, and she clipped it up by the bun on the top of her head. She pushed away from the desk and walked to the viewing platform, her heels clacking on the hard floor. Far below her lay the main floor of the Dome's atrium. Men and women strolled over white tiles, crisp uniforms at odds with their relaxed faces.

Except for one. Tall, broad, lanky, blond. He stalked next to one of the crew, face unreadable.

Her frown deepened as a quiet knock disturbed her thoughts.

"Enter."

The door slid open and Marcus Taylor walked in, a file clutched in his beefy hands. His eyes glinted behind the spectacles perched on his once-broken nose.

"I've brought you the file on the newest possible. Evan Hunter. Marine."

Her gaze darted back to the man below. Strength radiated from him.

"Has he signed the contract?"

"Not as of yet, ma'am. I thought at first, looking at his record, he might be too idealistic for Project Siren. But he's about to meet with Abraham. It might be he's damaged enough to jump at the chance to serve a higher good."

The words echoed in her head. In the end this would all be for the higher good. Whether everyone viewed her venture the same way was doubtful, but every day she girded herself with the knowledge she worked toward something better and greater. Something that would change the world. *The higher good.* "Might be? We need more than a perhaps. We need a signed contract."

Taylor inclined his head and passed her the slim folder. "Everything's in there."

She grasped the file and flipped open the manila cover. Hunter was younger than she thought. Twenty-seven. Two active tours. Heroic endeavours aplenty. She paused on one mission brief. Her eyes narrowed and her breath caught in her throat. Children. Failure. *Perfect.*

Her gaze shifted to Evan Hunter. His discomfort stood out in his rigid stride and the tightness of his arms. Despite his tension, he acknowledged the nods and greetings of those who passed him. A man who needed others. And better, one who carried guilt, always the easiest to secure. As she regarded him, considering, he and his escort left the platform, the steel doors sliding closed behind him.

She tapped her teeth. "This one could be a perfect match. He may need a special touch, though. You may leave me. I will arrange things."

"Yes, ma'am."

When silence rang instead of booted footsteps, she frowned. "And yet, you are still here."

"Do we organise a vessel? In case he decides no?"

A smile spread on her face, and the captain stepped back before catching himself and standing to attention again.

"I do not believe that will be necessary."

The captain saluted and left. She stared up at the water above her, stretching her hand and wishing her fingers could brush the fish searching for food where the lights shone. *Not yet.*

She let her gaze fall back to the people on the deck below as she unbuttoned her suit jacket. Every one of them had heard the call, decided to serve. They might not yet know who they truly served, but she did not doubt them. The new man's face swam into her mind. *Evan Hunter.* He would learn; they all learned. For the higher good to be achieved, sacrifices needed to be made.

Her hand caught the light, and for a moment, the webbing between her fingers flashed into view as scales shimmered in a shining pattern.

They all had to make sacrifices.

Chapter Seven

Gunmetal gray lined the windowless room. Shelves filled with neat filing boxes squatted behind a wooden desk. Photos of a graduation, a wedding, and a child's birthday party perched on the top of the shelves.

The grizzled man behind the desk stood, an affable smile stretching tanned and weathered features. He wore his silver hair in a buzzed regulation crop, and unlike some of the others in the Dome who, despite their khaki fatigues, wore no dogtags, he not only had tags but pips on the lapels of his shirt. A decorated soldier.

Muscle memory pulled at Evan's arm with the urge to salute, and he clasped his hands behind his back instead. The man's smile broadened.

"Welcome, son. I'm Commander Abraham. The crew call me Cap Ahab. I suspect they think they're funny. I don't mind much. What do you think of my Dome?"

His mind's eye flashed back over huge glass walls curving from the bottom of the ocean, the high level of tech in the medical bay, and the number of people housed in the monstrous snow-globe.

"It's impressive. Not like anything I've ever seen."

Abraham sauntered around to the front of the desk. "You won't see any place matching what we've got here, I guarantee you."

Evan glanced around the tidy room. Easy to forget they stood miles under the ocean's surface in a generic office like this. "And where is *here*, sir?"

The old man's arms spread wide. "The most advanced research facility on earth."

"What kind of research? Navy?"

Abraham leaned back on the desk. "We carry out a lot of things down here, not all of them at your clearance level, son. Now, what I want to know is, what's a former marine doing in this part of the world?"

His gaze flicked to the files piled on the desk. "I'm certain you read my medical file, sir. Everything's in there."

"Sailing? In this part of the ocean? That all?" The captain's eyes glinted stone-like above the ever-present smile.

The giant storm from nowhere. The fearful look on Dan's face. The secrecy of it all. He kept his expression blank and his voice steady.

"Yes, sir. Catching up with a college buddy."

Abraham's face dropped into a fleeting rictus of sympathy. "By all accounts a real nasty wreck. Sorry for your loss. I know what it's like to lose friends, son."

He wouldn't think of the pain. Wouldn't think of Dan's body bloated from the sea, food for the sharks. Wouldn't give this insincere man the merest hint of his grief.

"Yes, sir." The word rolled off his tongue. Some habits never break.

"Water under the bridge. We've looked you up, Evan. Quite the record. Medal of Honor, bravery under fire, honorable discharge."

The words fell around him like dust. Like any of

that mattered. When you were on the front line, you did what you did so you all survived. Anyone else would've done the same. The medals only reminded him who didn't come back.

Like Dan.

Lines wrinkled the other man's forehead as he raised a brow. "Modest too, I see."

The commander darted a glance into the corner of the ceiling. Evan remembered other times, other rooms, and cameras transmitting everything. He kept his face immobile, held his silence.

Your reaction is the test.

"I'll be upfront with you, son; you're the kind of recruit we need in this operation. Think you'd be interested?"

His skin crawled every time the officer called him son. They did it to infantilize you. Remind you who held the power. And they did so with a fatherly smile as they sent you into hell.

"I've done my service, sir. Were I to re-enlist, I'd only consider the marines." He smiled. "And since you've read my file, you'll know I'm past the cut-off age for enlistment."

"Yeah, *semper fi.* I get that, but let me ask you. What if you were given the chance to change the world for the better? Reduce casualties? Avoid civilian deaths?"

He clenched his jaw and focused on breathing through his nose, calming his racing pulse. "I'd say I would be sceptical any such chance existed, sir."

"Why do you say that, son?"

He caught himself standing at ease and shifted to lean into one hip and fold his arms. "I served my initial, then re-upped for another four, completed two tours in Iraq, sir. I've heard all there is to hear about changing the world for the better. That kind of talk tends to leave dead children behind."

Abraham's eyes narrowed and his smile soured. "No one ever wants collateral damage; you know that. Sometimes hard things are necessary to protect those closer to home. Regardless, this is different. This is a genuine higher cause. What we're doing here will change the face of warfare. Change it for the better."

"To be honest, I'm still not sure who the *we* is, in all this."

"Come now, Hunter, you know better. Classified material isn't handed out to every stray waif who washes up on our shore, no matter the honorable background."

"I understand, sir. But I'm uncomfortable joining an operation when I'm not clear on who's running the show."

"Well, we don't believe in unenthusiastic recruits. You have a choice. The next vessel headed for land doesn't leave for six weeks. If you decide you don't want to serve your country, you'll stay until then and you can return to the surface. After signing an NDA of course." The captain's teeth filled his face in what clearly aimed to be a reassuring avuncular smile.

Images of the soldiers in the corridors came to Evan's mind. Camaraderie. Unity. Brotherhood. Part of him cried out to belong again. But a quiet part of his mind no longer trusted those in authority, and his fingers clenched on his arms.

"What exactly does staying here involve? Is that information you could tell a stray waif, like me?"

The captain pursed his lip and hooked his thumbs in his belt. "Keeping fit, some logistics and supply stuff, depending on your skill set. You may be a good maintainer. Play it by ear, fill in where you're needed type stuff. Fairly standard."

"And with this you think you can change the nature of war?"

The captain's toothy grin flashed. "Oh, come now, son; don't expect me to give up all our secrets on the first date."

Typical skipper routine. The real answers are above my clearance. Roger that. Ooh—fucking—rah, sir. He stared down at his feet. Changing the face of warfare was hardly likely. He pulled his gaze from the floor. "You say what you do here will help avoid civilian casualties, but with respect, sir, I've heard that song before. What can you say to make me believe that's what you're working for?"

The captain's lips stretched wide but his eyes cut like flint. "My word not enough for you?"

His jaw tightened but he refused to flinch, refused to look away. "With respect, no, sir, it isn't."

"You and I might have different ideas of respect, Hunter." A muscle jumped in the tight cords of the man's neck, then he relaxed. "But it's a fair question. Think of the most elite force you've seen, then imagine how much more effective it could be when stronger, smarter, or different from anything the enemy might foresee. Targeted. Fewer casualties."

His gut tightened and he breathed out. "Bit of a fantasy if you ask me."

The captain laughed and shook his head. "Well, son, you're closer than you think to the truth of it."

He rubbed his jaw as he tried to get his thoughts in order. Super soldiers might save lives, but soldiers obeyed orders. What would stop them being misused?

"I won't deny I'm interested. Can I take a night? My mom always said a rushed decision would end up a bad decision."

The captain sat back in his chair, an air of geniality settling around him like a cloud. "Sounds like you got a wise momma. We'll catch up in the morning. Take some time and walk around, check out the facility. Talk to some folks. You'll find this is a great opportunity for you, son."

Chapter Eight

The captain kept to his word. Evan had free rein of most of the facility and wandered through corridors until he found a spacious atrium filled with people. He smiled and waved back at a few—they were nothing if not friendly down here. After a while, the people and the noise became too much, and he walked out, hoping to find his room, but ended up here, on a platform with inky depths surrounding him.

Thick plexiglass swept in a giant curve above him. Dim LED strip lighting dotted the steel grid of the dome like runway beacons. Outside the sphere's protection, the ocean swirled in ever-moving currents of darkness.

He let out a shallow breath, his footsteps loud in the silence as he stalked to the edge of the viewing platform. So much water above him. Flashes of memory reflected against the windows in his mind. Trapped under rubble, too scared to scream for help in case the oxygen ran out, the world pressing down on him. He uncurled his fist, joints stiff and resisting, and placed a hand on the glass. It hummed.

He focused beyond the reflection of his own eyes staring back at him, keeping his gaze fixed on the deeps. Strobes of light echoed through the water. Subs most likely. Divers perhaps. His breathing steadied and his shoulders relaxed.

A soft *whush* of the door opening brought his head around. The woman he'd bumped into earlier walked toward him, her cargos switched out for track pants. The eerie light cast a glow against her warm black skin, and a small smile curved her lips.

"A lot to wrap your head around, right?" Understanding shone in her eyes.

He withdrew his hand from the dome, his gaze flicking over the ink-black water once more. "Sure is. You been here long?"

"Nine months and counting. I came down with the first recruits. My name's Char Lewis. Former ranger. You?"

He shook her hand, smiling back at the warmth in her expression. "Evan Hunter. Marine."

She inclined her head then turned to the glass and the depths beyond. "Being here gets easier. You kinda forget for a bit until one day you look out and realize all over again you're living under the water"—her smile became a grin—"and your head spaces out once more."

Swirling water called to him with a promise of escape from the claustrophobic dome. He fought back the urge to smash through the glass, to escape.

Char stood tall, her shoulder below his. Her black hair was short and wound in two small knots on the top of her head. She raised her eyebrows at him with a smile, and he took the plunge.

"Mind if I ask you something?"

"Shoot."

"The commander said this venture is a chance to do something great, to benefit the world. Is that why you joined?"

She reached past him and laid her hand on the

dome. "I always loved the ocean. Ever since childhood." The shining dark of the water settled in her eyes. "Going home wasn't all I thought it would be. I figured this'd be a good way to serve without returning to the desert."

He knew the feeling. Alone in a gathering of people. Pretending everything was fine. Missing the fifteen-mile humps chanting old tunes about the Halls of Montezuma.

Char backed away from the glass and waved for him to follow. "Cap Ahab said you might want to see a bit of what we do down here. We're about to do some training, help out the research geeks. He said it'd be okay for you to join in. Problem-solving stuff, so it won't hurt your head, although I can't make any promises about your brain."

He touched the stitches and smiled, a rush of excitement in his blood. "Sure. Sounds good."

He cast a glance back at the high walls of the dome before the door slid shut behind them, narrowing his eyes at the shadow of a large tail against the glass. Deepwater fish sure grew big. Memories of arms around him holding him out of the water rose in his mind, and he pushed them away. Aftereffects of his head injury. Nothing else.

Walking with Char through the corridors of the underwater base, he saw things with different eyes. She knew everyone, and everyone wanted to say hello to her. By the time they got to their destination, a directory's worth of names jammed in his head. With each smiling face and firm handshake, the tight bands around his chest eased.

Twenty people filled the large room, some of

whom wore white coats and carried sturdy clipboards that shouted *researcher*. Char nodded at one of the whitecoats who peered at them from under long bangs and scribed a checkmark on her paper.

"Join group A," the researcher said. "They need all the help they can get."

They followed her derisive wave to joined a noisy group of three men and another woman. Introductions flew, and Evan's headache filtered away under the infectious energy of the crew. A warm sense of familiarity wound around him. The way they moved, the brisk focus when they got down to work, all of it pulled at memories of better times.

The tasks looked challenging but fun. Building bridges from sticks, testing the weight they held, whipping up pulley systems. All stuff he'd done at school. He raised a brow at Char and she smiled.

"They want to see how fast we can complete basic structural activities, how we work together, and who wins."

He grinned back. *Time to win, then.*

Char took point, assigning roles and giving instructions. The others in the group responded cheerfully and quickly; clearly they respected her judgement. Evan regarded her as he bound sticks together in a makeshift stand. She reminded him of one of his buddies, friendly but fierce. When he and Char got their team's pulley working first, he whooped, high-fiving her.

Time flew and when the researchers called an end to it, he was surprised to feel a twinge of regret.

Char held up a fist until he bumped it. "We make a good team. Come on, time for dinner. The food here's not too bad." Her grin flashed again. "Lots of fish."

Dinner was indeed fish. White and grilled and tasteless. He sat with Char and let the humming voices and sounds of clashing cutlery wash over him in a relaxing wave. Here in the busy chow hall, the ocean didn't intrude. He could have been anywhere. Char made him laugh. He'd forgotten what it was like to be around people who understood, who got it.

A petite blonde woman walked past, catching his eye. Her swinging ponytail shimmered in the light. When she turned to talk to someone, he froze with his cup halfway to the table, mesmerised by piercing blue eyes.

Char's elbow in his side brought him back to the present. She waved a napkin at him.

"Here. For the drool."

He fought down the flush of heat on his cheeks and laughed, tossing the napkin back at her.

"Seriously, Hunter? That girl's out of your league. Ana is different. No one knows what branch she's from, and my money's on Secret Service."

Secret service. Made sense. A place like this had to have an 'in' to those back in the Pentagon making the decisions. *She sure was pretty, though.*

Swapping stories with Char, he managed to avoid any detailed discussion of his last mission. His VA shrink encouraged him to talk about those memories more than enough, not that he could ever forget. The darkness of a stormy sea flooded his mind, and he shifted in his chair. Char nailed it though, better the sea than the sand. She prompted him to laugh several times, and he relaxed into a familiar camaraderie. The Dome didn't seem like such a bad deal, here and now.

At the end of the meal they left the hall together, Char walking him back toward the sleeping quarters "so you don't get lost." They neared the viewing platform, and she slowed her pace. Darting a glance at her, he caught a shadow of tension flicker over her face. She smiled.

"This way is faster." She pointed toward the platform, and he followed, the dark waters swirling above them.

About halfway to the exit, Char stopped altogether. Her bottom lip curled under her teeth and a frown line carved into the skin between her brows.

"What's up?"

"It was fun, today, working with you. I mean it, we make a good team."

He crossed his arms, a warning fluttering at the edge of his mind. "And this makes you frown why?"

The shifting inky water sent rippling reflections over her skin, hiding her expression. "Think about it Evan, about whether you want to stay down here. Don't rush a decision, don't be bullied into doing something you might regret."

Her smile flashed again but this time there was tension in her jaw. "Time for me to split. Night Evan. Take care of yourself, y'hear?"

She strode away, and he walked back to his room, thoughts whirling through his head.

Quiet filled the small unit. Somewhere in the distance a couple of clangs rang out. He leaned his back on the wall, the mattress hard under his legs. Habit pushed at the back of his mind, spreading a calm he fought against. Under the sea, friends missing, strange research facility. None of this should feel normal. But the military trappings, the routine, the set-up of the room, covered him like a blanket, deadening concern.

He clasped his hands together, staring at his fingers, remembering the metal rail slipping from his grasp and the depths taking him. He focused on the roiling waves so he wouldn't focus on the other memories—the ones sitting deep in his head, waiting. Perhaps Abraham had a point. To reduce civilian casualties, create a stronger set of soldiers to target the real enemy, and leave the rest of the people unharmed. How could that be a bad thing?

Abraham's smile nagged at him. Something hid behind his strained grin, something unsaid. He'd lay his life on it. But Char and the others stood against the unease. Decent people. Her last message passed through his mind and he shifted, a frown falling on his face.

Down here, there were merely people doing research. Clipboards and white coats. No enemy. No civilians caught up in the madness.

A sigh blew out his cheeks, and he collapsed backward on the narrow mattress. His feet touched the edge, and he shifted in resigned frustration. Lacing his fingers behind his head, he stared up at concrete and steel panels. The ceiling offered no more answers than the wall.

He sat in the dark and let his thoughts cascade.

****

In the morning he woke, showered, changed, and sat waiting for the knock on his door, his hands clenched tight together. Maybe Char was right, but something strange was happening. And maybe this was the thing Dan had been searching for with all that not-so-secret scanning. If he left, he'd always wonder.

When the knock finally came, he greeted the man the commander had sent with a tight smile. He followed the crewman down winding corridors to Abraham's gunmetal gray office. The officer greeted him with a wide grin, and Evan pushed away the image of a shark smiling at its prey.

"You've made your choice, son?"

His shoulders twitched, but he nodded. "Yes, sir. I don't want to turn down a chance to make a difference. Seems like this is an operation I can get behind."

Abraham held out his hand and Evan shook it, the other man's grip firm and strong.

"Excellent! Take a seat, Hunter, we'll go over the contract."

Evan's lips pressed tight. So, not enlistment papers, a contract. This really was some kind of covert op. The urge to tell Abraham he'd changed his mind sat on the tip of his tongue, but he swallowed it and sat down as the man pulled out a thick white roll of paper from his drawer.

Evan read through several times and tried to squash unnecessary qualms. Thick paper shifted under his hands, more the kind of thing certificates were made from than a standard contract. A one-year term of service with a company called Deep Sea Endeavours. More cover-ups. His gut clenched and he kept reading. Contact to be made by the organization to reassure family. Kelly would be okay then, nothing to worry about there. An NDA stating he wouldn't discuss Project Siren with anyone. He frowned. He'd expected to see treason indicated if the NDA was breached but this talked of forfeit of life. *Guess it was the same thing, just someone trying to sound fancy, like the paper.*

His fingers tightened on the metal casing of the old ink pen, the nib hovering over the dotted line. Kelly kept saying he needed to find a new purpose. Maybe this could be it. The shame twisting Grace's expression the last time he saw her—she cast him off, and now there was so little to go back to on the surface.

"Take your time, son." The walls closed in a little. Evan inhaled and set pen to paper. When he wrote the date, the ink sputtered. He wiped the nib on the palm of his hand and scrawled a clean signature.

He passed the paper back to Abraham. "Why Siren? Like an alarm?"

The officer smiled as he rolled up the contract. "I guess you could say that. We're creating the first line of defense."

His signature disappeared into the roll of paper, and shivers tracked down his spine. Like he'd crossed a line and turning back would be impossible.

Standing, the commander held out a hand to shake his. "Welcome to your new life, Hunter."

Chapter Nine

The uniform fit well, almost too comfortable. Stubble met his hand as he stroked his jaw. *Better find a razor.* He tugged at his belt, then rolled his eyes. Talk about putting things off. How bad could another medical check be? He jabbed at the lock and the door slid open. People crowded the corridor, all walking with purpose, most chatting with each other. He dove in to join the flow.

Not as many curious glances as he expected came his way. The skin around his brow tightened. Maybe the sea tossed up people all the time. *The ocean didn't give Dan back.* Chasing the thoughts of Dan came the curling worry about his sister that he'd pushed away since he got here. *Kelly is strong, she'll be fine. They'll let her know where I am. Won't they?*

The identical hallways were confusing but he gritted his teeth and tried to work out the way himself. When he ended up at a T-section for the second time, he paused, rubbing at the headache in his temple.

"Need a map?"

He turned and the woman from the sub smiled back at him.

"Esther, right? The coffee fiend."

She laughed. "Yep. Are you lost?"

"I'm supposed to be heading to medical, but I keep ending up here." He jabbed a hand at the offending intersection.

A faint line appeared between her brows but she smiled and pointed to the left. "Down this way. Come on, I'll show you."

Her ponytail swung as they walked, and her shoulder nearly came up to his. He smiled at her.

"My friend's sister is called Esther. I didn't think I'd ever meet another one."

A sardonic glance darted his way. "Try visiting the local supermarket in a Korean suburb in New York. You'll meet plenty of us there. I've not met another Evan though."

"It's Welsh. My mom's from there."

"Do you speak any Welsh?"

"Ever seen how it's spelled?"

"I take it that's a no."

"*Helo, sut wyt ti?*"

"Okay, I'm guessing the first meant hello?"

He laughed. "The only Welsh I learned, hello, how are you."

"*An yeonghaseyo, dangsin-eun eotteoseyo?*" she replied in Korean.

"*Naneun joh-eun gamsa haeyo.*"

She raised her brows. "Whoa, not bad!"

"Yeah, my friend Dan taught me." His face closed down.

"Oh." She stopped and laid a hand on his arm. "The friend whose boat you were on?"

"Yeah."

"I'm sorry."

"Can I ask you something?"

She pulled back, her arms crossed. "I guess. Sure."

"The commander said they found no sign of Dan's

body or the crew. He asked a lot of questions about our trip. You rode in the sub. I need to know; did you search for Dan? For any of them? See anything?"

Her gaze slid away, and a muscle flickered in her jaw. "We always scan. Anyone would, right? We didn't find anyone in the debris. We found you because we passed the cavern, and the scanners showed a heat signature where none should have been."

She glanced back at him, her face stern but kind. "I don't know a polite way to say this: when these things happen, if we don't find survivors, a body often washes up a few days later."

Dan's smile flashed into his mind, and a familiar darkness spread through him. Esther reached out again.

"Whatever happened on the boat, with the storm? I'm not surprised you capsized. It happens a lot here. Rough seas. The wreck wasn't your fault."

His mouth twisted. "I know. But knowing and feeling are different."

"I get you."

Her steady sympathy helped drive away some of the darkness. "We're here anyway. Down the hall on your right. And Evan—you need anything in the next few days you shout out, all right? Most everyone down here's decent folk. My crew are the better ones. So hit us up if you need to."

She stretched out her hand, and he smiled as he clasped it.

"Thanks, Esther. I appreciate the help and the offer."

She walked away with a little wave. He tried to keep the warmth of new friends with him as he strode toward the ward. A series of closed doors greeted him, and he scanned the nameplates by the door for Room 15 and C. Mitchell. One of the doors opened, and a man dressed in a white coat came out. Before the door shut again, Evan glimpsed unfamiliar machines and beeping monitors.

"Are you here for the initial medical?"

"Yes, to see Dr. Mitchell."

"Celine. She's over here." The man walked him a couple of doors down the hallway. "She'll be expecting you, go on in."

An edge of nausea swam in his stomach. The doctor walked over to him as he opened the door, a bony hand held out and a wide smile on her lined face. He shook her hand and she cocked her head, graying hair escaping from a messy bun.

"Evan, right? Nice to meet you. I'm Celine. Did they explain what we'll be doing today?"

He found himself relaxing under her friendly gaze. "Not so much, no. Communication doesn't appear to be a strength in this place."

A deep laugh sprang out of her, earthy and contagious. "You're right. This is simply a more thorough medical check. I know you've been checked out for your head injury, but now you're staying longer we need to gather a baseline for your health and fitness, so as the training goes on we can track improvements in specific areas like speed and reaction time."

The machines lost their looming air. Just a physical then. Pushing away the edginess that lingered no matter what, he tried to relax.

He stripped to his shorts when she asked him to and stood for photos and measurements. The process seemed a lot more pedantic than he remembered from enlistment days but he guessed the research required stricter measurements. *I'm under the ocean, of course everything's different.*

The treadmill run and the heart beat test relaxed him with their familiarity. A desire to push himself, to impress this older lady with the laughing eyes, snuck through him. She arched a brow and he shrugged with a laugh. After the reflex tests, she brought out the syringes. He grimaced. *Why did there always have to be blood tests?*

Her fingers touched his skin with a gentle pressure, and the needle slid in smoothly.

"You must do this a lot."

She nodded, gaze on the blood sample. "Sure do. We want to keep an eye on you all, make sure you're healthy."

He stared at the ceiling as vials filled with red blood.

Finally Dr. Mitchell withdrew the needle and dabbed on a tiny plaster. "There you go, all done." She carried the samples to the counter and gestured at his clothes. "Time to get dressed."

His arm prickled, like a pincushion, as he pulled on his shirt and his trousers. He was buckling his belt when she came back with a dark bottle.

"Last thing before you go. Special tonic formulated just for you. You'll be given a weekly dose of this with your regular check-ups."

Clear syrup with a greenish tinge oozed from the bottle into the measuring cup. Celine passed the dose to him with a smile and warm sympathy in her eyes.

"Sorry. This stuff tastes awful. Best to swig it back fast."

His face screwed up and he sniffed at the liquid. A salty tang hid under a cough medicine aniseed kind of smell. He raised his brows at her.

"Do I have to?"

She laughed again and he found himself twinkling at her.

"Yes, you do, you big baby. Living in the artificial light with limited food sources, you need to consume a range of proper nutrients to counter the effects. It might be disgusting but the tonic keeps you well."

He brought the syrup up to his lips, then paused as an odd shadow passed over her expression. She smiled and prodded his arm.

"Come on, drink up so you can get on to the fun parts."

They'd hardly poison him when they could shoot him. Not like anyone else knew he was here. He swigged back the medicine, gagging as a bitter aftertaste assaulted his taste buds.

A cup of water appeared in front of his face, and he snatched at it gratefully. Drinking didn't quite rid the saltiness from his mouth, but it stopped him wanting to vomit.

"Told you the stuff is awful."

He wiped his chin, his mouth twisting. "And I really have to drink this weekly?"

"For starters. The longer you're here, the more you need to have."

He stood, drying his fingers on his trousers. "So we're done?"

"We're done. Head to the training gym. Someone there will take you under their wing."

He extended his hand and, after a slight hesitation,

she clasped it.

"Thanks Celine, I guess I'll see you next week."

The shadow flicked over her face again and although she smiled, the lines around her eyes tightened. "Sure will."

He searched her face but the twinkle came back into her eyes, and he told himself to stop imagining things.

"Behave until then, Mr. Hunter."

"I'll try."

The door closed behind him and he scanned the corridor. He always thought he had a strong sense of direction. But this place meandered like a maze, and everything looked the same. He turned left and hoped for the best. Hope died when he reached a dead end. Grimacing, he turned to head back the other way. A door opened, and a disturbing sound between a shriek and a shout escaped. He froze as a voice rode over the sounds of distress.

"There's no need for the fuss, this will be over soon. Clark, make sure you record all reactions."

The bare hallway held no places to hide, and he tried to figure out if he should look the other way or what. The noise increased, and the person holding the door let go and it shut, cutting off whatever happened inside.

Evan headed the other way, keeping his footsteps light. The positive vibes he'd left the clinic with faded.

What the hell have I got myself into?

Chapter Ten

Long ropes hung from the ceiling in the cavernous training room. Two men wrestled in one corner. One threw the other off the mats and onto the padding beneath the gymnastic equipment. So mundane, so familiar. All of this seemed a world away from the creepy screams in the medical center. *Maybe I imagined it.* But deep inside sank the certainty he hadn't.

At least the water wasn't visible from here. The longer the cheerful focus of the men and women training washed around him, the more he relaxed. Unlike the clear plexiglass with dark water fighting to seep inside, this he understood. He stretched his shoulders. Char landed on the mat from the vault, wiped her brow and waved at him with a grin. He waved back and headed in her direction.

Four men stepped into his way. Evan stopped and crossed his arms. *Ridiculous. Like some little kids on the playground.* He stared them down, not trying hard to stop his lip from curling.

Silence spread around them as people broke from their training to gawk. Always the same, wherever you went. Always one jerk who wanted to be the biggest dog in the pack. He'd bet anything this grinning lump never saw active service. Once you'd been under fire, all the posturing became not only unnecessary but dumb.

"So, newbie, think you got what it takes?"

A grin spread on his face. *Newbie. Whatever.* "Wouldn't be here if I didn't."

The guy's jerkwad pal nudged. "Thinks he can challenge you, Blake. Whaddya say? Bit of a contest?"

Blake shrugged with his arms out. "I don't like to take candy from a baby."

Evan chuckled. "Is that supposed to rile me? Being called a baby?"

The men shifted, muscles flexing, and he tried hard not to roll his eyes.

"I'm here to start training. You guys want to piss on lamp-posts, go do it without me."

The smile wiped off Blake's face. "Sounds like you're chicken to me."

Oh man. These jerks wouldn't let it lie. He scanned the room. Everyone was waiting to see what he did.

"Not so much chicken as bored. This what you all do for fun?"

"Scared to show us what you got? Once round the circuit, first one back wins."

He caught Char's gaze and she shrugged. He turned back to Blake and his cronies. "What the hell. Show me the course."

"Up the ropes, swing to the ledge, leap frog down the posts, somersault down to the pad, over the rings, the vault horse. First man at the square chooses gloves or batons."

"A fight at the end of the course?"

"Sparring. Why? Not up to the challenge?"

He swallowed a sigh. "Let's go."

In an unsurprising move, Blake started before the

signal. Evan pulled himself up the ropes at a steady rate and caught up to the other man's scramble with little effort. At the top of the rope a buzzer and light sat in a box in the ceiling. He smashed the buzzer before swinging back to eye the ledge. A little far but he'd made further.

He swung the rope, taking his time, then leaped. He grabbed the edge with his fingers and used his momentum to swing his legs up and over, while Blake scrabbled at the wall below. He shook out his hands, heart thudding in his chest, and scoped out the posts which staggered downward. His arms swinging forward as he jumped, he landed on two feet, knees bent. The next post stood further away and he stumbled a step. Blake caught up, landing next to him.

Two more posts, two more heavy jumps. The final one wobbled, and he paused a moment to catch his breath and his balance. The pad below might be thick but he remembered another place another time and the impact if you fell wrong. Evan centered himself and dove, flipping at the half-way point so he would land on his feet. He straightened and leaped off the pad the same moment Blake lighted on the one next to him.

He sprinted to the rings, feet tapping inside each one in a steady rhythm, muscle memory taking over. His speed placed him in the lead but he pushed himself to race to the vault, taking a flying leap over. He touched down and dove into a somersault, reaching the square as Blake careened over the vault horse.

He panted, heart racing, and licked the sweat from his lip.

Blake stalked into the square. "Well? Gloves or batons?"

"Neither. This is dumb enough as is, hand-to-hand first hit."

Blake nodded, walking the perimeter. He scooped up a baton, a narrow black club spreading out at the end.

"How about no."

He ducked the first swipe, a chorus of hisses coming from those around them. He drove his shoulder into Blake's gut, pushing him backward. The baton crashed down on his back, and he winced but twisted away. A third smash came from his blind side, smacking into his head. Evan rolled with the impact and sprang to his knees, shaking his head to clear his vision. Boos sounded from the bystanders. Blake scowled, eyes flashing. He raised the baton, and Evan steadied himself, ready to jump.

A lithe form appeared behind the soldier. With an almost blurring speed, the woman round-house kicked Blake to the ground, smacking her elbow into his jaw as he fell.

"Ambushing is fun, right?" she said.

Evan stared up at her, wiping blood from his mouth. The blonde from the chow hall. Petite and shorter than expected for a soldier. Maybe Char was right about secret service. White blond hair swung from a high pony-tail. She might be slight and lean but she clearly packed a punch. Blake lay on the floor nursing his jaw, glaring daggers at her, but surprisingly he didn't say anything. Fair enough, Evan wouldn't either.

He brushed away her outstretched hand and pushed to his feet himself, ignoring the pull in his kneecap. Standing, she came up to his shoulder.

"Thanks," he said.

She lifted her chin, pale ice blue eyes ringed with indigo meeting his. "What, no 'Could have fought him myself'?"

He rubbed his elbow and grinned. "Nope. My vision blurred and he doesn't fight fair. The help is appreciated."

A smile tugged at the corner of her lips. This time, when she stretched out her hand, he shook it.

"You can call me Ana."

"Evan."

He became aware of Char at his shoulder, and he shifted to include her. "You know each other, I guess?"

Char's eyes flashed and she lowered her lids. "Sure do. Nice kick, Ana."

The blonde smiled, glancing up at Evan through her lashes. "Doing my part to keep the bullies down."

He sucked in a breath and stepped back, a flush rising on his neck. "Well, thanks again. Perhaps one day we can spar. You can teach me how to be super-fast."

She ran an assessing gaze over him, and he fought down the heat rushing to his cheeks. "You're too big. Best stick to power over speed."

Char snorted. Ana flicked a last smile at him, then strode away. Char dug an elbow into his side.

"Come on, Romeo, let's get you cleaned up."

****

The chow hall filled with the clatter of cutlery and the loud tones of people all trying to speak over each other. Fish lost all appeal after the first few times, but it was food, and his muscles cried out for protein. Char and Khalid kept up a rapid fire banter throughout the meal, and he listened with a smile while scanning the room.

He wondered at first if there would be recruits from other nations, but they all appeared to be from the U.S., no matter how diverse. An undefinable sense of camaraderie threaded through the room, connecting each distinct group together. Except Blake's crew.

At last he saw her. She stood by the coffee machine at the end of the hall, her face screwed up in concentration. He ruffled a hand over his hair, hoping he looked respectable, wishing for a comb.

"You guys want a coffee?"

Char glanced up then over at Ana, and a twinkle lit her deep brown eyes. "Yeah, sounds good. You want me to go fetch it? I don't mind."

He shot up from the table. "Thanks but I got this."

"I'm sure you do," said Khalid into his mug.

Char snickered but Evan ignored them, rubbing at the heat creeping up his neck.

The aroma of capsule coffee hung in a welcoming miasma in the corner of the room. He swiped a cup from the stack on the nearby trolley and strolled to the machine.

"Need some help?"

Ana glanced up, her frown clearing. "This new machine is so confusing! Why don't they use words instead of these symbols?"

He smiled, trying to act nonchalant. "Ah, that would make things too easy!"

She cocked her head, puzzlement falling back on her face, and he cleared his throat.

"I think you select the strength here," he pointed at a plus and minus symbol next to a flashing run of bars, "and the type of coffee here." His finger traced over the different symbols. "I think this is a cappuccino because of the fluff on the top."

She leaned in to squint at the picture. "I thought that was a muffin."

A laugh escaped from his throat but he choked the sound back when she flushed. "It looks like one for sure. I'm not sure I'd be sorry if I got a muffin instead of a coffee."

A smile crept over her face. "I think I might kill someone if that happened."

He grinned back. "A coffee addict, are you?"

"Let's say, don't get in the way of me and my coffee." She pushed the final button and a stream of hot caffeinated water shot into her cup. "Humanity's best invention."

"I'm not disagreeing, but there's one problem. Where'd you hide the bodies in a place like this?"

Her smile froze under wide eyes.

"Hey, sorry. Bad taste?"

She shook herself, much like she was trying to reset. "No, no it's fine. I just—" The machine beeped and picked up her cappuccino. "All yours now!"

Kicking himself, he smiled and pushed a random button. "Cheers. And hey—"

She turned back, her mug cradled between fine hands.

"Thank you again for today. You were pretty amazing."

Heat flared on her cheeks, and she bit her lip as she smiled. "Oh. You're welcome. No trouble at all."

Breath hitched in his throat at the clarity of the blue in her irises. A smile spread over his cheeks as he stared. The aroma of coffee enveloped him. She grimaced and pointed at the machine. His cup overflowed with inky black liquid.

"Oh crap!"

Reproachful beeps rang out as he stabbed at the buttons until water stopped flowing. After snatching some napkins, he mopped up what he could. When he glanced up, she had gone.

Great. He continued to make excellent impressions on her. Wiping his wet fingers on his trousers, he headed back to where Char and Khalid silently applauded him.

Jerks.

Chapter Eleven

Ana turned into the quiet corridor at the far end of the residential quarters. The door to her unit sat tucked away right at the back under a once sputtering light that now never worked. Not that she minded. The shadows surrounding her doorway comforted her, shielding her from curious eyes.

Evan's face flashed into her mind, and she shoved at the door harder than she needed to. Her hand went to her cheek, remembering the heat suffusing her face as his smile twinkled at her. She had blushed. She hadn't known she could.

This is no time to get distracted. Evan might be charming but he's only another soldier. But as she pulled up her computer and started her night's work the words blurred into his smile, his shoulders, and his arms as he pulled himself up the rope in the gym. With a huff, she pushed the computer away, her hands rising to her temples. *Ridiculous. Focus.*

She let her arms fall, drawing her feet up on the chair, hugging her knees to her chest. *He smiled at me as if he liked me.* Others like him noticed her, their gazes roving over her body, and their hands never straying more than once. But so few people liked her. He joked with her. Her brother used to joke with her.

The thought halted her wandering mind with the sudden weight of an anchor. Her mission didn't include mooning over Evan.

Green light lit the welcome logo as she opened the laptop again. What her brother started, she would finish.

Blueprints scrolled on the screen, and she scribbled notes in a red journal retrieved from under her mattress. Positions and locations of hatch points and access ways filled the pages in a messy scrawl.

Her fingers hovered over the keyboard, and she tugged at her lip. In a rush, she typed, "port cities America sightings phenomena."

Result after result came up but she homed in on one she remembered from before. The page loaded, with screen caps of tabloid headlines juxtaposed with charts of figures and graphs relating to warming seas, disturbances in current, and changes in seabed. She scrolled to the end, to the photo of the author, focusing on the caption with his name. Daniel Kim. Her fingers curled into her palm, as if doing so would squeeze out the tension shooting through her.

Coincidence.

She jabbed at the off switch. The screen winked out and darkness swept in. She blinked and things took form again—the shapeless lump of her jacket tossed over the chair back and the hard edges of the steel cabinet. Her pulse pushed at her throat. She jumped onto the bed then leaned over the edge to fumble the night light on.

Rough wool scratched her skin as she pulled a blanket around her shoulders. One day she would conquer the darkness but tonight black thoughts crept around the edges of her mind, searching for an entrance. She kept her gaze on the circle of light on the ceiling and waited for morning.

****

Ana paused at the door to the crowded pool, breathing in the scent of the water. The chlorine of the pool irritated her skin, but the touch of the water was still better than the stagnant air of the Dome she walked through every day.

Shouted instructions bounced off the high ceiling. She tuned them out, heading straight to the edge and diving. Barely a ripple surrounded her as she closed her eyes against the sting of the chemicals, trusting her sense of direction.

She rose up a half length along, and water cascaded down her neck from her ponytail. Wiping drips off her face, she opened her eyes to Blake's smirking face as he leaned back on the edge of the pool, his shoulders above the surface of the water. The purple bruise marring his cheekbone gave her a rippling moment of pleasure.

He stood, flexing his arms, and she didn't hide the curl of her lip.

"Nice of you to join us," he said.

"I've been busy with other duties."

A lurking leer crept over his face, and he darted a glance to the side. "Duties, eh?"

No need to follow where his gaze went. Evan's presence at the other end of the pool acted like a burning light she didn't know how to turn off.

"You need to stay in your own lane, Blake."

A smirk twisted his face, and he pointed to the coil separating the swimming lane from the training section of the pool. "I'm in the right place. Are you?"

The question hit home in a way he couldn't have

intended. This time when she dove under the water she kicked her legs hard and sprayed water into his face.

Two laps in, her shoulders loosened in the welcoming embrace of the water, and she swam over to the others. One group of about eight sat underwater, weights on their arms, holding their breath for incrementally longer periods. Another group practiced combat moves in the resistance of the water. A sergeant paced the side of the pool, barking insults and instructions in equal measure. She grinned as the sergeant arrowed in on Blake.

"Don't dick around in the water. This isn't synchronized swimming, ladies. This ain't kiddie hour at the local pool. What, are you playing chicken, Blake? When you babies are out there in the ocean, there's things that'll make you piss your pants. Better get used to it now."

Her grin faded. The sergeant was more accurate than he realized. Hanging her arms on the stone edging, she checked in with the instructor. Evan kept drawing her gaze as he ducked and weaved, sparring against Khalid. Water streamed over lean muscles, and he powered through the churning wake to land several accurate hits.

Char darted over and grabbed a water bottle from the stash near the ladder. "Put your eyes back in before they fall out."

Heat flashed over her cheeks. She fought the urge to duck under the water. "I'm observing. Watching the strategy. It's an important part of my research."

"Okay, sure."

She glanced at Char, who grinned around the sipper of the bottle.

"How's your sparring going? I heard you won the last round."

Char tossed the bottle to the trainer. "Yep, last three rounds. Want to try me?"

Prickles ran up her neck but the other woman's playful expression relaxed her. Something else she didn't expect here.

"Why not?"

They moved into the center of the pool, and she beckoned Char, who grinned and jabbed a hit.

She kept her movements contained, pulling back on the power until she judged the other woman's strength. Char fought well, moving *with* the water not against it. Well-defined arms rippled in fluid motions. Ana ducked a jab from the right and coiled through the water to come up on the other side. Char spun, water rippling away from her. Ana smiled. Playing was fun. She feinted to the left then the right. Char expected the feint and blocked the hit but not Ana's leg wrapping around her knee and yanking her forward, off balance and under the surface.

Ana scanned the water, anticipating the rising attack. When Char shot out of the water, Ana jerked to the side, water spraying, and chopped down at her opponent's outstretched arm with the side of her hand. The other woman collapsed under the impact and raised her other hand.

"Yield!"

She wiped chemical scented water from her face as a grin tugged at her cheeks.

"Thanks for the bout," she said.

Char grinned as she held out her hand and clasped her forearm. "No, thank *you*, I enjoyed myself."

There were shouts from behind. A crowd gathered, celebrating someone's long count underwater. She exchanged a glance with Char, and they swam toward the fuss. A woman rose from underwater and passed over a weighted belt to a trainer, beaming at her record time.

Evan stepped up next and Ana's heart skipped a beat. His muscles flexed in a ripple of water-soaked skin as he accepted the weights from the instructor. He shook his head a little, blinking, and she frowned. Their gazes met, and electric shocks tingled over her skin. Ridiculous, she didn't even know him. But her glance lingered, caught by an invisible thread connecting them together.

The man next to him prodded him toward where a painted circle lay on the bottom of the pool. He inhaled deeply and ducked under the surface, clear water closing over his hair and ripples spreading as he sank.

She bit her lip and focused on his still form under the water. The little shake of his head kept playing in her head, the blinking to clear a foggy mind. He'd been training hard, boxing. She scanned the faces until her gaze lit on Blake. His jaw clenched tight, and he glared at Evan's wavering shape under the water. He didn't like being shown up. Had they fought again today?

Evan stayed underwater. Cheers and hollers of encouragement beat at her ears. Anxiety threaded a dark coil through her veins. The voice in her head shouted at her, and she stepped toward the middle of the ring.

"How long has he been under?"

"Four minutes and some." Char's voice was clipped, a frown between her brows. "I don't think he's all right."

She ducked under, swimming down to his seated form, weights on his lap, his arms floating out by his side. Jagged rips, like shells on skin, tore through her chest, and she kicked faster.

Treading water, she reached out to cup his face. When he didn't respond, instinct took over. She bent her face down and fastened her mouth on his. Soft lips opened and she blew air into him. His chest lay hard beneath her hand, and she didn't feel it rise with her breath. Bubbles escaped and she pressed closer, trying to stop them leaking, her heart racing.

Her eyes wanted to shut against the sting of the chlorine but she kept them open and fixed on his. When his lids flew open and his lungs inflated under her hand, she waited a moment more, giving him the last of her air. His mouth moved under her lips, sparking her blood, and his eyes widened. She tugged him up, kicking off the weights, pulling him to the surface.

Helping hands grabbed him, lifted him out of the pool. She hooked her arm around the plastic coil divider. A medic checked him out, pushing his hair aside, exposing a welt on his temple. His gaze didn't leave hers and something shone in his eyes. He almost drowned before the sub found him.

She wondered, not for the first time, how he survived.

Chapter Twelve

Evan ducked his head and stepped into the tiny submersible. A whole month of training and he still couldn't get used to these hobbit holes where everything existed lower and smaller than it should be. His chest tightened and his breathing shallowed. Snatching onto the thought patterns his VA therapist gave him, he controlled his panicked breathing. He focused on the feel of the metal beneath his fingers, chilled and humming with the engine, and counted five things he could hear, five things he could see.

Ana walked in behind him, a perfect size for the sub with no need to duck. She shot him a glance as she squeezed past, and his face warmed. Clearly he didn't hide stress as well as he hoped.

Esther waved at him from the pilot seat as Khalid maneuvred himself into the copilot chair. He strapped himself into the space opposite Char and Ana, bumping fists with the man next to him. Hudson? Something like that.

"Don't worry, man," Hudson said, "it's weird the first time you're in one of these bugs, but Esther's the real deal when it comes to driving them."

"Piloting…"

Hudson winked at Evan. "She doesn't like me talking about her driving."

"I swear to God, Hudson, you make one more

sexist joke, and I'm kicking your ass out to the sharks."

The man leaned back, a grin splitting his face. "You know you love me really."

"Yeah, you and your ego are taking up too much room. Might need to—"

Evan tuned out, letting the familiar banter wash over him as water closed over the bubble of glass, and beams of light spread in front of them. The doors slid open, and the mini sub jetted out into the ocean.

Lit in patches from their headlights, the depths held shadows and shifting movement that scraped at his nerves. Evan huffed out a breath, his hands tightening on the harness straps. He glanced at Hudson who cradled one of the underwater guns, the ADS amphibious rifle looking alien and futuristic. No one explained why they needed weapons under the ocean. His own smaller gun sat heavy in the holster on his thigh.

They'd said this was a patrol, a routine check on the waters to make sure nobody was out there who shouldn't be. His thoughts flashed to Dan and he shifted in his seat. His trousers caught on the metal and he frowned. Char had shrugged when he asked why they weren't wearing wetsuits and told him he'd get used to it. His frown threatened to turn to a scowl.

More secret super-soldier crap.

Across from him, Ana leaned back and stared through the roof of the small dome. The inky depths reflected in her eyes, turning the bright blue to almost green. Heat flushed his cheeks at the remembered softness of her mouth as she blew air into his lungs, the way he roused to her lips on his. He tore his gaze away. Char's brows lifted over a twisted smirk. She made a

74

kissy face at him, and he pressed his mouth on a smile and turned away.

He focused through the water streaming past them as the sub chugged along what must be the perimeter. Massive boulders littered the ocean floor.

Hudson nudged him. "Crazy landscape down here right?"

The sub skimmed the base of one of the outcroppings of oyster encrusted rock.

"Sure is."

"Like a giant played skipping stones with mountains," Char said, flushing as he quirked a brow at her. "What? Just because you guys don't read doesn't mean I can't be poetic if I want."

He tried to take in as much of the bizarre underwater landscape as possible. Being able to pinpoint the Dome on a map would be useful.

If I ever get out.

Evan shifted on his seat, reaching down to fiddle with a buckle on his boot to cover the discomfort. Foolish. Of course he would. He signed an ordinary contract, a term of service, not something mysterious in blood. He would do his time, his part for a higher cause, and then go home. Setting his shoulders back, he pushed away the nagging questions. These were good people.

Esther brought the sub-bug to a halt, hovering in a swirl of bubbly wake.

"Tanks on, fishies," she said, gesturing over her shoulder at the oxygen tanks lining the wall of the sub.

Evan grinned at Khalid, wondering at the shadow passing over Ana's face.

Securing his earpiece and adjusting the

mouthpiece, he stood in line to exit the airlock. He braced against the ice-bath shock as swirling water soaked through his clothes.

The current pulled at his trousers, dragging at the holster. His muscles burned as he treaded water. As they sank lower to the sea bed, the chill seeped through fabric and skin, settling into his bones. Super soldiers be fucked. This shit was cold without a wetsuit. Esther's voice buzzed in his ear, the tin-like tones of the earpiece reassuringly familiar.

"Char, take point. Khalid at the back. Hudson to the west, and Evan, since this is your first time on patrol, Ana will show you the ropes."

He ignored Khalid's brows waggling above his goggles. At least the cold water hid the heat rising in his face. His friends shot off, cutting through the water as if the dragging weight of their uniforms was nothing. Ana gestured for him to follow and swam off.

She glided through the water with smooth effortless strokes. He pulled himself after her, his shoulders complaining. As they went deeper, the water darkened, despite the fact it appeared shallower at this point than where the Dome sat. The seabed rose and fell in swells of sand and stone beneath them. Shoals of fish veered out of their way as the beams of their flashlights hit them, darting through patches of waving seaweed lying scattered like overgrown gardens.

The drag of his clothes, the chill of the water, and the awkwardness of swimming without fins, all faded. For the first time, he saw this underwater realm as more than an obstacle. Joy could be found here also. Ana's legs kicked out and she dove. He changed course and followed.

Movement caught the corner of his vision and he tensed. Sharks might leave them alone but he pulled ahead to be in front of Ana, regardless. She turned to him, her eyes flashing through the goggles. He pointed to where a section of kelp still waved against the movement of the rest. Bubbles drifted between them as she breathed out, hiding her face. She shook her head, her braid floating in the current. He couldn't tell if she was saying nothing was there or she didn't want to check. Frustration licked at the edge of his mind. The helmet might have a built in microphone but either his wasn't working or they were a piece of crap.

A buzzing sounded in his earpiece—Esther's voice shouting a warning. Adrenaline spiked through him. He swung round in the water, bubbles rushing over his head. A little distance away, Khalid struggled, trying to rip off some kind of snaring weed tethering him to one of the overhanging boulders on the seabed. A stream of bubbles shot from his detached oxygen tank.

Evan swam toward him, cutting through the water as Khalid's movements grew more feeble. Chills raced through Evan's blood. *Not another one lost. Not if I can help it.*

The sub maneuvred closer, but the air from the rotors swirled up sand from the seabed, and Esther cut the engine.

Darting past him, Ana tore off her mask and held it to Khalid's mouth. Evan caught up to them and snatched at the knife as she passed him. His pulse thundered in his ears as he hacked at the weed, tangled and knotted. A half-forgotten image flashed into his mind—the village they stayed at, going with the elder as he checked his snares, heavy fiber woven into loops.

He frowned.

No, these couldn't be snares. The weeds must grow that way. He sliced through the last knot and glanced up as Ana pulled Khalid out. She swam with him toward the sub. He breathed out a stream of bubbles. Ana must've swapped the mouthpiece back again or she had better breath control than him.

He stared at the rock, the weeds at the bottom waving in the currents. His fingers clutched the tangle of weed that appeared too much like a snare for comfort. Coincidence.

A hand touched his shoulder and he jerked back, feet pushing at the water. Char lifted her hands palm out, eyes showing white behind the goggles. He lowered the knife, his heartbeat thudding in his throat. She scanned the boulder, the weeds, and her jaw tightened around the mouthpiece, her cheekbones standing out. Tugging at his arm, she jerked her head toward the sub-bug.

He opened his fingers, letting the current take the snared weed. His skin crawled and he stared into the shadows. Something moved, then stilled. Char tapped him on the arm again, and he followed her to the sub. The sensation of being watched followed him the whole way.

They filtered in, one by one through the air lock. Evan waited until the end. Khalid lay propped against the wall, a mask on his face and Hudson checking his pulse. Esther punched at the controls and turned the sub back to the Dome. She and Char shared a glance, tight lines framing their eyes. Ana sat with her knees up to her chest, biting her thumbnail, a frown settling on her brow.

Evan stooped and padded over to Khalid, laying a hand on his shoulder, relief flooding him as the other man's eyes fluttered open. He tightened his grip for a second, then straightened as much as the cramped roof would allow. Avoiding Ana, he sank into a seat on the other side of the sub.

He stared at his hands the whole journey back to the Dome. Heavy wet fabric clung to his body, and he shivered despite the heating in the sub turning the enclosed space into a sauna.

The uplifting sense of camaraderie from the last few days bled away, leaving chilled suspicion behind. White marks lined his hands from where his grip cut off the blood. He eased up a little, and as the blood seeped back, he thought of shifting kelp, watching eyes, and a half-remembered sensation of arms lifting him out of the water.

Something had been out there, and no one would talk about it.

Chapter Thirteen

Evan left Khalid recovering in the sickbay and joined the rest of the crew in the training room. Khalid had laughed off his questions, blaming himself for getting caught in the weeds. But the red marks on his skin left doubts lingering in Evan's mind.

A range of different height posts dotted the back of the room. Ana stood in horse stance, balanced between two posts. He tore his gaze from her and joined Char. Some sparring would hopefully bleed out some of the tension pulling at his chest.

Char grinned and flicked her hand at him. "Come on, devil dog."

He lunged and she dodged, spinning back at the same time as a shout rang out. The post Ana stood on had split at the base. The loosened post wavered and shuddered as she sought to keep her balance. He stepped forward, colliding with Char's outflung arm.

"Wait, Evan, there isn't anything you can do. Ana's tough, she'll make the jump."

He shook off her hand and ran forward. Ana met his gaze, her own wide open. She bent her legs and jumped from the top, landing with a roll. The post tumbled down, smashing into a stand of weights. Dumbbells and metal bars spun and clattered across the floor.

Reverberations thundered through his head and he

flinched, shaking as if he could clear away the echoes. The air shimmered in a haze of heat and silver steel transformed into sand and brick. Shouting voices turned into harsh battlefield calls and grunts. Evan hunkered down behind the broken wall, sweat tracking lines in the dust caking his skin.

Trapped.

The only way out of the street was the way they came in. Cadavers of buildings spilled on the road behind them, blocking escape.

"Where the hell is air support?"

"Cover!"

"Sniper on the left!"

He rolled to the edge of the bricks, tattered knee guards pressing into shards of glass, sighting down the AK-57. A spray of bullets ripped through metal and mortar. The returning gunfire died from the left, but the rebels circled round the other side.

Concrete exploded in a fountain of blood-soaked powder, and Sajeed screamed as a grenade blew off his leg. They dragged him to the side, tourniquet out, motions mechanical, as the shock set in. Engines sounded in the sky. A grim smile cracked the grime on Evan's cheeks.

"Finally. Birds in the air."

Billy "Bosun" Chase grinned back, adjusting the strap under his chin. With a start, his eyes widened, horror freezing the lines of his face. Evan wheeled around. The door on the other side of the street creaked open and a woman, dusky pink scarf held up to her mouth, cast a glance around the square. A child, then another, and another, piled out behind her. Holding hands. A long line. Everyone gripping their buddy tight.

"There aren't supposed to be any schools in this area! Sam, radio control and tell them to abort!"

The whine of the planes grew louder, and the woman stared at the sky, then back at the older girl who closed the door and grasped the hand of the last pre-schooler. They started running as fast as toddler legs could go.

"Abort, damn them!"

"They say no. Destroying the cell is prime directive. Collateral damage will be minimal."

Collateral damage. The hell with that. He pushed to his feet, and the girl at the back startled, shoving with frantic rapid pats on the back of the small boy in front of her. His little sandals kicked up dirt. Evan waved his arm and pointed at the sky, yelling at them to run. The girl scooped up the little boy and dragged another child along by her shoulder.

Silence surrounded them. Big eyes full of fear stared back at him over the girl's shoulder but the boy made no sound as bombs rained down with precision on the street.

Screams. Dust. Fallen masonry.

Bosun shouted at him, pulling on his arm until he collapsed to the shattered concrete, the child's dead accusing eyes filling his vision.

He came to in the middle of the training hall, on his knees, sweat soaking his t-shirt, fingers cramped from gripping vise-like on someone's arms. Char. She knelt in front of him, her quiet words a mantra he clung to.

"It's okay. I got you. It's okay."

He let go and collapsed on the floor, drawing his legs up to his chest and resting his head in his hands as he focused on breathing.

Ana's voice came from over his shoulder, and her light touch on his hair sent shame spiralling through him.

"What's wrong with him?"

"Flashback. Lots of us get them. This one seemed bad."

He risked a glance up. The room was empty save for the two women.

"Thanks. For, well, y'know."

Char clasped his shoulder, her brown eyes warm in the shadows. "No biggie. Happens to all of us."

His gaze fell to the floor again. Ridiculous to feel shame, but hot embarrassment spiralled through him in a sick wave anyway.

"Yeah, but I thought I got past them."

"Oh man, I don't know about you, but I doubt we'll ever make it past those suckers."

She stood and he focused on her shoes, the white sport socks with the cartoon characters another little way she held onto herself. He didn't think he had much self to hold on to anymore.

"Can you stay with him? I'll fetch some water."

Ana's murmured assent settled on his hunched back. Char's footsteps echoed on the wooden floor, and he gripped his hands tighter.

Ana moved away for a moment, and he fought against a sense of abandonment. When she returned, she knelt next to him, and a dark towel entered his vision.

"Here. For the sweat."

Evan accepted it with a grateful mumble and buried his face in the soft fabric before rubbing his hair and the back of his neck. He draped it around his shoulders and darted a glance at her.

"Are you okay? After the posts, I mean. Did you hurt yourself?"

She shook her head. "I'm fine." Her eyes stretched into pools of an emotion he couldn't quite name. "What do you see? When you have one of these flashbacks."

He sucked in a breath. This more than anything made it clear she hadn't served. You took for granted everyone wrestled with demons, and you didn't ask them to name them. Something of this must've shown in his expression. A blush crept on her cheeks and she bit her lip.

"Sorry. I just wondered."

"Oh hey, it's okay. You surprised me, that's all."

A hint of a smile glinted in her blue eyes. "You surprised me. I always thought of soldiers as without feelings, but your feelings seem so large."

He fidgeted with the end of the towel. "I don't know what kind of soldiers you hang out with." He thought of Cody Blake and his ilk. "Yeah, there are some sociopaths but the rest of us have emotions the same as everyone else."

The blush crept back and she stared down at her feet. "Sorry. I said the wrong thing again."

"Don't worry about it."

Her hair escaped from her ponytail, light strands falling over her face. With a grunt, he pushed himself up, drawing the towel from around him.

"I'll wash this for you. Thanks."

She scrambled to her feet. "I didn't do anything, except pry."

Her face closed down. She looked so frail and small he found himself pausing, words pushing at his lips.

"The children."

She froze a moment before lifting her gaze to his face. He reached out and tucked the escapee locks of hair behind her ears. He didn't know why he told her, but the words had been released now and wouldn't be stopped.

"Sometimes the old people, or the young soldier with his face shot off, or my friends sprawled on a road I couldn't get to in time. But mostly I see the children. Every time a flashback finishes, I wonder if I could've done something else if only I'd been faster. But I wasn't. And they died."

"I'm sorry."

He waved his hand, glad it didn't tremble. "Don't be. Not your fault. Besides, I'm the one who's still here. The least I can do is remember them."

She stepped closer, her head tilted to gaze up into his face, her eyes intent and shining. "I've witnessed your bravery but now I see your compassion."

A flush spread up his neck. His gaze fell to her lips, full and inviting. He leaned down, his hand brushing against her arm, but he jerked away as the door banged open.

"Sorry it took me so long, Khalid waylaid me with some story about—" Char's voice cut off and he pasted on a smile.

"Thanks, I'm all good now. Better go, get a shower before chow." He picked up the water bottle from her outstretched hand and on impulse, gave her a quick hug around the shoulders. "I meant what I said, thank you."

She smiled at him but her gaze slid to Ana standing behind them.

He headed to his quarters, blue eyes tangling with the darkness in his head.

Chapter Fourteen

Early rising for a new morning duty turned out to be enjoyable. Breakfast still tasted like cardboard but hot and fresh cardboard. Silent anticipation filled the Dome as it waited for people to wake, fill the halls with clomping footsteps and the never-ending hum of chatter.

Evan licked the final bit of knock-off butter from his fingers before chugging back tepid coffee. He eyed Hudson. The man's usually cheerful expression lay flat and sullen, with heavy lines tugging at his brow. *Not a morning person then.*

"I haven't been to Area 8 before. Have you?"

Hudson glanced at him before staring at his toast, stabbing at the plate with his fork. "Couple times."

Definitely not a morning person. "Right." Evan swallowed his questions with the dregs of his coffee and rose to his feet. "Best get going, you think?"

Hudson grunted but swiped his breakfast tray off the table and headed to the counter.

Evan flashed a smile at the cooks as he walked out the door. One waved back with a grin. So many friendly people. So many things staying hidden beneath the surface. He grimaced and followed Hudson toward Area 8.

Tanks filled the space from floor to ceiling. Pipes filtering the sea water and siphoning out the oxygen bound them together in a massive network. He'd seen similar things on some larger submarines but the monstrosity of these metal beasts stole his breath. He stood, gaping, until a book slammed into his chest and he snatched at the ruffled pages before it fell to the floor.

"What's this?"

"Homework."

"Oh man, and here I thought I escaped school."

"Funny guy." Hudson patted one of the tanks. "These here are the heart of the Dome. Without these, we all die a slow horrible death."

"Oh. Good to know."

Hudson chuckled, and Evan grinned at his lightened expression.

"Yup. Hope you're ready for the responsibility. Maintenance might be boring but in this case it's the difference between life or death."

"Yeah, I've never been great with responsibility."

He thumbed through the book, eyes glazing at the pages of specs and complex instructions. With a sigh, he folded the manual into a fat wedge and shoved in his back pocket. "How about you tell me what to do."

Hudson motioned him to follow and strolled to a large cabinet filled with gauges and switches. "This is the place to start."

Every instruction, every turn of each dial soaked into Evan's brain. He repeated the instructions in his head, willing himself to remember.

The next few hours were filled with switches and the soothing hum of machines, and a good amount of banter. Hudson was good company, despite the cloud still marring his expression, and Evan found himself relaxing into the rhythm of the maintenance checks.

A soft chuckle came from the doorway, and he glanced over to see Cody Blake. His buzzcut appeared fresh, and his face red and scrubbed, like he just got up. Evan straightened and stared him down.

Blake leaned on the frame of the door, arms crossed and lips curled in a sneer. The idiot wore toughness like a kid wore a monster costume; both believed they scared people, and both were wrong.

"A little bird told me about your new role, Hudson," Blake said. "Should've read the contract. Hope you've written your will."

Evan frowned. *What the hell?* He stared at Hudson whose brows lowered over darkening eyes.

"Back off, Blake," Evan said.

A muscle twitched in the other man's jaw. "Wasn't talking to you, Hunter."

"You should be keeping your jerk mouth shut, full stop."

Blake pushed off the wall and squared up in front of him. "Your girlfriend isn't here to protect you, still want to mouth off?"

He smiled. "Not my girlfriend. If you ask me, she didn't so much step in to help me as she snatched the opportunity to teach you a lesson."

Hudson gripped his shoulder, an unmistakable signal to shut up. Evan raised his hands and stepped back. Not his fight.

Hudson stood in front of Blake, not quite nose-to-nose but close. "He's right, you're a jerk. You're also a waste of time and space, so clear out and let us do our jobs."

The smirk slid back on Blake's face. "Don't like to

argue with a condemned man."

Hudson's hand shot out and grabbed Blake around the neck slamming him against the wall. "Fuck you."

Blake tugged on Hudson's grip, his scowl deepening and his voice rasping out, "Not my fault you didn't read the contract."

The pulse thudded in Blake's forehead. He'd step in if necessary but this was Hudson's deal.

"Get out." Hudson released Blake and stepped back, wiping his hands.

Blake drew a ragged breath and rubbed at his neck. "You're lucky you won't be coming back."

Hudson flipped him the bird, and he pushed out the door. Evan crossed his arms, frowning at Hudson.

"What did he mean, about the contract, and all the condemned bullshit?"

Hudson sighed, rubbing the sweat from his shiny head. "Did you read the contract before you signed?"

"Of course."

The other man's glance found his, an eyebrow raised in scepticism.

"All right," Evan said. "I skimmed, sue me. Does anyone ever read each section?"

"If they're still here, you can guarantee they didn't."

The carved lines around Hudson's mouth drove chills through Evan's veins. "This doesn't sound positive."

"Let's say I'm not surprised Blake talked about drawing up my will."

"Jesus, Hudson, what the hell will they make you do?"

The other man's jaw tightened and his eyes

darkened. "Not the best idea to talk about it. What can you do, right? Got us over a barrel."

Whatever this was about, the man had to fight back. "Contracts can be broken. They're broken all the time."

Hudson shrank in front of him, his shoulders caving in. "Not these ones. It's probably all drama, I'm sure it'll be fine." He looked up at Evan. "But if it isn't, can you give this to Esther? She'll know what to do." He passed him a small envelope, bare but for the name Shelley.

Evan turned the thin paper over between his fingers, a chill spiking into his chest and his pulse thundering as his mouth moved on automatic. "Sure. No problem."

The envelope slid into the pocket not stuffed full of manual. He pressed his mouth closed on the questions pushing to escape. A shutter like iron covered Hudson's face.

Maybe it was some kind of underwater thing, like the bends. Maybe Hudson hadn't been taking those rank vitamins. Maybe it was all some medical issue that could be fixed. Maybe something worse.

Following the other man back to the gauges, he stumbled as the building vibrated, massive thumps echoing through the wall. Loud shrilling tones of an alarm cut through the silence. Dials spun as the pressure dropped without warning.

"What the crap?"

Hudson grabbed his shoulder and dragged him at a trot to the other side of the array. Cracks appeared in one of the pipes.

"Shit."

Hudson flipped out the radio from his belt and contacted engineering. "We have a breach in Tank Array 5. We need divers outside, now."

Another thump echoed through the air, and the floor shuddered.

"What the hell is happening, Hudson?"

"We need to let some of the pressure out. Reroute it. There's been damage to the outer array leading to a feedback loop in here."

Water hissed out of one of the pipes closest to them.

"Holy shit! That doesn't look good."

Hudson pointed at a small cabinet recessed into the wall. "Should be duct tape and tools in there."

He ran over and wrenched open the cupboard. He threw the tape at Hudson, who snatched the loop out of the air. Rummaging around in the dark space, he withdrew a clanking bag and raced back, opening the zipper as he went.

"None of this will be any use if we can't fix the pressure."

"There must be a failsafe, a safety valve?"

"Got destroyed a couple weeks ago. We're waiting on replacements."

"Destroyed how?"

Hudson swore and sucked at a burned finger, then held his hand out for a wrench. Evan handed him the tool, swapping for the tape. He raced over to a hissing hose and ripped at the tape with his teeth. Then wound black around the seam where the hose met the metal.

One down.

Clanks and curses floated through the air, competing with the whine of metal under stress. The next pipe rattled in a rising cacophony, water bubbling through the welded spaces. He shook his head and wrapped tape around and around, his hands juddering as water built up with nowhere to escape.

He followed the clicks and screeches, tracking the sound growing in intensity. The dials over this tank screamed into the red.

"Hudson! I think I found a starting point!"

More clanks as Hudson tripped over the bag of tools in his haste. His face turned to granite, and he stared at the dial.

"That bad, huh?"

The radio beeped, and Evan fished it off his hip, passing it to Hudson. The thunder and clangs of the pipes obscured the noise; but Hudson held the speaker up to his ear, his finger pressed tight in his other ear, and his face relaxed.

"Roger that." He clipped the radio to his belt and flashed a smile at Evan. "They fixed the external problem. The situation should settle down soon."

Evan taped up the hoses, relishing the increasing quiet as the hissing faded into condensation. When the final hiss and rattle left silence behind, they tossed the tools back in the cupboard and Hudson grimaced.

"Seems about right this shit would happen at the end of our shift, not on the next."

Following smart on the heels of his grumbling, the door opened and their replacements arrived.

Hudson shook hands with one of the new guys and gestured at the room. "This mess is all yours. I'll ask Mac to send some of his engineering crew down for a proper service."

The two of them walked past the replacement crew

into the corridor and the door closed with a dull thunk. Evan wiped sweat off his face and shook a hand through clammy hair.

"Talk about better workplace stories."

Hudson chuckled, rolling his shoulders back. "We've never had such a drama before. Must be your influence."

"Yeah, sure." His smile faded and his thoughts went to the thuds, the shaking floor. "I still don't understand how this happened in the first place."

Hudson eyed him sidelong. "I forget you've not been here long." He tossed the bag back to Evan before setting off down the hall. "Damn fish grow big around here."

Chapter Fifteen

Ana strode down the corridor, dry musty air catching in her throat and her nerves prickling under her skin. Her ponytail swung as she wheeled round the corner to the docking bay—a smaller one, seldom used. Casting a glance around, she slipped out a swipe card and opened the door. After closing it behind her, she leaned her back on the metal and breathed until her chest expanded.

Salt. Seaweed. The tang of stale ocean air.

She bit her lip as a smile spread. The prickle under her skin turned to a burning fever, and she yanked her t-shirt over her head. After fumbling at her belt, she kicked her boots off and stripped. Her skin breathed in the sea air like the sand soaked up the tide.

Holding the amulet around her neck, she padded down the metal ramp into the water. Her skin shifted and glistened. She arched her back in delight and dove forward into the dark depths.

Human legs fused, and shining luminescent scales rippled upward as her tail reappeared. Streaming fins floated behind her like the plumage of the birds the pirates loved. She pulled the band off her ponytail and slipped the elastic around her wrist for later. Humans were right. Those things disappeared. Her hair floated out in a sheaf of white.

She rolled and twirled and flipped through a drift

of bubbles. Her gills opened as if to take in as much as possible, everything her human form denied them.

Sliding through the water, she closed her eyes and listened. Echoes in the currents, the high pitched whistle of a dolphin, and nearer, the soft murmur of someone circling in the waves. Her eyes opened, glancing to the side. Her hands flexed, and a dull glow appeared between her fingers. Electricity coursed through her arms. Twisting her tail she spun, hair floating around her and her hands outstretched.

"It's only me."

She drew her hands back, curling her fingers over the glow until it vanished.

"Sister. You're too sneaky for your own good. One day I'll zap you."

Amatheia laughed and bubbles spiralled upward. She pushed her hair from her face, the indigo streaks richer in tone under the water, as changeable as a Badis.

"You'd have to catch me first."

Light swirled around her arms, and she raised her brows, a smile teasing at her lips. *"Do you really want to test me?"*

"We both know who would win, little sister."

She let the energy dissipate into the tide. *"I can't stay out for long, but the ocean called to me."*

Amatheia zigzagged to her side, her hand soft on Ana's cheek. *"Sariana, I am glad you came. Too long without the sea is harmful, and the council has waited a long while to hear from you."*

Lead sank into her tail, dragging it down as her smile faded. *"I don't know how much longer I can do this."*

She leaned into her sister's ready embrace, closing

her eyes to the specter of the missing sibling over Amatheia's shoulder. Amatheia pulled away and swept her hair off her face.

"Are you ready?"

She summoned up a smile. *"More than you, anyway."*

Amatheia swam alongside her as the water parted in front of them. A kelp forest waved in the current, and she eyed her sister in a challenge. A spark lit in Amatheia's eyes. Iridescent hues shimmered down her scales and she darted off.

Joy filled Sariana like the bubbles her sister left in her wake. She tossed her head, and small fins sprang out at the side of her neck and down the back of her arms. Her own rippling colors weren't as bright as Amatheia's; they had always been a deeper tone. She stared at the newer deeper crimson blending to the color of dark blood. A flip of her tail and she dragged her gaze away from the dark streaks. It didn't mean anything.

Zipping through waving fronds, she let her fingers trail through the water, the webbing allowing small movements to redirect her body.

Amatheia was nowhere in sight, and Sariana pulled up, her body moving in small waves to keep her in one place. She searched sidelong through her floating hair and caught a glimpse of bright red and purple. Rolling into a dive, she headed down before shooting upward, surprising her sister in an ambush.

They tumbled in a tangle of tails and fins, bubbles tickling her skin.

When at last they righted, her sister smiled, silver eyes warm with affection.

"I enjoyed our play, sister, but the council is waiting."

She drew back, chills running over her scales, her tail whipping the water. *"Let them wait."*

Amatheia's head cocked and she frowned. *"Don't be silly. They place a lot of trust in you."*

The thought of the council members and their sanctimonious faces sparked a dark inky anger inside her. Not a hot rage this, more a cold loathing.

"I can't forgive them."

Amatheia's tail waved gently in the current, her face softening. *"You don't need to. You don't do this for them, Sariana, you do this for all of us."*

Ana followed her sister toward the rocky outcrop hiding the enclave, the words like oyster shells in her skin.

I'm doing this for myself, for my own peace. But swimming after her sister brought back too many childhood memories. The specter of their missing brother loomed in a shadow that never left her.

Pillars rose from the massive platform jutting out over the cavern in the seabed. Lights fluttered below but she turned away from them. Far too long since she'd called the caves and crannies home.

The enclave council lounged on wide benches carved from sandstone, still except for the gentle rocking of the current. The same intricate carvings decorating the benches wound their way up the columns. She searched for her childhood favorite, the mermaid saving the sailor. Her eyes narrowed. Times changed.

Her sister's mate raised an arm in greeting. She stared over his head. Myrndir had been one who agreed to let Baruthial speak to the humans, to make an arrangement with them. He'd been one of the first to search for Baru when he vanished, true, but forgiveness came hard.

Her brother's face swam in her mind, his conviction that working together with the humans they could find a way to combat the effects of the warming oceans, a way to survive.

Survival.

They deserved more than a clinging existence like barnacles on the ploughing ship of humanity. She believed in a partnership too, once. But not anymore.

"Sariana, welcome. It has been too long since you came to visit us."

"It's not like I can leave whenever I like."

Amatheia poked her and she tried to still the sharp flapping of her fins, to show more patience, more respect. Even if they didn't deserve it.

"Are they still treating you well? As one of their own?"

"Yes. Nobody suspects." Evan's face swam into her mind, his ridiculous jokes about the coffee machine. *"What of the one who calls herself the Siren? Have you learned any more of her?"*

Her tail shimmered in the water as she shook her head. *"She only speaks to those directly under her. They control the rest. I tried to get them to talk to me."* She thought of Blake, how satisfying it had been when her elbow connected with his face. *"But they aren't very intelligent."*

"What of the procedures? Do they continue?"

She eyed the Mer who spoke. He was old, his long hair rough with kelp and roped with shells, his bone trident displayed notches from at least seven leadership cycles. Contempt soured her tongue with a bitter taste.

"Experiments. Torture. Are those the procedures of which you speak?"

The elder belonged to the group who decided Baruthial should participate in the experiments, find out what they could learn. One of the first to agree Ana should observe as a spy, without offering assistance to the captured mer. Hypocritical whaleson. If justice existed, he would also be at the front of those facing retribution.

Amatheia swam to her side, caution shining in her eyes. Sariana's fins rippled down her back where no one would see, and she plastered on a rueful expression.

"My apologies, councilman. I find the situation difficult, as close to their pain as I am."

"Of course, Sariana."

The questions continued. Pointless. She had nothing more to tell them. Things would continue as they were until the Siren succeeded or the Dome collapsed. Either way, the Mer's way of life would be changed forever. She eyed the fools on the council who had sold out her brother. Until then, she would do what she had to do: complete Baruthial's mission to use the human's knowledge against them.

Then she would wreak vengeance.

Chapter Sixteen

Evan turned, fingers tightening on a cool metal lunch tray laden with steamed fish and rice. People crowded behind him at the serving counter and sat crammed together at the tables. It was like a lead blanket lay over them. There was none of the noise he had become accustomed to. *Subdued. That was the word.* His eyes narrowed.

Several days had passed since he and Hudson had stopped the pipes exploding but he hadn't seen the big guy since. The day after, Evan had turned up for duty, and another crewman had taken Hudson's place. No explanation. Par for the course with this place, but when he thought about Blake's bad taste jokes about wills, his spine crawled.

He tore off a hunk of bread with his teeth and chewed as he strode to the nearest table. Esther raised a mug of coffee and smiled, but darkness hooded her eyes. He liked Esther. She regarded the world with a cynical detachment he appreciated. But today she turned back to her plate and poked at her fish.

He ate half of his before pointing at her untouched food. "You don't like it?"

She grimaced at the pale fillet. "You'd think they'd do something different with the fish after all this time. My mother used to make an amazing Maeuntang, a spicy fish soup. It's not hard." She sighed and laid her fork down. "It's all right. I'm not hungry today."

"Looks like no one is. What's up?"

"Nothing." Lines spread from her mouth and around her eyes.

"Well, that's a lie. What's the deal? Something above my clearance level?"

She eyed him sidelong. "Yeah, let's call it that."

Anger sat in him like a sullen beast. He leashed it. "Not a lot of trust in a place like this."

Her black braid swung forward as she shoved herself up, away from the table. "Word of warning, Evan, because I like you. Don't push too hard for answers. Once you know, you can't pretend anymore."

Bitter coffee warmed his mouth, and he shifted his stare from her departing back to the tables around them. He kept his face immobile while his mind raced. Not everyone ate at the same time. Sometimes duties meant later rotations. But crews often ate together. Which meant more people than Hudson were missing.

The table rocked as Khalid slid his legs under, his tray clattering on the metal top. His face wore the same careful nothingness Evan pasted on his own. *Well, screw this.*

"Seen much of Matthews?"

Khalid choked on his rice, waving his hand at Evan and grabbing at the water cup. "Bro, you got to not startle a guy when he's got a mouthful."

"Doesn't seem a question to startle a guy. I figured I haven't seen him in a few days."

The other man's lips pressed together, and he darted a glance down the table. "Saw him Wednesday. He headed off to medical and research."

"What about Hudson? Same for him?"

Khalid licked his lips, his arm going around his food like a wall. "Probably. I don't think too much about it. Neither should you."

Anger curled in his stomach. Like hell he wouldn't. "I'm not great at doing what I'm told."

Khalid hunched further over his plate. "Seems like a bad habit in a marine."

He leaned back in the chair, the plastic back bending under the pressure. "There's a reason I'm not a marine anymore."

"Newsflash, down here what you are doesn't matter. You sign a contract, and the contract doesn't need you to think, just follow orders."

His hand tightened on his cup as memories of a series of bad orders flickered through his mind. "Not how I play anymore."

Khalid glanced up from his plate at last, brown eyes glinting with a fierce intent. "Evan, seriously, bro, you need to drop this. You think Blake's not looking for one more reason to have a go?"

"Blake can take a flying leap. So can everyone else. I don't like secrets, don't like lies, and I don't follow orders simply because. Not any more."

Khalid's jaw dropped. "Shit. You're serious."

"Dead right I'm serious. I'm fed up with all the mystery. If no one will give me straight answers, I'll go find them myself." He held his friend's gaze, his teeth clenching together.

Khalid wiped his chin and made a smacking sound with his mouth. "Okay, man. But if you scope stuff out, make sure you be careful, a'ight?"

"Only 'cause you asked nicely." He reached out his hand, and Khalid gripped it in a firm shake.

He picked up his plates, raised his brows at Khalid, and headed to the counter and out.

****

He lay in bed for a while, staring at the ceiling. What if Esther and Khalid were right? Knowing something was a wasp's nest should mean you stopped poking. But Hudson's face when Blake taunted him about the contract played over in his mind. Blake mentioned something about a new role and a will, and soon afterward, Hudson vanished. Those thumps too. No one explained or even mentioned the incident that might have left them all without air. He told Char and she only nodded.

Something was up, and medical seemed to be where everything centered. That's where Matthews went, according to Khalid. He remembered the shouts of distress, the strange machines in the medical quarters.

Shifting weeds in the water, and a torn oxygen hose flashed into his mind.

He sat up. *Screw this.* The small clock indicated it was almost midnight. A good time for nefarious deeds.

He pushed off the bed, pulled on his hoodie, then grabbed a flashlight and his key card. If he got caught what was the worst they would do? He squashed Blake's voice yabbering about a contract and the chill fear edging around his mind.

The weekly medicals meant he knew his way around now. Evan sidestepped cameras and stuck to the shadows. But when he couldn't, he strode with measured steps. Walk with purpose and nine times out of ten people assumed you had a right to be where you were.

A keypad sat next to the doors to the center. He rubbed at his chin then shrugged. May as well try. He punched in the code Celine had used to open the secure cabinet in the clinic where they stored the toxic tasting vitamin drink. He held his breath and after a second, the doors slid open. Darkness swallowed him as he strode over the threshold. A bitter scent of pine and something sour hit him, and he screwed up his nose.

Evan walked past the clinic doors, dismissing the rooms beyond as a possible location for mysterious deeds. He headed down the corridor he had walked down by accident his first day here.

The corridor ended in another window. Unlike the viewing platform, no lights studded the base or the strips alongside the glass. On either side of the window, on opposite sides of the passageway, two metal doors filled the wall, the viewing slots bolted shut. He stood for a moment, undecided. A quick glance over his shoulder showed only a dark empty hall. Choosing at random, he tried the handle on the left door. It didn't shift. Not a big surprise.

He contemplated for a second longer before crossing to the other door. This handle didn't move either, but the door did. Someone had left in a hurry, locking but not shutting it properly.

Silence spilled from the room. His pulse returned to normal, and he spread fingers on the door, pushing gently. The dim light from the hallway flowed in behind him, pooling in front of the doorway, not strong enough to chase away the shadows clouding the room. He fumbled for the flashlight in his pocket. The cool beam swept over an aluminium bench at the side of the room closest to him.

His eyes widened at the array of instruments picked out by the light. Clipboards and notebooks sat in neat stacks next to machines with too many dials, squatting unpleasantly against the wall. An empty floor stretched in front of him with a grate embedded in the dipped center of the tiled surface, grooves running toward the iron grid. Four hooks sat on the floor in a rectangle—about the size of a trolley bed—as if to hold said trolley bed in place. His pulse pushed at his throat and he swallowed. Dread curled through him and he tried to ignore it.

They said they're a research facility.

Dark glass filled the back wall of the room. He walked over, dodging to avoid hitting his head on an adjustable hanging lamp, the kind they had in operating theaters. The window reflected back the beam of the flashlight, and he focused on dim shapes in the adjoining room.

Evan clicked his tongue in frustration. The feeble beam struggled to show what hid beyond. He chewed the inside of his lip, tapping his fingers on his leg. *Screw it, I didn't come this far to not find out.*

He stepped back and ran the flashlight over the sides of the window until he spotted a switch. Holding his breath, not certain he wanted to see, he flipped it.

Neon lights sputtered and spread a clinical illumination over a room full of beds. Men lay in those beds.

What was left of them.

Bile rose in the back of his throat, and he swallowed. He'd seen worse. His fingers clenched on the flashlight, and he breathed out, chasing away the images of a tented field hospital always creeping at the back of his mind. Pale bodies spread out like meat on slabs. An arm hung off the side of one of the beds. A strange black pattern mottled white skin. He peered closer, pressed up to the glass. The wavy lines reminded him of scales. *What were they doing in here?*

If a viral outbreak was imminent, they ought to warn everyone. He tore his gaze away from the strange pattern teasing at something in his memory. No black rash marred the brown skin of the body in the next bed, but strange cuts at regular intervals marred his arms and legs. Evan swore and leaped back as the body spasmed, the man arching his back in a soundless scream, his body twisting as the cuts opened and shut.

Like gills.

His heart thundered against his ribs as he recognised Hudson's friendly smile under the contorted grimace. The flashlight dropped from his slackened grip, clattered dully on the floor.

The thing that had been Hudson convulsed and twisted until he fell off the bed. As soon as the body hit the floor a high-pitched beeping sounded from the monitor. Evan lunged to the door, fumbled at the handle and burst into the room. A fetid stench hit his nose but he held his breath and raced to his friend's side.

Hudson flopped on the floor. *Like a fish out of water.* He slid his arms under him and hauled him up. Panting, almost gagging with the feel of Hudson's scaly skin and the smells of antiseptic mixed with rancid sweat, he heaved him onto the bed. Brown eyes met his, a kind of despairing pain clouding them.

"Hudson. Can you hear me? What happened?"

The mutated body shuddered and fell back on the blue plastic mattress. Hudson's chest still rose and fell in a ragged rhythm, but his eyes shut.

Evan stood for a moment, frozen and uncertain. He'd never seen an illness like this, but he'd never been under the ocean before. His gaze lifted from the broken man and scanned the room. *Too many machines. Where are the nurses if this was an illness?*

He fought against an urge to stay. There was nothing he could do here to help. Evan slammed the switch off, scooped up his flashlight, turned off the beam. He paused a moment.

"I won't leave you like this," he said to the bodies lying in the gloom. "I'll figure this shit out. I'll come back."

Once in the corridor, he took a shuddering breath, but the air still seemed tainted with the stench of the small ward. His hands shook, and he gripped them on top of his head, trying to make his breaths slow and regular.

How could that monstrous thing be Hudson? Is this an illness or is this what the *contract* does? Esther's gaze sliding from his. Khalid telling him not to push too hard. Bitter anger twisted with fear in his mind.

A distant light flickered in the dark water outside the window. He stared at the glass, his mind still filled with the memories of contorted, mutated bodies. Scales, fins, screams. There had to be something he could do, someone he could ask. Wild thoughts of raiding the doctor's office whirled in his head.

The light pulsed, the water glowing pale green. He dropped his arms and moved closer to the window. A figure moved in the light. A diver? Dolphin? The figure slowed, twisted, a long tail flipping close to the glass. Heat rushing through his veins, he reached his hand up to the glass. The tail flicked over and a woman's form arose.

This can't be happening.

Silver curls floated in the water, purple tints stronger in the water than they had been on land. He knew her.

The mermaid from the cavern. Amatheia. Chills laced his blood.

She was real.

A glow lit her face, seemingly coming from within her. No lines pulled at her brow, no human signs of care carved into her translucent skin, but her eyes were wells of sadness. She shook her fins, fine ribbons rippling through the water as she stared through the glass at him. He recoiled from the reproach in her face. No, *she* knocked him over. Left him to rot in a cave. She had no right to reproach him.

The gills on the side of her neck pulsed, and he thought of the marks on Hudson's limbs. A horrified thought slid out from the depths of his mind. She hovered in the water, her tail waving in small motions to keep her in place against the current. The floor shifted under his feet, and he flung up a hand to rest on the wall. The cool panelling helped ground him.

I'm in a dome under the water.

She couldn't be real.

Hudson has gills on his legs. Matthews has scales on his arms.

Her gaze bored into his and ragged breath filled his lungs. He stumbled forward but she turned, her tail moving with slow grace and slid away into the depths.

Inky dark water obscured everything beyond the glass. He stayed for a while, staring, fingers pushed against the surface of the dome as his mind whirled.

Nothing moved now except fish. He shoved hands into his pockets and turned back, trying to ward off the chill seeping from his core.

He managed to round the corner of the corridor a moment before footsteps rushed down the hall. Intent voices and half-heard words. Evan's clutching fingers closed around a door handle, and he slipped into a supply room a second before they came into view.

"The outcomes are improving, despite these setbacks, ma'am. When we find a better specimen, I'm convinced we will see some positive results."

Rage burned away the chill, and he leaned his forehead on the door. This was like some mad scientist's lair.

The second person's voice came out muffled, but still the lighter tones of a woman. He hoped like hell she wasn't Celine. The need to know if the nice doctor who'd teased him was part of all this, pulled at him until he surrendered and cracked the door open.

The hooded figure cast a slender silhouette. Not Celine. The couple arrived at the locked door and swiped a card then disappeared into the darkness. He slipped out the door and padded as fast as possible out of the center. The taint of what he left behind curled in his mind, a bitter taste of bile creeping into his mouth.

He needed answers.

Neat black ink stating Char's name filled his head as he stared at the tag next to her door. He weighed up who he should talk to, Char or Khalid, but Khalid didn't want to talk at lunch and more cover-ups weren't what he needed. He knocked, a brisk rat-a-tat. The door opened, and an expression he couldn't fathom shuttered her face. She tugged at her tank top and smoothed a night wrap over her hair.

"Can I come in?"

A smile pulled at her lips. "Sure."

Her unit was as small as his but somehow the space felt like more. Char's presence and personality filled the room, through the pictures tacked up on the wall by her bed, the books piled on the small bedside table, and the flowers on the table. He stared at the bright daisies, incongruous in the stark little room.

"Fake."

"What?"

"The flowers. They're fake. I like flowers. Figured I'd be here for a while, may as well give myself something I like to look at."

She appeared softer, here. All at once he was conscious of his hands and the smallness of the unit meant he didn't know where to stand.

"So. Social call? Or something else?"

I saw a mermaid. Oh man. This wouldn't be easy.

"I needed to talk to someone. About something I saw."

The softness fled her face and her shoulders hunched. "Oh. You sure you want to talk?"

His heart sank. *Not Char too.* "Yeah, I am. That bother you?"

Her chin tilted and a fire sparked in her eyes. "Nope. Go ahead, devil dog."

Crap. He huffed out a breath and pulled his hands down his face, trying to reset. "I found Matthews. And Hudson. And some others I didn't recognize." *Couldn't* recognize.

She crossed her arms, seeming to shrink into

herself. "Are they, I mean—"

"They're alive. But changed. Really changed."

Her eyes glistened with unshed tears and regret tore at him. She'd known them much longer than he.

"But that's not all. Call me crazy but I saw something. In the water."

"Probably another fish, Evan."

"No. Not this time. It was a mermaid."

Part of him hoped she would scoff, or appear concerned, or anything other than the silence filling the air with the surety this was not the first time she heard the word.

"You knew?"

Her lips screwed up. "It's complicated."

Anger rose, spreading fire under his skin. "How can it be more complicated than the fact you knew something rotten is happening here, and you never told me."

She squared up to him, her hands dropping to her hips, raising her face to his. "This isn't something we talk about to the new people. We find it's kind of easier when you find out for yourself. How would you have reacted if I started telling you about mermaids?"

His eyebrows flicked up. "Okay, fair point. But what about the rest? What happened to Matthews and Hudson?"

"I've never seen what happens to the men who disappear. I figured they'd been pushed too hard, hoped maybe they left. We don't ask questions here; we aren't the only ones who might get hurt. The truth hurts sometimes, marine."

His lungs constricted and he leaned back on the wall; everything he thought he knew was crumbling about him. "Tell me the truth. All of it."

She sank onto the bed. Her hands pulled the blanket toward her. "Project Siren. Research to create better and stronger armies to target the enemy in a more focused and deadly way. That's what they told you, right?"

"Yeah. And what are you telling me?"

"The mermaids. That's how they hope to achieve their plan. Crossing mermaid DNA with human to fuse human and mer powers and abilities."

He stared at her.

She shrugged. "Think about it. Humans dominate the world, we possess many strengths, but mermaids have things we can't imagine, breathing underwater, their vision and speed better than ours. The scientists discover new things all the time. They think they might control energy as well, like shape it into blasts. Think of how that would benefit our infantry." Her eyes remained calm but her fingers pulled and twisted at the corner of the blanket.

"What else aren't you telling me?"

"The mermaids don't exactly volunteer."

His fingers steepled on his forehead. "Jesus. So they're captured? And used like-like lab rats?"

She nodded, her mouth scrunched up.

"And knowing this, you stay here?"

"Blake says the mermaids aren't sentient. They're more like dolphins, like animals."

"Unbelievable. *Blake* says? Since when did you listen to that cretin?"

"I've never met a mermaid. I wouldn't know."

"I have."

Her gaze shot up to his, shock writ large on her

face. "When?"

"She saved my life. She has a name, Char. A name. Amatheia. She's no animal." He pushed off the wall. "I expected something different from you."

Her face crumpled but she stood, her shoulders back. "I didn't know they weren't animals. I didn't know what they did to the humans. I don't like it but I believe there must be a reason for it."

"Tell yourself that to help you sleep at night. I'm done with excusing things in the name of some mythical higher good. There's no such thing."

He stalked out, anger easier than the hurt lying beneath. She didn't call for him to wait. He didn't know if he was relieved or disappointed.

He turned to the passageway to his room and stopped short. Outside his door, a man in olive green drab leaned on the wall, his arms crossed, staring at the floor. Evan's shoulders loosened as he relaxed into a walk which could at any moment turn into an attack. The man glanced up at his approach, his face closed and eyes flat.

"Hunter?"

"Yes. And you are?"

"Waiting for you. The Siren wants to see you."

"Who?"

"The Siren. She's not patient so best we go now."

"Whoa, pal I'm not following you anywhere until you explain a bit more."

The man's lip curled. "You might be new here but I doubt she'll care. When the Siren calls, you come. Her quarters are through the command center, and you won't get in without me, so are you coming or not?"

His skin prickled like electricity coursing through

him. He'd be unlikely to get a better chance to scope command out than this. He smiled. "Sure. Lead the way."

Chapter Seventeen

Green light dappled the metal floor, breaking up the gloom. A long metal desk stretched out on the other end of the chamber. Beyond sat a woman shrouded in darkness. Her jewelled pendant caught the light, but her face hid in the gloom. Evan halted a few feet from the table, fighting the urge to salute. He was not hers to command. Fixing his gaze on a point above her head, he waited. Silence didn't rattle him.

The woman shifted, and he darted a glance at her shadowed face, features indistinguishable, hair swept upward. Her fingers flicked over the pendant and she leaned forward.

"We've been observing your progress with interest, Mr. Hunter."

Not being able to see her face bugged him. Her voice came out as a monotone, indistinguishable from AI voices at call centers. His lips pressed together and he waited.

"Agility, stamina, leadership. You have what it takes to succeed in this Project. Except of course for your unfortunate tendency to turn up in areas you aren't supposed to be."

Lead sank in his gut. *Shit.*

"I have no interest in succeeding in your project."

"May I ask why?"

Hudson's silent screams. The mermaid's

116

reproachful eyes that wouldn't leave him.

"Let's say it isn't aligned to my personal values."

"You'll need to make peace with that. Your potential for Project Siren is too important."

His lip curled. "I don't think so. I'll be leaving next vessel out of here." *As far as possible from your crazy labs and super soldiers.* "Thanks anyway."

For the first time she dropped the monotone. "You think we would let you leave?"

Dark walls closed in on him. He blinked and they settled back to dim panels. "I think you'll have trouble stopping me."

A screen slid down from the ceiling, settling close to him. He glared toward where the woman sat. Irritation spiked with fear stoked through him.

"I heard the propaganda show already."

"Your sister. Her name is Kelly? Such a pretty garden she has now. Daisies. Always so lovely."

Ice speared his chest and he stopped breathing. "What do you know about my family?"

The dark figure gestured, and the screen lit up beside Evan. Photos covered the monitor. Working in her garden. Smiling at the cashier as she ordered a coffee. Rushing into her office. Coming out of the hospital, brushing tears from her eyes. A rising fury heated his blood. If they follow her to the hospital they might follow her in. Kelly might not be the only one in danger.

"We know quite a bit, as you can see."

He forced himself to breathe, for his pulse to slow to normal. The woman in the shadows tilted her head.

"What do you want me to do?" His throat clenched tight and speaking hurt.

A moment of silence sat in the air, heavy and cold.

"We want for you to uphold your contract. Continue your service to your country. Keep out of areas that aren't your concern. Nothing untoward."

Evan fixed on his sister's face, the pain lurking behind her smile. She didn't deserve this. He gripped his hands behind his back, fighting the rising panic which would do him no good here. His muscles pulled, and he focused on the tension and the pain, breathed in and held it, exhaled.

"You control yourself well, Hunter. This is one of the reasons you show such promise. You owe it to your country to keep doing so."

His jaw tightened, words tasting bitter on the tip of his tongue. He kept them in. He only owed something to some people: to his family, to his comrades dead and alive, and to small children ripped apart by bombs. Could he work with people who would capture sentient beings—mer and human both—and torture them for their own purposes? Even for Kelly? Surely they wouldn't harm a civilian. He pushed away memories of destroyed cities and thought instead about the men lying on a table, twisted and mutated. He shook his head.

"I can't uphold something which goes against everything I value."

The shadows deepened. The woman leaned forward.

Show your face, you coward.

"Such a shame about your mother. So sad when memories die. Do you think she'll remember who her daughter is when they take her to Kelly's funeral?"

Fire raced through his veins, burning out thought.

Ten steps and he could wrap his hands around her throat, choke the threats from her lips.

He couldn't even curse. His words tangled in a blanket of rage. He lunged forward. A criss-cross of lasers appeared, forming a barrier between him and the desk, and he stumbled to a halt.

"You would act rather than think? Perhaps I mistook your potential."

Bile churned in his stomach. She was right. He needed to think. He was stuck in a dome under the sea, in the middle of nowhere. Stealing a sub wouldn't work; those things needed a crew. Maybe he could work on Char, Khalid, and perhaps Esther. Surely none of them wanted to be here. The thought lit a candle in the darkness roiling in his mind. Keep your head down. Stay out of sight. Keep out of trouble. Until you couldn't any longer. Then you fought back and ran. Long years taught him he couldn't rescue everyone.

He couldn't save Hudson or Matthews, and God knows what they did to the mermaids here, but if he could make it back, persuade someone to believe him, maybe the Dome would get shut down.

Char's words echoed in his head *They want to create super soldiers.* His hands curled into fists. If Plan A failed and no one agreed to leave, there would be nothing left but to swim out of here. To swim he needed to breathe underwater. Turned out he might end up having to engage in those experiments himself.

Plan B for Bad Idea.

Participate in the evil to shut it down later? A few lives now to preserve more later? He glared at the shadowy figure.

"I'll stay. But if you harm my family I will unleash

hell on you."

"Big words for a little soldier. You keep up your end of the bargain, and we won't have to test them."

The door opened behind him and two men in uniform entered. "Remember, Evan. You signed a contract. The words are important, but so is the deed. You signed and now we own you."

The chair swivelled around to face the wall of dark water behind the desk. *Yeah. Audience over.*

He spun on his heel, brushed off the hands of the guards, and stalked from the room.

Chapter Eighteen

Evan wiped the sweat from his brow and aimed another blow at the punching bag. The impact radiated up from his knuckles, dissipating some of the fire racing through him. Too many images flashed behind his eyes and he jabbed out at each one, only for it to be replaced by another.

Hudson's convulsing body...

A punch sent the bag circling.

Disembodied limbs scattered over a Kabul square...

His hand smacked into the canvas with enough force to draw blood.

Char's face twisted in a half truth...

A rapid tattoo of swings stole his breath. His arms shuddered.

"Hey, Evan."

He caught at the bag, stopped its wild movements. A few feet away stood Ana, towel on her shoulder and kick pads under one arm. He inclined his chin in a brusque greeting. He wasn't in any mood for small talk this morning.

"Ana."

He hadn't talked to her in a couple of days, not since he stumbled on the dark truth of this place. She walked past in the distance and he watched her talk with the crew, wondering if she, like Char, knew about

Project Siren.

She lifted her hand, boxing gloves dangling. "Want to spar?"

"I'm not sure that's the best idea."

"Think you'd leave me as dented as the bag?"

He straightened the bindings on his hand. "Not intentionally."

A small smile tugged at the corner of her mouth, and he stared at her lips.

"Who says I'd let you? I'm not a bad boxer. Plus you already took out most of your anger on the bag."

"I'll be pulling back."

"See how far that gets you. Come on, devil dog." She tossed the gloves and he snatched them from the air, heat flushing his neck. Char's nickname for him sounded a lot more flirtatious on Ana's tongue.

"Okay. One round."

She was quick. He started off holding back but when every jab missed her he pushed forward until his muscles used their full power. Only once did he come close enough to graze her hair as she ducked. She spun, and her leg connected with his waist. He winced as pain arced out from his side.

Next time she kicked he jumped back and darted forward as she overbalanced, grabbing her heel and flipping her. She arched, landed on her hands, and shoved off, flicking her legs out. Her foot connected with his chin and he fell backward. Sweeping his leg out, he hooked her ankle and dropped her.

Her eyes snapped wide, and her mouth gaped until she laughed. The light melodic sound floated up overhead. He grinned, and warmth spread through his chest.

"Nice to know you fight dirty when you're outmatched," she said.

Evan leaned up on his elbows. She lay, staring up at the ceiling, a small smile still on her face and the tiniest of laugh lines around her eyes. Taking advantage of her focus being elsewhere, he let his gaze roam over her, attention catching on the pale whorls of ink on her left shoulder. The start of a tattoo. Curiosity pushed at him, and he glanced up to find her staring at him, her eyes blue and piercing.

He raised his brows, ignoring the pulse thundering in his ears. "Cool ink. What is it?"

She rolled her shoulder forward and showed him the rest. A delicate waving frond of some kind of plant. "A reminder."

"A reminder of something good or something bad?"

Her eyes shadowed. "Of something."

Evan swallowed a sigh. He got that. Sometimes you remembered because it formed a part of you, good and bad. It was all the same person. He glanced at the frown on her face. *Hope it's more good than bad for her.*

She sat up and nudged his leg with her toes. "Do you feel better?"

His muscles pulled as he stretched out his triceps. "Yeah, I do. Thanks."

"So do you want to tell me why you're trying to murder the poor punching bag?"

He rested his forearms on his knees, frowning at the floor. "This place. Do you ever wonder if it's more than it seems?"

Her head cocked, and a puzzled frown lay between

her eyes. "Do you mean more than a giant dome under the sea where they're trying to train an elite task force?"

He huffed a broken laugh. "Yeah, more though—this sounds crazy—but have you seen any...experiments?"

"They do research here. Is that what you're talking about?"

"In a way."

He stared back at the floor. He didn't want to see her lie to him.

"It doesn't matter. I was edgy but I'm better now. Thanks to you and your ninja kicks."

He jumped to his feet and held out a hand. "Come on. We both better head back to quarters."

She clasped his hand, and electricity skipped up his arm. He pulled her up. For a moment, they stood a mere hand's width apart, but she stumbled back and he dropped her arm, heat flaming in the tips of his ears.

"I'll walk you back."

A hesitant smile curled the corner of her mouth, and she cocked her head. "Let's walk each other back."

Their path led them through the viewing platform. They talked easily before they reached the door to the platform. As the door slid open with a gentle hiss, her lips pressed together.

Silence filled the platform. Their footsteps echoed, and inky water swirled above them. She paused, and he raised his brows at her as they stopped in a shadow. Gloom swallowed her features.

"Pretty, isn't it?" His gaze stayed on her. "Beautiful."

Stillness surrounded her before she tossed her hair back and walked toward the glass rising up to create the dome. She placed her hand on the dark glass and leaned to stare outward.

He recognized the longing in her expression. The same urge wound through him. Miles under the sea, they lived in a cage and the weight of the glass closed in on them. Green light reflected in her eyes. So beautiful.

He reached out and tucked a stray strand of white blond hair behind her ear. She startled, almost as if she forgot he stood there. A smile curving his lips, he stepped closer, his heart drumming in his chest.

"What do you see, Ana, when you look into the depths?"

A cloud crossed her face, followed so quickly by a smile he doubted himself.

"So much is hidden, out in the ocean. So much unknown. One day I want to explore everything."

"Is that why you joined Project Siren?"

Her hesitation was almost imperceptible but he recognised the sliding stare, the flicker of the eyelids, the tightening of her jaw. He did that himself.

"Yes."

He fought away the niggling dissatisfaction. She would confide in him in her own time. She didn't owe him anything.

"What about you, Evan? Do you want to explore?"

He shifted to the glass, his shoulder nudging hers. "I don't know if I want to explore the depths of the sea. There's a hell of a lot of mystery out there but I think I'd be happier watching someone else figure it out. I always wanted to travel around the world when I was young. One of the reasons I signed up." His gut twisted, and he turned away from the water. "But I don't like planes much anymore."

"Home is always better, in any case."

"Yeah. Home's great."

She didn't say anything, her silence filling the room in an expectant hush. He resisted but found himself answering her anyway.

"Nowhere's felt like home in a long time. After my father died, my mom had a nervous breakdown. Since then, it was just me and Kel. She wasn't happy when I went to combat, and even less so when I signed up for a second tour."

Kelly's tears had soaked his t-shirt. He'd shoved down the impatience, and let her cry. With the invincibility of a twenty-year-old flooding through him, he thought her fears ridiculous. Six years and several tours later and he carried in his mind the scars of her tears.

"Coming back you think it will be easy. But everything's too real and too mundane, and nobody understands. You end up smiling at a barbecue and feeling caged by isolation. No one wants to hear about your experience. The pain, the guilt, or the fear. So you keep on going on."

He cut a glance at her, uncertain about her silence, memories of Grace changing the subject and calling him weak burning in his mind. Ana's face froze, and her gaze bored into his.

"And if you could make them understand, to *know,* maybe things would be different. Maybe you could get the family back. The home. But they never do understand."

Tension bled out of his muscles, and he breathed deeply. She got it. "Yes."

He couldn't work her out. An irrational wish she would tell him flashed into his head, and he filed it away. He of all people was not one to prod at pain. He'd wondered if she knew more, if he could trust her, but right now all he cared about was the connection he'd felt since the beginning, a thread pulling him toward her, reeling him in.

He held out a hand. She hesitated and his chest hitched. But she reached out, and he enfolded his fingers over her small hand. Delicate but strong. Like the rest of her.

A smile flickered over her face, uncertain and tremulous. The warmth of her, so close to him... His pulse raced. He stroked a thumb over her wrist. Her mouth was soft and enticing. When she reached out to cup his jaw, his stomach tightened. He slid a hand around her waist and drew her toward him, ready to stop at the slightest sign of her discomfort.

Her thumb traced his mouth and he smiled. She blinked at him, something reflecting deep in her eyes. Her body stilled for a long second, then she melted against him.

His hand tightened on her waist, the sweat from her top drying but still damp. Each beat of his heart pounded against his ribs. He bent his head and took her mouth with his. Her lips parted, almost in surprise, and he pulled back.

"Okay?"

Her eyes shone and her body trembled in his arms but she nodded tightly. "Yes. Just, surprising."

"I hope not so surprising it doesn't happen again."

She smiled, light glowing in her face. "I hope not too."

Fire spread through him, and he cupped his palm around her face, butterflies leaping in his stomach. "I think you're wonderful, Ana."

A curtain fell from her eyes. and instead of blue ice they burned with a deep silver flame. His hand stroked through her hair, the fine silky strands whispering over his fingers. He tried not to count every second until she replied.

"I didn't expect this. Here. With you. But you do something to my heart I haven't experienced before."

He clasped her tight to his chest, his face buried in her hair. His own heart swelled, cascading joy through his bloodstream. Her hand stole up around his neck, and she pulled his face down to hers. Their lips met, and fire slammed through him.

The taste of her, the musky scent of sweat, the softness of her against his chest... He tightened his arms and held her closer, as if to consume her. Dark water swirled around them, and darker images battled in his mind.

But for this moment he pushed them aside, for the woman in his arms who was fast stealing his heart.

Chapter Nineteen

His alarm sounded, cutting into dreams of Ana interspersed with visions of Hudson and Matthews. Guilt about kissing her last night, for enjoying himself when his friends lay damaged and ruined, threaded through him.

Ana sent his heart racing and set his blood on fire. He hadn't known her long, but every time he met her he felt a connection, like only the two of them existed. He rolled his eyes at the ceiling. *Ridiculous.* He wasn't a teenage boy to moon over a crush. But warmth flooded through his chest for the feel of her body under his hands and the open joy in her smile.

The alarm sounded again. He threw a pillow and missed. Shit. He pushed out of bed and stumbled to the head.

A knock on the door interrupted his shower. Evan reached for a towel, then padded through the small unit, wiping beads of water from his forehead. *This better be important.*

The woman behind the door froze when he opened it, and he was suddenly conscious of every drip sliding down his bare torso. Her gaze stayed fixed on his face, and a blush crept up her neck. With a mumble, she thrust a paper at him and strode off.

His heart sank at the familiar-looking envelope, and he ripped the brown paper open. The order to present himself at the research center didn't change no matter how many times he read the statement. Hudson's twisted body and soundless scream flashed through his mind, and his clenching fingers crumpled the sheet. He could refuse.

But he remembered what Hudson said about the contract, how they had him over a barrel. He had wondered what he meant. No one had given him a copy of the contract he'd signed, which was weird. Hudson clearly knew what he headed toward, and he still went. Shivers ran down his bare back. *Kelly.* He thought of the letter Hudson had given him. *Shit. No wonder no one resisted.*

The only way to escape was to participate.

He tossed the paper on the table and reached for a shirt. Either way he ran the risk of dying down here. If he played along, pretended to do what they wanted, he might learn enough to get the chance to help.

****

The door slid open, and the harsh lights of the corridor gave way to a dim room lit with green lamps, and a couple of beam lights in the center of the ceiling. A tank sat in the middle of the floor.

A tank with a mermaid.

The mer turned to face him and he breathed out. Not Amatheia. Her hair shimmered in multiple hues, floating in the still water. A deep shadow lay in her eyes, and she bared sharp teeth in a snarl. She moved as if to shield something, and a small hand crept around her waist where her tail began. Numbness spread through his limbs. A child. They did this to children?

"Hunter?"

He tore his gaze from the trapped mers, focusing

on the man approaching him as his stomach roiled. White coat, clipboard, with a cheerful, reassuring smile plastered on his young face. Hard to connect this unassuming scientist with the horrors of the other day.

Habit directed his hand to shake the other man's even though his mind shouted about the trapped mers.

"That's right. And you are?"

"Call me Doctor Jones."

He smiled, anger fusing like steel down his spine. "Nice to see we're all so open and aboveboard here."

The doctor ignored or missed his sarcasm and gestured to the corner of the room where a woman stepped forward. A hollow feeling spread through his chest. Esther. She kept her face averted.

"The two of you are helping today. We'll start the corresponding research in the next few days."

His mouth went dry. "Helping with what?"

Irritation flickered over the doctor's face, disrupting the amiable scientist facade for a moment before he regained control. "No need for impatience, all in due time."

Jones approached the tank, thin clipboard clutched to his chest like a shield. The mermaid lunged toward the glass, her hand clawing at the sides. Evan forced himself to stand still as the urge to comfort her and to free her, raced through him. The doctor cocked his head, and a smile played on his lips.

"They don't respond well to sedation, although the medication does slow them down. We find restraints, and the right incentive more effective."

Fire burned through Evan's skin and his hands curled into fists. "Can you hear yourself? Restraints and sedation? What the hell is going on?"

"Shut up, Evan," Esther hissed.

He glared at her. "You're okay with this?"

A shutter closed on her face. "It's complicated."

He drew a shaky breath as images of his family flashed into his mind. *Yeah. The whole stinking business was complicated.* Clenching his jaw, he turned back to where the doctor regarded him with an intense focus.

"Ready? Or should I prepare for more moralizing?"

His lip curled. "Tell me this, doc, how does any of this fit with your code of ethics?"

"Easily. They're not human. They're animals, and there's no PETA here under the sea."

His gaze went to the mer in the tank; the child's face peeping around its mother. Pale skin, almost green in the light, wide silver eyes, and hair the color of flame. The mother's webbed hand stroked back the hair from the child's face, staring into its eyes. The water between them rippled, and the mermaid's skin pulsed with the glow he last saw on Amatheia. These were no animals. They were magnificent, strange, and eerie creatures. But not animals.

Bile rose at the back of his throat. He had to do this. Not only for Kelly but to make sure he had a chance to bring the whole Dome down. Getting himself killed or worse now wouldn't help anyone.

I still won't be able to forgive myself.

He summoned the part of him, the ability to detach, that served him well in war. Until the moment it didn't. He pushed those memories away, harder to do with another child staring at him, fins trembling in irregular bursts.

Esther followed the directions of Dr. Jones and

moved a machine with a nozzle to hang over the tank. Jones fiddled with some dials and flipped a switch. A fine spray like a shower scattered from the nozzle to filter through the water. The mermaid twitched, trying to find somewhere the spray didn't reach, sheltering her child. After several long minutes, the sedative slowed the frantic flipping of her tail. The child sagged, blinking, long before she gave in to the dulling medication.

Sweat beaded on his forehead and trickled down the back of his neck. *Think of Kelly. Do it for her.* But the mermaid's arm was tight around her listless child, and disgust at his actions flooded him.

A metal panel on the floor of the tank moved upward, water draining through holes like a colander. His stomach turned. Switching off the part of his mind that continued to shout at him, he followed the doctor's curt instructions. He and Esther moved a step ladder to the side of the tank. He clutched the child first, floppy and silent but with terror swimming in his blinking eyes. He passed the small mer down to Esther as shards of shame speared his chest.

The mother pushed at him as he grasped her arm, her touch feeble. Blinking away the tears springing to his eyes, he gentled his grip and moved higher on the ladder, changing his stance to scoop her up. Her tail dangled, heavier than he expected and he almost unbalanced on the steps. Holding her close, her scales shifting, he breathed in the scent of the chemicals they infused into the water. No salty tang. He didn't pass her down to Esther but backed down the steps, clutching her to him.

"On the bed."

The metal slab reminded him too much like a butchery. He hesitated for a moment and her twitching strengthened in force.

"Faster, Hunter! She must be in the restraints before the sedative wears off."

He lay her down down then stood back as Esther and the doctor hustled to buckle straps around her. His focus shifted from Esther to the child, restrained on a bench next to his mother.

The mother thrashed in small, feeble motions. Her hands scrabbled at the restraints, and her face turned to her limp child. Evan's pulse thundered in his ears, as the doctor approached the small mer. Jones held a scalpel. Such a little thing to be so terrifying. The mother stilled, her tail sinking to the metal surface, bright fins fading to a dull gray, her eyes sparking hatred.

"As I said, Hunter. The right incentive."

A vice squeezed his lungs, every breath shallow and painful. He moved as in slow motion to pull the scanner over and attach the electropads to the mermaid's temples. He brushed her hair off her face, tucking wet strands behind her pointed ear. She closed her eyes, her mouth twisting. Stepping back, he raised his face to meet Esther's gaze. Tight lines pulled at her eyes, and she blinked away tears. Part of him wondered who back home was threatened as the lever for her actions. Husband? Parents?

The doctor came to the head of the bench, a syringe in his hand. "Change."

The mermaid pressed her lips together, her eyes snapping open.

"I know you understand. Change."

The mermaid's voice rasped against his ears like a whisper of surf. "You are a beast."

Jones shook his head. "No, that would be you. Change."

The child shifted, a small whimper escaping its throat. Her eyes luminous opals, the mermaid shuddered and changed, fins shrinking and disappearing, her tail fading in a shimmer of green until she lay human-looking with legs and naked except for an amulet glowing purple.

Was the pendant around her neck, magic? His heart hammered against his chest, as his mind struggled to accept what he saw.

Jones withdrew the syringe he'd inserted as she began changing. A thick substance filled the vessel, and he busied himself emptying it bit by bit into a series of test tubes.

Bright red trickled down the puncture point on the mermaid's arm. Guilt stabbed at Evan's chest. After searching for a cotton swab and finding nothing, Evan reached out and wiped the blood off with his thumb.

The mermaid stared at him and her voice rasped against his nerves. "Why do you do this to us?"

He shook his head. He didn't know, God help him. His eyes burned. This was wrong.

She shuddered and closed her eyes. Esther appeared at his side.

"Here. Lay this over her."

He grasped the sweatshirt she handed him and draped the soft fabric over as much of the mermaid's body as possible.

Jones glanced up and away. "You don't need to bother. Cold-blooded. Fish don't mind a bit of a chill."

His fingers tightened on the sweatshirt, as the urge to punch Jones's smirk down his throat raced through him.

The mermaid's mouth twisted, sharp little teeth appearing. He touched her shoulder tentatively, and she flinched, her eyes snapping open.

"I'm sorry."

Her gaze bored into his. "A soft word with no weight."

Leaden guilt dragged at his stomach. "You're right. But I'm still sorry."

Jones approached and the mermaid shrank away from him. "Almost done, one more trial, and we can call this a day."

The doctor jabbed a needle into the mermaid's arm, injecting her with a bright red serum. She shivered, and he pulled out the syringe.

"Now we see if you can keep those legs, little fish."

Before Evan could stop him, the doctor ripped off the amulet. The mermaid convulsed, changing back into her natural form. Her back arched from the bed, pulling against the restraints until they tore. The bed toppled, falling on its side. It landed with a thud and knocked over a chair. The mermaid's tail swept against Evan's legs. The sound of high-pitched terror filled the air in a nerve-jangling scream, and the child pulled against the restraints. Esther stared between him and Jones before lunging to stand in front of the merchild.

Jones frowned and tossed the amulet on the floor. "Another failure."

Failure? What the hell was he hoping to achieve?

Evan fell to his knees, reaching out to the thrashing

mermaid. Fear pulsed at the back of his head. Her gills sucked at the air, and her mouth gulped. Webbed hands clutched at her throat, as if they could push air into her lungs.

"You see?" said Jones, "Just like a fish."

Rage mixed with horror. "Shut the hell up."

Her movements grew smaller as the energy faded from her muscles. Soft hair fell over his shoulder as he lifted her from the floor, holding her close to his chest, hoping against hope he could get her into the water before she stopped breathing. She stared at him, her throat working and her tail flipping. He reached the stepladder by the tank before she choked and fell still.

He held her dead body with the screams of her child filling his head as guilt burned a hole in his chest.

Chapter Twenty

Cold metal cut into his shoulder as he leaned on the doorframe. Stepping inside was the last thing he wanted to do. The merchild lay in a small tank, tail twitching, eyes squeezed shut against the harsh lights of the laboratory.

The silent screams of the mer's mother still echoed in his head, as did her expression as she died in his arms. He massaged the tension cording his neck muscles.

A film reel of guilt ran in his head. He doubted the end justified the means anymore. Blinking away images of the past, he opened his eyes to the new shame. At the very least, the child deserved to not be on his own.

Steel scraped against concrete. A stool moving. He drew back from the door. A figure in track pants and a baggy sweater moved into his line of sight.

Char stood next to the tank, arms crossed and fingers pulling at her sleeve. The merchild opened his eyes as she blocked the light, scrambling away from the side, his tail moving in weak flutters. She knelt, her fingers splayed on the glass. The merchild uncurled and reached out a hand, silvery webbing translucent in the reflected light. His fingers touched the glass opposite hers. Evan held his breath. Char smiled, but tears tracked down her cheeks.

"Hey little guy. I don't know if you can hear me.

But you aren't alone."

An ache spread through his chest. "No, he isn't."

Char whipped round and she stared. "What are you doing here?"

"Same as you. I wanted to check on him."

She shook her head, a fierce light in her eyes. "I don't think he needs to see you, of all people."

He thought of arguing, of saying if she told him earlier what was going on he wouldn't be here now, but she was right.

"I understand." The frame of the door chilled his fingers, the grooves biting into his skin as he held on. "I won't come closer."

A shadow passed over her face, and she turned back to the tank. Dark water settled into stillness once more, and the merchild pushed up on his tail, his gaze fixed on Evan. Sterile air chilled the small room and he breathed against tight lungs.

"I'm sorry for what happened." *For what will happen.*

Minutes passed into an hour. They didn't talk. The child appeared to gain some comfort from not being alone. Gradually his eyes closed, and he slipped into slumber.

A quiet beeping from his wrist snagged Evan's attention. Duty called. He hesitated then caught her glance. She padded over to him.

"I don't like leaving him, but at least he's sleeping now."

She brushed past him, and he fought back the urge to hug her. She didn't want comfort from him.

Quiet filled the corridor, even their footsteps sounding muffled as they strode toward the living quarters.

"Is this the first child you've seen?"

"No."

"Jesus, how do you cope?"

She flashed a glance at him."Who says I cope?"

He grabbed her arm and stopped them both. "It shouldn't be like this."

She shifted away from his grip and pulled her sweater around her, like she sought comfort from the fluffy blue wool. "When has life ever been what we want it to be?"

He stroked his jaw. Tension threaded through his muscles. "What if, this time, we could change it?"

She scowled at the floor. "How?"

"You're trapped too, aren't you?"

Her shoulders hunched and she half shrugged. "I think we all are. We signed a contract and now they own us."

"The contract is only a piece of paper."

She stared up at him, lips parting then pressing together in a sharp line.

Darting a glance down the still deserted corridor, he shifted closer. "Regardless, they only control us for now. I'm not content to stay here like some kind of lab rat waiting to see if I die or not."

Skepticism emanated from every line of her face. "And you think you can find a way to avoid that? Good luck."

"I'm figuring one out."

"Are you? Or all talk?"

"For real. There must be a way out of this hell under the waves. We could steal a sub."

If her eyes rolled any more they'd fall on the floor.

"That's the plan? Steal a massive sub, and try to pilot it with two people and somehow outgun anything they send after us?"

"There are smaller subs."

"And exactly how far do you think we'd get?"

He crossed his arms. "I said I would figure out a plan, not that I had one figured out. What about the communications?"

"What about them?"

"They need some way to communicate with people on the surface, to co-ordinate things. It might be as simple as us sending out a message."

"A message? Hi, I'm under the ocean with a bunch of mermaids. Can't wait to see how you spin that one."

"We'll need to get proof."

She bit her lip. "You say that like it's easy. This whole idea is crazy."

"You know what's crazy? Hudson with black scales on his legs, mermaids being tortured for their DNA, their magic or whatever. *That* is crazy."

"Do you trust me, or am I simply the only one you could turn to?"

He stared down into her warm brown eyes, dark with a fierce emotion he couldn't name. "I trust you with my life."

Char blinked, tears welling, and her mouth twisted into a trembling smile. "I don't think you're very wise."

He gripped her shoulder. "You're being ridiculous. Why shouldn't I?"

She hunched in a half-shrug. "We don't all have your stellar record, Evan."

Tiny bodies strewn across a bloodied street flashed into his mind. "None of us are truly without guilt."

A shudder wracked her frame, and he pulled her into a hard one-armed embrace.

"You're right though; we can't do this just the two of us. Who else do you think we can trust?"

She stiffened and pulled back, her fingers twisting in her sweater. A lead weight filled his chest.

"A couple of people but I think we need to keep this—whatever this is—under wraps. And that means—Evan I know you won't like this—but this means you shouldn't tell Ana."

"Why not?"

"She's a nice person, I like her, and I know *you* like her, Romeo, but there's something about her I can't figure out. Not the kind of thing I want in someone who is supposed to have my back."

He glared at the floor, as if the mottled concrete held the answers. Everything in his heart wanted to argue but his head agreed with her. Hot prickles spread through his chest and he sighed out through puffed cheeks.

"Okay."

Surprise flashed across her eyes before her expression shuttered. "Easier than I expected."

"Let's not go into it."

"Gotcha." She tugged at an earlobe. "Khalid's a trustworthy guy. He's useful too. Knows a lot about this place."

He scanned the corridor, the endless uniformity no longer reassuring. Chilled stale air dragged at his lungs. His muscles twitched with the urge to run.

"I'll talk to him tomorrow."

A light sputtered and shadows danced over her face. She chewed her lip. "If we do this, it might end real bad."

Evan sighed, his head full of echoes of screams. "I think it will end badly regardless. At least this way we will know we tried."

Chapter Twenty-One

The next morning Ana entered the chow hall and his brow lightened at the sight of her, blonde ponytail messy today, and a tiny smile dancing on her face when she saw him. He kicked out a chair on the other side of the table and gestured. Heat rushed over his own skin at the blush creeping up her neck.

Ana curled up on the hard chair, grimacing as her knee knocked the table. He smiled at her and rescued his mug.

"Sorry."

"No, you're good. See, no spills."

She bit her lip, and he tore his gaze away from her mouth. He stirred his coffee, focusing on the whirlpool created by the spoon.

"I talked to Esther," she said.

The spoon clattered on the edge of the cup, and he wiped the splashes off his hand. "Oh?"

A fresh fragrance like sea air wafted as she leaned toward him. He stared at the table.

"Is it true? Did they capture a child?"

The hot tin of the mug burned his fingers as his hand tightened. Forcing his gaze up to hers, he nodded. Her eyes shone with an intensity he didn't expect. Everyone else seemed so inured to the evils here, so caught. Harsh lines framed her mouth as she inhaled sharply. He reached out and tucked a strand of hair behind her ears, wishing he could smooth away the frown.

"What happened to the child?"

"Nothing. Not like—" He swigged the hot coffee, letting the heat burn away the lump in his throat.

The mermaid's dead eyes followed him everywhere now.

She frowned down at her hands, gripped in her lap.

"He's okay. Char and I visited him."

She stared intently at him. "Where?"

He waved a hand in the direction of the medical center, and his lip curled as bile rose. "He's in a tank."

A shudder went through her, and he reached out a hand without thinking. Frail fingers clutched at his.

"They're not supposed to do that, not on children." Her voice came out hoarse.

He scootched his chair around the table to sit next to her, stroking his thumb over her wrist.

"I'm sorry, Ana. I figured you knew. Everyone seemed to know but me." He couldn't keep the bitterness from lacing his tongue.

She withdrew her hand and ran it through her hair, glancing around. His fingers drew back on his palm, and he ignored a flicker of hurt. It shouldn't surprise him she pulled away. They always did in the end. Grace was just the worst.

"I didn't know about the children."

He rubbed his palms over his eyes and pinched the bridge of his nose. No matter what he did, the wails of the merchild played on repeat in his head.

"Char says he isn't the first. This place is crazy wrong."

Ana's face hardened, her eyes like blue flint. "They

145

should let him go."

"I don't think these guys care much about *should*."

A curtain descended on her expression. A chill spread through him as she shut him out. The coffee had cooled but he sipped the tepid liquid anyway. The urge to tell her of his plan pushed at the back of his throat but something held him back.

"I have to go."

He checked his watch. "Night duty doesn't start for another hour at least. I thought maybe we could hang out for a while."

She uncurled and stood, pushing her chair back. "I can't. Another time."

His pushed a smile onto his face and nodded stiffly.

Her mouth twisted, and she glanced around quickly before brushing a kiss across his cheek. "I mean it, another time."

Ponytail swinging, she marched from the room and he frowned into his mug. Char had said she didn't trust Ana, and he hated that Ana kept giving him reasons to agree with her.

****

Ana paused before the entrance to the medical center. Chills raced along the line on her arms where fins lay hidden. Her hand hovered over the handle. Darkness obscured the glass, but the hall beyond appeared deserted. No one would question why she was here. No reason not to go in.

Evan's face swam into her mind. The curl of his lip, the darkness in his eyes. His disgust had been palpable. Her hand trembled. Everyone else seemed to accept the experimental side of Project Siren, but an edge of fury laced his quiet words.

She gritted her teeth and opened the door, the sterile scent of antiseptic floating through the aircon. Voices came from the small room to the left, soft murmurs and laughs. Walking past, ignoring them, required a lot of restraint.

There were many tanks, many holding pens. She didn't come down this way too often, but she possessed blueprints; she knew which room was the likeliest.

She strode down the corridor, trying to ignore the doors lining either side. Insistent thoughts of who might be confined behind the locks battered at the shield in her mind.

The door she searched for hid at the end of the hall, concealed by dim light. A numeric lock sat heavy on the metal frame. She slid her small notebook with the codes from her back pocket. Her breath caught as the light flicked from red to green, and she turned the handle.

At the center of the room sat the tank. Her stomach flipped. Dim yellow light reflected off the water. Smears coated the glass in small handprints. The child huddled in the small space, his tail curled and shoulders hunched. His fins drooped at his side in the still water. All color leached from the once bright ribbons. Slivers of shell sliced through her heart, breaking the hard surface she worked so hard at maintaining. He didn't look up as she approached but curled in on himself more tightly.

Prickles ran along her skin—her true self itching to escape. She sank down by the side of the tank closest to his head.

"Youngling. Can you hear me still?"

His head lifted and he stared, wide eyes she didn't recognise.

She let her gills flash for a second.

"Have you come to save me?"

Urgency rang through her mind, his thoughts shoving like a hammerhead into hers.

Dull marks showed on his arms where he'd been restrained, and anger burned away her fears. *"Yes, youngling. But you must be patient."*

He gazed at her unblinking, his fins fluttering in the water.

Smiling, she stood and walked to the side of the door, right beneath the monitoring camera. She pulled the amulet out from under her t-shirt, let her arm shift and change. She held out her hand, palm upward, and concentrated. Electricity gathered in a charge, pulsing from glands along her torso, spreading down her skin, and gathering in a fizzing ball above her fingers. Punching upward, she sent the sparks into the base of the camera. The acrid scent of burnt plastic and fused wiring floated through the air.

She stumbled backward, a shudder wracking her body. It had been a long time since she'd used so much power. The boy perched up on his tail, his hands against the glass. A claw machine hovered over the tank. She scanned the controls and started up the motor, wincing at the humming grind of the metal cutting through the silence. The boy shivered, his fins whipping in agitation. Dark bruises lined his torso, and she stared from him to the mechanical claws matching the marks.

"It will only be a moment. It is the best way."

His fins settled, and his little mouth closed. Water cascaded from him as she maneuvered the claws to pick him up, as gently as possible, and bring him over the side.

His amulet still lay around his neck, and she pointed. "Can you change?"

He flinched at the spoken words but grasped the pendant in a trembling hand. The air around him flickered and hazed and his scales retreated and two human legs replaced them. Would he need clothes? She worried at her lip. This s what being impulsive gets you. He shuddered, and she rubbed his arm.

"Are you cold? Wait here."

Two cupboards lined the wall near the door. She opened one of them and smiled at the long white coat hanging on the back panel. *Perfect.*

The coat swallowed the boy's small frame, highlighting the pallor of his skin. He needed the ocean. He needed home.

Ana opened the door and startled as the boy's hand stole into hers. Her heart constricted. She hustled him down the empty hall, holding her hand up to the side of her head for silence.

Heavy doors lined the walls. She refused to glance at them, refused to think about who lay beyond them. They were adults. They could cope with the harshness of the experiments. But the youngling needed the ocean.

A small access hatch sat halfway up the wall at the end of the corridor. Ana ignored the yellow danger sign and the "Authorized and Emergency Access Only" plastered above the iron handle. She'd disabled the cameras here long ago.

She twisted it open and helped the boy clamber through into the narrow airlock.

After sealing the hatch behind her, she tapped in the access override code for the outer door. The metal below them slid open, and the small space filled with the tang of salt. Water from the chilled depths seeped around their feet. A glint shone in the boy's eyes. He shrugged off the baggy coat as scales rippled up his legs, turning to a tail growing brighter as the water touched him.

Ana stripped and cached her clothes with the coat in the highest space. Light shimmered up her legs and she inhaled the aroma of home as her fins shifted from her skin. The water closed around them, and a warm ache spread through her chest as the boy darted and flipped and somersaulted.

"You need to come with me. I will take you to someone who will help."

He swam to her side, and she stroked down his tail, tugging on the feathery ribbons.

"Stay by me. You are still not safe under the shadow of the dome. We must go the way of the kelp forest."

Her tail pushed through the water, and she dove into tall waving fronds, her arms making a path for the smaller mer behind her. Rough strands caught on her hair, and she twisted her way out of their determined grasp. Going through the kelp would slow them down, but watchers didn't stay in the Dome.

The row of doors flashed into her mind, as did the imagined screams of those behind them. She dove lower, twisting and turning through the kelp, bringing the child up beneath her. But outrunning guilt never worked. The boy escaped, that could be enough.

They reached the edge of the Merfolk border, the

part closest to the Dome, most likely to be patrolled. The long figure of her sister's mate glided into view. Half relieved, half anxious, she tugged the boy by his shoulder and swam out to meet him. She batted the water in a warning pattern.

Myrndir's trident glittered in the sun's rays filtering through the depths. Matted hair threaded with shells rested on his broad back, shifting with a rippling vibration as he turned.

His eyes widened as they lit on the child, and he swam with rapid strokes toward them.

"Shodica's youngling. We searched everywhere. Is she safe also?"

Her fins rippled and an impulse to lie, to say she didn't know, sparked through her. The boy keened, the sharp note jabbing into her mind. He shuddered and curled in on himself, his tail shielding his face. She closed her eyes for a moment, then turned to Myrndir, his face shadowed with a knowledge she didn't want to speak.

"No, she isn't."

His strong arms reached for the youngling and scooped him tight against his chest. He met her gaze over the trembling form of the boy. *"You should come, speak to the council."*

She stroked backward, shaking her head, hair swirling in her wake. *"No. I need to return before I am missed, and they connect my disappearance with his."*

Myrndir frowned but nodded, the shells clattering in ripples again.

Her gaze went to the boy, and her hand floated up as if to reach out, but she curled her fingers back and spun around.

"Give Theia my greetings."

"Be careful, Sariana."

The current streaming around her, she swam back to the Dome. Back to duty. Back to her mission.

"I always am."

Chapter Twenty-Two

The door slid open into the Dome's arboretum. Evan caught his breath at the different world in front of him. Ultraviolet lights hummed in long strips hanging down from the ceiling, beaming through misty air. Rows of bright green shoots reached up from a grid of planters. Lettuce, tomato, carrots, and a leaf he didn't recognize. He rubbed it between his fingers.

Khalid's voice came over his shoulder. "Potato."

"What?"

"Potatoes. What you're squashing under your hand."

Evan let go of the plant and brushed his hand on his trousers. "This place is unbelievable."

"Isn't it? That's why I don't mind this being my shift."

"Peaceful. You could almost forget you're under the sea."

The lights in the ceiling were like in a massive warehouse. This place was a constant surprise.

Khalid wiped his hands on the towel, walking toward Evan. "Char told me about the boy."

Evan leaned back against the wall, hands behind his head, fixed on the carefully tended plants. Inside his head, the mer youngling screamed. "Yeah. It sucks."

"Do you think they'll, you know, let him go?"

He quirked his brows and stared at Khalid until the other man shrugged and waved his hands.

"All right, all right, I know. Of course they won't. Bastards."

Khalid's tone was light, detached, but his eyes told the real story. You learned to read eyes pretty smartly out in the field. You also learned when to look away from people's pain. This was not one of those times.

"They won't because they don't give a shit. They see them as animals."

The towel twisted between Khalid's fingers, betraying the calm shuttering his face. "And aren't they?"

Evan pushed down rising anger. "No more than we are."

"Look, man, I know you don't like it, I don't like it either, but what can we do?"

He rubbed his jaw. It was a rhetorical question but this was why he'd come in the first place. Char was right, they could trust Khalid. But first they had to convince him.

"If we could get out, we could make contact with the government. If the world knew—"

"If the world knew, they'd be putting in tourist attractions and a theme park."

Evan gritted his teeth; he could see it all too clearly. Instead of a dome, there would be cages and zoos.

"Humans suck."

"That they do."

"There's gotta be someone in the government who could stop this, something we can do to get the word out to them."

An thoughtful expression flickered over Khalid's face, gone quickly. Evan straightened, his hands resting on his hips, using his height over the other man. "You know something."

"Nope. Nothing."

He stared at Khalid. "The boy screamed. The whole time his mother died in front of him. He screamed, thinking he was next."

"You play dirty."

"I'm not playing."

"Fine. I don't know much, all right? It's practically nothing."

Something is better than nothing. "So tell me."

"I was in the communications room this one time, I'd been sent to deliver a box of files. People don't always notice me, I don't know why."

Khalid often seemed to slip under the radar, which was strange. He was larger than life, tall, although not as tall as Evan. Loud. And yet when he didn't want to be seen he wasn't. "Sniper?"

Khalid grinned. "Eight years."

"So what did you hear? Or see?"

The grin faded, and Khalid closed in on himself. "There was talk of a watcher. They'd picked up some frequencies they weren't expecting, someone piggy-backing in on their transmissions."

"A hacker?"

"Sounded like more than that, like someone after information. You should ask your girlfriend. She was there, talking to Blake. She might know more."

Heat flashed in his chest and his stomach sank. "Are you sure?"

"How many petite blondes with killer eyes do we have down here?"

His brows raised in acknowledgment even as his

heart screamed denial. Ana seemed to often be where she wasn't expected to be.

"It doesn't mean anything."

"I never said it did. The fact you say that tells me you worry it does, though."

"Yeah, but it's true. It doesn't mean anything."

Khalid scratched at a piece of mud hardening on his arm. "Yeah. Fair enough. I wouldn't necessarily tell her what you've been planning, though."

Tension ran through his shoulders, and he rubbed at his cheek. "What plans?"

"For what it's worth, I think you could be on to something. If you can find out about this watcher, you might have a chance to get a communication out to someone on the outside. Whether that helps is a whole different issue."

"Meaning?"

"Meaning unless you have a whole lotta proof, there ain't nobody who's gonna believe you. They're more likely to certify your ass. That is, if they could find you. Which they won't, because you're stuck down in this dump."

His fingers tracked through the soil, and he gazed around the plants. All this to feed all those people so they could...what? Get turned into some mad scientist vision of a super soldier? He thought of Hansel and Gretel and the witch fattening the children up before she consumed them.

"You never told me why you joined Project Siren."

Khalid leaned back on the bench, staring at the fan on the ceiling. "I joined the army because I believed. I *still* believe, someone has to stand up for those who need protection. That serving your country is an honorable privilege." He glanced back at Evan. "Turns out a lot of it is about money and power and bullying on an international scale. I got sick of fighting for things I didn't believe in. When the opportunity came to transfer here, I took it. Something different, something where I could maybe make a real change, serve my country in a way I could believe in." Bitterness dripped from his usually cheerful voice. "Turns out I was wrong about that too."

"If you'd told me there was a secret base where crazy unethical experiments were being carried out by ex-army personnel, I'll be honest, I'd have expected most of the crew to be like Blake. But they're not. It confused me but I think we all joined for the promise of serving a higher cause. And now we're trapped."

"For now, right? You say you got that plan."

His plan was nowhere near concrete, and he could tell the other man knew, but he smiled back and thumped his chest. "Oh yeah, brother, I got that plan."

****

His footsteps sounded a slow tempo against the metal grids crisscrossing the hallway. Khalid had given him a lot to think about. Somehow he needed to get into the command center, see what he could find out. There would be no point contacting someone when he had so little knowledge about the enterprise.

Adrenaline rushed through him at the thought of breaking into the command center. This place held too many secrets.

Time to bust some of them out.

Chapter Twenty-Three

Evan tightened the Kevlar vest he'd smuggled out from the armory Khalid had told him about. He shrugged his hoodie on over it. A beanie low on his forehead with the hood drawn forward should shield his face enough from security cameras. Before sliding he gun into the holster, he checked the safety on it.

Evan strode down the hall, steady even steps making barely any noise. Night lamps shone dimly at even intervals on opposite sides of the hall. He crossed diagonally before each one, staying out of direct light as much as possible. He knew the patrol times, knew the positions. There were two points at which he might have trouble.

If only he had a camera, or if he hadn't lost his cell phone in the wreck. Hopefully he'd find out more of the truth tonight but unless he stole any information he found, who would believe him? Each step of the mission would have its own trials. No point borrowing trouble.

He rounded the corner of the corridor heading toward the command center. The need to fight someone pounded against the base of his neck. He was almost disappointed when he reached the end of the corridor unchallenged.

The handle into the main office didn't budge. He hadn't really expected it to. He'd come prepared this time. Evan pulled the wrench from where it dragged at the pocket of his cargos. Silence filled the corridor. He brought the wrench down hard on the lock and burst the quiet with a single clang. Evan waited one moment, then a final smash, and the lock split. Swinging the door open, he swapped the wrench for his flashlight.

Three large filing cabinets sat at the back of the room. Moving swiftly, he crossed and scanned the labels with the beam of his flashlight until he found "H". He pulled out his file, frowning at the unexpected thickness of it.

After putting the flashlight between his teeth, he flipped open the file and shuffled through the pages. Medical records. Training records. Military service.

Assessment notes?

He scanned the printed pages, his brows contracting and anger rising.

Evan Hunter is a prime candidate. Physically fit but emotionally damaged, he has a strong streak of loyalty that can be worked on with his sense of isolation and need for comradeship.

He nearly spat out the flashlight but kept reading. Seeing yourself laid bare by someone who thought they had a bead on you was weird. They wrote positively about his strength and agility, and he wondered about watching eyes in the training rooms.

Celine's neat handwriting filled in pages of notes of medical exams and results. She was doing her job, but it felt like a betrayal.

At the very end was a copy of the contract with a paper-clipped note attached about the meeting he'd had with the Siren, or whatever she called herself.

The words *Reaffirmed. Consequences outlined,*

jumped out at him, and anger coiled at the thought of Kelly in their sights.

A noise filtered through the room, a distant door closing. He switched off the flashlight and froze, waiting in the darkness. Blindness faded into gray gloom, and he counted each heartbeat. After a minute of no further noise, he risked the light again.

The contract was deceptively simple. Terms of service covered length of time—six months with option to extend—and pay—a stipend to be paid into a designated account. Further down in the fine print, he found what he searched for: duty of service to include participation in research of any kind. Period of service could be extended at any time by the contractor if deemed beneficial to the project. Failure to abide by contract would lead to repercussions not exclusive to the contracted, and liability could extend to family members. Under all of this sat his signature.

He remembered the strange feeling that spread up his arm when he signed. Something told him more than the words on the page bound him. Everyone talked about this damn contract as if it was unbreakable. Maybe in a world where mermaids were real, some kind of hocus pocus could be cast on a contract. None of it mattered now anyway. He'd chosen his course.

Evan shoved the file back in the cabinet, pausing as he saw *Hudson, Michael* on the label of the file behind his. Drawing it out, he held his breath. In it were photographs, records, and progress notes. Bile rose in his throat. The photographs laid out in horrific detail everything that had been done to the former soldier. The man's once strong frame was reduced to twisted muscles and bizarre deformities. Notes under the photographs recorded the dissatisfaction of the research team with what they called the transition phase. His fingers gripped so hard on the file the paper crumpled, and he forced himself to relax before he ripped it accidentally.

He'd tried not to think about what must have happened to Hudson and Matthews. Deep in his gut he'd known they wouldn't make it, but it was different seeing it laid out in this sickeningly clinical style. The last update was dated yesterday. They were still alive. Jesus. They were observing to see how long they'd last before dying. His jaw clenched as he folded the file and turned the flashlight off.

They were right about him. But wrong in one essential thing. His loyalty might pull him toward his comrades, but it had never conflicted with his integrity. No man left behind. Hudson's jokes and Matthews' calm good sense whirled in his mind, interposed with memories of mutated screaming bodies.

He wouldn't leave them like that. Couldn't.

He scanned the room for signs anyone had been here, apart from the smashed lock. Nothing to trace it to him though.

The corridor was still deserted and cold. He stuck to the edges and flitted down the hall, steel forming reinforcements around his mind. This had always been part of his calling, doing the hard things because they were the right things.

They clearly didn't expect trouble down here. Hardly any patrols at night. The cameras were easily avoided. It was like they relied on other means to keep people in control. The threats against family embedded in those contracts, for instance.

Medical and Research were not far from the main admin center. He punched in Celine's code, hoping it hadn't changed. Hefting the wrench, he stalked down the corridor, almost hoping someone would check. The photographs burned images in his head, and he wanted to break someone.

The door at the end was shut properly this time, and he wasted no time in smashing the lock and pushing open the door.

Evan paused in the outer room, his fists clenched. Had to be something in here he could use. He stared at the lock pad on a cabinet. *Worth a try.* He punched in Celine's number and it hissed open. A ragged breath tore from his lips. The right thing was always the hard thing.

Bottles clinked as he sorted through them with a shaking hand and grabbed several. Syringes were in a box in the open cupboard next to the cabinet.

The door to the inner room sat sullen and dark at the end of the room. He twisted the handle. A foul stench of rotting skin and acrid chemicals sent him recoiling, his arm shielding his face. He breathed through his sleeve, then fumbled with his hood to tighten the cords so the fabric covered his nose and mouth. The flashlight beam flickered, and he hit the side of it on his hip, shaking the batteries.

The two men lay where he'd last seen them. Matthews was closest to him. His eyes were shut and a deep line scored between his brows, echoing the lines carved into his face. Every breath the man took was a shuddering convulsion of his thin chest. The air rattled in the back of his throat. An IV line pumped who knew what into his veins, and a machine hooked up pads on his temple. A line with a locked valve was taped to his inner arm, bruises marring the pale skin around it.

Evan wiped shaking hands on his trousers. It was easier now Matthews lay in front of him. No one should be left like this. He held the bottle of morphine in whitened fingers and drew it out into one of the syringes. No need to tap it.

He leaned over the man's drawn face and whispered, "Sorry."

Unhooking the IV line from the bag of murky fluid, he then injected the morphine into the line. He kept his gaze on the liquid making its way into the weakened body covered in black flaking scales. A second bottle followed the first.

Matthews' breathing slowed and eased. His mutated body, covered in scales and gill-like cuts, slumped, the machine quietly flatlining. Evan wiped his face and yanked off the cardio monitor pads. The machine shut off.

He patted Matthews's feet and stumbled around the bed to Hudson. He froze. Hudson stared up at him from a face contorted into a frozen rictus. Brown eyes full of anguish blinked at him from under creeping scales, and his mouth tried to form a word. Evan gripped his shoulder and leaned close.

"Please…" The word was a whisper of breath.

"Hudson. I'm so sorry."

"End it…please."

He jerked a nod. "I'll get your letter to Shelley; don't you worry about it."

He filled the syringe, injected it into the line, then kept his gaze on Hudson's and his hand on the other man's arm while the drug claimed him. The gills on

Hudson's legs and arms sucked in air with disturbing rapidity until they fluttered and stopped. The light flickered out in Hudson's eyes and a fire flared inside Evan.

The report in his file claimed he was a prime candidate. *Screw them!* If he had to blow up the whole place with him inside, he would stop this. A tear slid down the side of his face. He stuffed another couple of bottles of morphine and a syringe packet into his pockets. The wrench he wiped with alcohol and left in a cupboard.

He paused at the door. In his heart, he knew he'd done the right thing but guilt twinged. He didn't promise vengeance or anything a movie hero would have. He was no hero.

But he silently vowed to not forget and to do what he could to get out.

Chapter Twenty-Four

Ana sat on the rocky ledge, her tail curled under her, fins fluttering in the water lapping at the stone. Shells clicked through her fingers. She breathed in as memories flashed through her head in time with the shifting net. Doubt ate at the corners of her mind, and she clicked faster, each memory pushing uncertainty a little further away.

Baruthial's face the last time she'd seen him was the constant image pasted behind her eyes. His grin, the determination in his eyes, all wiped clean in a pale rictus of death. She'd been numb for days after his body washed up, the marks on his neck and arms raw and bloated, and no amulet around his neck.

Click. Click.

Back further, to her uncle, his love for a human leading him to forsake the ocean until one day they found him, starved, clinging to life on a dinghy, the power to change long forgotten.

Click, click, click.

Her grandfather, his eye socket a ragged hole in his head, great scars on his tail from the chunks torn out by sailors a century ago as they sought fame and fortune.

Click.

He'd beaten them. Escaped. Taught his family never to trust. Humans brought nothing but pain.

Evan.

She closed her eyes and let his face fill her mind, chasing away the darkness. The guilt stayed, a curling sickness in her gut. But his smile and the kindness in his face, the feeling of his skin... they stayed too.

Ripples arrowed toward her and she sighed, rolling the net of shells into a tight ball and placing it behind her back.

Amatheia's head rose from the water, drops wending their way to the surface. "Sariana, why are you here? Did something happen?"

Her gaze slid away from her sister's piercing stare. "Nothing. And everything. I needed somewhere to think. Somewhere to be myself."

Amatheia ducked under the water and surfaced close to the ledge, pulled herself up, and flipped her tail to the opposite side to Ana. The shells poked Ana's hip as she shifted to give Amatheia room, and her sister darted a glance, concern writ large in the lines of her face.

"Sariana, remembering isn't always the best thing to do."

"You've all been trying so hard to forget. Someone has to remember him."

Amatheia's fins shuddered, and a dark pit opened in Ana's chest.

"Sorry. I didn't mean that."

"Baruthial made his own choice. No one pushed him to work with the humans."

Ana held up a hand, her gills opening and closing fast. "I don't need to hear it again, sister. You and I don't see eye to eye on this, but I know you loved him too."

"So why did you come? Surely not merely to count

the shells for Baru?"

The crisp tangy scent of the ocean wound around her, and she stared into the inky depths as her hands twisted together.

"There is a man. One of the soldiers. He is different." She glanced at Amatheia but the fierce silver glow in her sister's eyes drove her gaze away. "He confuses me."

Amatheia reached forward and laid a hand on hers, the fine webbing tingling over her skin. "You mean he confuses your heart."

"I don't know what to do!" The words broke from her, and she pressed her lips tight against any others.

Amatheia sighed, her tail swishing down into the water where it waved back and forth. Foamy ridges rippled outward. "I know you remember our uncle. I know you know this won't end well. No wonder you are confused. He must be quite a man to get past your loathing for the humans."

She shook her head, her stomach flipping and twisting in time with her thoughts. "I don't loathe them all. I wish I did. I loathe humanity. But there are some individuals I like a lot. Char, she is funny and kind and strong. You would like her."

"And him? The man? Who is he?"

"His name is Evan." She couldn't stop her lips turning up as she said his name. Her fingers curled into her palms.

"Evan Hunter?"

She turned and stared. "Yes. How do you—"

"You must not tell the others. I have only told Myrndir. I saved your Evan from the wreck. I carried him to the cavern, and that's where the humans found him."

Thoughts whirled in her head, feelings battling for supremacy. "The others? Did you see them?"

"No." The word was definite but Amatheia's gaze slipped from hers, and her fins fluttered.

"Would you tell me if you had?" Bitterness laced her voice, acrid on her tongue.

"Sariana—"

"The council doesn't always know best, sister. You and I both know that."

Her sister arched an eyebrow. "Do you perhaps forget my bond partner is on the council?"

"As if I could ever forget. He reminds me all the time in that deep *I am so important* tone of his. But neither do I forget you are a key keeper. We both know some secrets are kept even from the council."

Amatheia's hand gently pushed the mass of shells and beads around her neck, until her fingers closed on the keys. "You speak truth."

"You admit you keep secrets, and yet you deny hiding the truth from me."

Amatheia sighed, a flutter of fins rising with the sound. "Things are more complicated than that, Sariana. Come, follow me. There is something you need to see."

Amatheia slipped off the rock, her hair fanning out on the surface in a sheaf of silver before she sank into the depths. Ana followed, silky water closing over her skin and the chill calming her roiling thoughts.

Her sister didn't head out into the reef as she'd expected. Amatheia swam around the base of the ledge, heading deeper into the cavern, ribbony fins curling in the water behind her like a beckoning finger.

The farther they got into the cavern, the more

squid-ink black the water became. The light from the sun did not reach this far. A glow spread through the water as their bodies luminesced, pulsing energy warming her skin. Amatheia swam deeper, icy cold closing over them. Ana's tail shivered, and she shot forward to touch her sister's shoulder.

"Where are we going?"

Amatheia gestured behind her. *"There."*

Ana turned to look. As their pale glow spread to the water ahead of them, shadows deepened around a door in the rock wall. Hewn from the stone and surrounded by a frame of carved motifs, the slab of the entryway was ornamented only by a massive lock. Ana coiled back, her tail rising in front of her and the sharp fins on her arms standing high. Amatheia drew out the key from around her neck.

"You spoke of secrets. This is one I have shared with no one else. Not even Myrndir."

A jolt shot through Ana's blood. Her hand flew up in an urge to stop Amatheia, to keep her from breaking her oath. The webbing between her fingers pulsed. But she curled her arm back in a stroke through the water, pulling herself closer to the door. Her gills opened and closed with the rapidity of her heartbeat. Amatheia cast her an opaque glance and slid the key into the lock. The door opened with the merest push.

Darkness spilled out in streaking tendrils of sluggish water. The oily murk clogged her gills. She gritted her teeth and pushed through the discomfort, sliding in through the doorway. Ripples of light flickered along the edges of the circular room, mosses and weeds responding to their luminescence with their own weak light. Bubbles floated up from the bottom of the room as small shoals of jellyfish investigated. She twisted her tail, spinning slowly in the water, trying to take it all in. So many carvings. Her heart thundered against her ribs. This place was a warning.

Amatheia's tail flashed and disappeared around a column. Ana swam toward it, a prickling running up her spine. The column marked a dip, a well in the floor. A fin slid into it as Ana stared.

"Theia?"

"Follow me, sister. It isn't as bad as you think."

The sides of the shaft scraped against her elbows, and her hips bumped the rock as a sharp corner came up too fast. She clenched her jaw and thrust with her tail, seeking the end of this cramped space that stole her air. The bright flash of Amatheia's tail called her on.

Walls closed in on her at the end of the tunnel. It was a small space with a heavy stone slab at the center. Symbols and pictographs covered the smooth stone.

"I know you're used to computers and books now, Sariana, but this rock bears our history. Here is the story of our uncle. The real story. It is tragedy and warning both."

She traced the carvings, the pain lying within the story shooting fire up through her webbing as the sensitive fibers brushed over the motifs.

Her heart slowed to a painful ache. Marobian had loved his human so intensely. Every chisel stroke betrayed his feelings. He had been drawn in by her beauty and snared by her kindness. He visited her in human form and their love blossomed, but the sea called him, and to the sea he returned every few days. Her brothers would not allow her to marry a man with no dowry, no abode, no family. So he signed a contract with the eldest. He did not know it was bound by magics. The next time he tried to enter the sea, his legs burned with a pain of a thousand knife cuts. Try as he might, he could not change; his mer form was lost to him.

"Why is this kept so secret? We know about Marobian, he is a constant warning to young mer."

"Because of the pain. Even near death he loved his human still. Until his last breath he spoke of her. He lived a half-life and it destroyed him, but here in this chamber he poured out his love for her."

She drew her fingers away, chills cascading down her spine. *"And so you seek to warn me."*

Theia darted close to her, sweeping her hair aside. *"I have met your Evan. I believe he may be a good man. But he is human. And the humans do not understand us."*

Her fins drooped, floating without resistance in the barely perceptible current. The imprint of Evan's arms around her settled on her waist, and the tender light in his eyes burned in her mind. But he didn't know she was mer. She lifted her chin and faced her sister, closing her feelings inside where they belonged.

"You are right. He is not mer. But this one will be different. You will see."

Chapter Twenty Five

His feet pounding on the treadmill, sweat dripping down the back of his singlet, Evan kept his focus on the doctors and their clipboards.

This was the fifth day of concurrent tests covering his fitness and his response time. They'd increased the doses of the toxic-tasting vitamin drink. He thought of the mermaid and the syringe depositing her DNA into test tubes and fought back bile. Thinking of it as a vitamin drink was easier to handle.

He was already faster.

He'd pulled back but let himself do enough to raise a sweat and to assuage their interest. For his plan to work he had to keep them interested in using him as a test subject but he shied away from showing them the extent of the new strength and speed he experienced. His cardio response had improved, and his reflexes were noticeably quicker.

"Thanks, Hunter. You can hop off now."

He punched the minus button, slowing down the treadmill to a stroll, walking off the heat in his muscles. One of Jones's many assistants came up to him, gestured sharply for him to get off. He wondered where Celine was, guilt at using her key code rising in him.

He jumped off and reached for a towel, rubbed it over his head and shoulders.

"Take a seat."

The chair was different from those he'd been in before, this was more like what he'd seen at a dentist, that long reclining back that put people at the mercy of those around them.

He stared between the chair and the assistant, everything in him reluctant to make himself so vulnerable. The white coat raised his eyebrows and jerked a hand.

"Come on, Hunter, we don't have all day."

The leather was sticky under the sweat of his torso, and he shifted uncomfortably as they attached pads to his skin.

It was hard to not feel like a slab of meat with muscles prodded, and electrodes attached to skin and measurements taken. He started consciously trying to catch the gazes of the scientists but not one looked at his face. Memories of Hudson's twisted form flashed into his head.

Doctor Jones approached with a syringe, and he eyed the needle, his fists clenching.

"More blood tests?" He flinched as the doctor ignored his proffered arm and swabbed the base of his neck next to his shoulder. *What the hell?*

"Hold still please, Hunter."

"Exactly how much blood do you need?"

"Oh no, we aren't taking this time. We are giving."

He tried to pull away but two of the burlier assistants held him down. The doctor frowned.

"I'm a bit disappointed, I have to say. You've been doing so well up until now. You do remember the contract you signed?"

Kelly's face swam behind his eyes. "You're an asshole, Jones." He yanked his shoulder from the grip of one of the orderlies and exposed his neck. "Get it over with."

The needle slid into his vein with a sharp sting.

"Ready?"

"Yes."

"I wasn't asking you."

Arms like iron folded around his torso. "Don't move. It's important you hold still, buddy."

His heart thudded against his ribs, and he clenched his fingers, trying to keep his neck still as the skin around the needle began to throb with a sickening ache. "Jesus, hurry up."

Jones flicked his eyebrows at the man behind him, and the grip tightened as the doctor pushed down the plunger in the syringe.

Hot fire seared through his veins, and he bit back a scream, willing himself to stay still, thankful for the vise-like grip on his chest. A curling pain threaded through his torso from the needle point as it slid slowly out. His teeth chattered as shock set in, and he fought down the feeling of not being able to breathe. *Feel the oxygen, there is air in your lungs, you're not dying, you can breathe. You can breathe.* The self-talk helped take the edge off, but his limbs shook and nausea clouded his mind.

He was too weak to push away the arms that lifted and guided him to a bed. The hard mattress pushed on skin suddenly painful to the touch. His body contorted and he turned his head to vomit. Shudders wracked him. and he curled his knees up to his chest. focusing on each breath in, each breath out. Sharp knives attacked his mind, ripping into his brain. His eyes blurred and his vision shimmered green, then opaque gray. Heat blossomed and pulsated from the puncture on his neck, wrapping his body in skin-crawling warmth.

Blackness spread over his mind. He fought it, desperate not to sink into an unknown dark beyond.

I can't go. I have people depending on me.

You always fail. You let them down.

They died because of you. It's best if you go too. You don't deserve to go, don't deserve the peace.

Kelly, she doesn't deserve more pain.

Inch by inch he fought against clinging nothingness. His eyes flew open, and harsh neon light speared into his sight, driving away the dark. Burning breaths tore at his lungs and his back arched against the plastic mattress. Every muscle contracted, as if electricity coursed through him.

At last he fell back onto the bed, shuddering and weak. He blinked at the blurry faces hovering over him. Muffled voices floated in the air, and he squeezed his eyes shut as they battered at his ears.

The blankness in his head gave way to a slide show of memories. Too weak to push them back into the dark where they belonged, he sank into the leaden weight of guilt.

****

Waking some time later, he almost wished he hadn't. His skin stretched over aching muscles as if it belonged to someone else, not quite fitting and pulling at his nerves. Wires ran from pads on his temple to a machine hovering above him, lights and bars flickering in patterns he didn't understand. His pulse picked up, rapid, weak, and shallow.

Muted light fell on the room's white walls. He gritted his teeth and turned his head, trying to see. A woman in a white coat straightened from where she leaned over an array of blue lit test tubes. Pushing back her safety goggles, she walked over to him. A smile softened the fierce lines of her face.

"You're awake."

He tried to talk but the words stuck in his dry mouth, and he coughed. A plastic cup filled with ice chips appeared in front of his face. The frozen water slipped down his throat, spreading relief.

"How long?"

She dug her hands in her coat pockets and tilted her head. "Since you blacked out? About four hours. You're doing well, too. Better than others we've had."

Anger burned sluggish under his skin. "Great, so I'm not dying."

A tight line drew between her brows. "I have a few tests to run before we release you."

He lay his pounding head back on the pillow. Nausea tugged at his stomach. All the worst symptoms of a hangover without any of the fun.

"Better get on with it then."

A hot ache pulsed at the base of his neck, radiating down his left shoulder. His eyelids kept trying to sink shut but he forced them open and studied the woman's every move. Gloved hands tapped a needle and his arm began shaking. She raised a brow.

"Don't worry, Hunter. This one's for the pain."

Taking his hand, she injected the drug into the IV port. Ice flooded his burning veins. Another needle appeared.

"And this one's for the blood."

She drew out three samples in total, pausing between each one to write out labels in a rapid scrawl.

After the samples, she flashed a light in his eyes, took his pulse, checked his lungs, and finished with some skin scrapings.

"Excellent. All looking good so far. I'll get Doctor Jones. He might have questions for you, then you can go back to your quarters."

She patted his arm, and he flinched as it set off another spiral of pain from the puncture on his neck. With an apologetic grimace, she tucked her pen in a pocket and left, her heels clattering on the tiles.

For a moment he focused on simply breathing. The stuff they'd injected into him, that must be what they shoved into Hudson and Matthews. Images of himself lying twisted and screaming churned in his head.

No way he was waiting here for that to happen to him, plan or no plan. Jones could kiss his ass.

He yanked the electrodes off, wincing as hair came up with the tape. The room swam as he pushed up on his elbow. *One breath. Two.* Footsteps echoed down the corridor. Bracing himself, he pulled the IV out and tossed the line on the bed behind him.

The metal frame of the bed chilled his fingers as he gripped it, levering himself up. Jelly filled his legs, and he leaned for a moment to catch his breath. Each step to the open door was a victory. He blinked at his boots, on the floor next to a chair with a folded pile of his discarded clothes. If he stooped he might not make it up again. He gripped the back of the plastic seat and reached as far as he could, his breath catching. He snagged a lace in an outstretched finger and pulled the boots up. Leaving the clothes, he staggered out of the door.

"Hunter! Where are you going?"

He flipped an elaborate salute to Doctor Jones. "I've had enough for today, Doc. Find another pincushion."

The manic grin vanished from his face as he turned, his eyes blurring. He refused to stop, to stumble, to reach grasping fingers to the wall. Pride reinforced his muscles, kept him moving down the hall, from pools of light through shadow and back.

Jones called out once more but didn't follow. It wasn't as if he could go anywhere the doctor couldn't find him later.

Neither the shaking legs nor the constant pain caused the lump of lead dragging at his stomach. His skin prickled in the shadows. His vision shifted, every dot in every panel visible, every etched letter in the signs. He swallowed the bile pooling at the back of his throat. *Aftereffects. That was all.*

Hudson's twisting body screamed into his mind, and he stumbled.

Not all. Not by a long shot.

Chapter Twenty-Six

Evan rounded the corner, his shoulder pressed into the wall, and his arms curled up against his torso. A shadow moved by his door, and his muscles froze. Blinking away the fog blurring his vision, he used the last of his strength to stand his full height.

The shadow bled toward him, solidifying into the welcome sight of Ana.

She shuffled toward him, arms crossed, eyes wide as they took in his state.

"Hey. Sorry, I wasn't expecting company, or I would have scrubbed up."

She didn't smile at his poor attempt at humor. He reached out a hand. A long moment passed before she clasped it.

"I shouldn't be here," she said. "I don't know why I *am* here."

He pulled her to him and held her rigid body close. The cinnamon soapy scent of her drove out the stale sterility of the lab. She clutched at his sweater, and his heart ached at her trembling.

"Do I look that bad?"

Her words came out muffled against his chest. "No, of course not. I wasn't expecting it. The bruising. And the rest."

His pulse spiked, and he breathed out the residual panic. The ache in the side of his neck wouldn't let him forget everything would be different now.

He pulled back, sliding his hands down her arms and clasping her fingers. "I need to sit down before I fall down."

She bit her lip and moved to let him past to the door. Holding on to one of her hands, he punched in his code. The door slid open and he sighed. *Funny how somewhere so bare could feel so much like home so soon.* He walked in, reaching to turn the light on. Ana pulled back against his fingers, and he let her go.

"Won't you come in?"

Her gaze flicked up to his face and away. "I really shouldn't. I only came to make sure you—"

"That I what? That I came back?"

Her shrug turned to a shudder, and he leaned against the bunk. His eyes closed, and the words slid out through the fatigue like someone turned on a tap.

"I did come back and I'm mostly fine, but I really need some tea or coffee or even some goddamn water, and I'd love for you to stay so I don't feel so alone, and because you make me happy, but I understand if you have to go—"

A rush of air touched his face, and he opened his eyes to see Ana in front of him.

She stared up at his face, eyes fierce sapphires, then flung her arm around his neck and leaned up on her toes. "Tell me you're okay."

He bent his lips to her raised mouth, and let her kiss him better.

Her fingers slid over his shoulders, and the pain eased where she touched. Soft cotton scrunched under his fingers, as he tightened his arm around her waist. Her body was strong and soft in his arms. He sank into her mouth with a need for something more than merely touch. He kissed her as if he could draw her into himself, keep her in his heart for always, let her chase away his darkness.

Her hands drifted up into his hair and sent tingles over his scalp.

Evan left her lips and kissed down her neck, indulging himself on her soft skin. Her fingers went to the puncture wound, and his muscles went rigid as pain speared through them.

"Is this what they did to you?"

He drew back, his forehead bent to hers. "Among other things. I don't really want to talk about it today." The pain throbbed, sapping his energy. His knees shook, and he collapsed down on to the bed. "I think I need to sleep."

She stroked his hair, cupped his face. "I'll leave you to sleep, then."

"Stay with me."

The intake of breath was small but audible. Her eyes widened.

"Sleeping. Just sleeping. Scout's honor." He gave a small salute. "I really don't want to be alone."

The darkness crossed her face again and he wished he could take it away.

"Then I'll stay."

He hadn't realized how tense he was until floppiness at her answer ran through him. He grinned at her. "Good."

He slid down the wall 'til he lay sideways on the narrow bed. She stared at him, her face carved in grave lines. He patted the bed, and she smiled, one of her rare heartbreakingly beautiful smiles spreading sunshine in her face. Unfolding her body down onto the mattress, she lay carefully next to him, her face close to his.

He smiled and kissed her forehead, stroking soft hair from her face, then closed his eyes, his arm resting on her shoulder.

****

Ana lay in the darkness, tracing the lines of his face with her gaze. Warmth wrapped around her, and the weight of his arm over her shoulders anchored her whirling thoughts. Angry bruises marred his strong jaw. Fresh lines were carved around his eyes, like arrows to the dark circles fading into his skin.

She moved her hand from where it lay between them, reaching to hover over the inflamed puncture site on his neck. He shifted and she froze. His arm slid from her shoulders to her waist, his hand pulling her closer to him. Heat flooded her, and her pulse thundered in her ears. He remained asleep, and her heart rate slowed to a humming thud. His skin beneath hers sent electric shocks running through her veins.

None of this was supposed to happen. What if he knew? He would hate me.

A hot, tight ache spread through her chest, and she lowered her head to nestle into him. Her hand crept around his waist, and she listened to his breathing. She hadn't meant to fall in love with him. She should leave.

But she stayed, his heartbeat beneath her fingers and her heart in his hands.

Chapter Twenty-Seven

The Siren leaned close to the surface of the Dome, her fingers tracing the swirls of water on the outside. The file sat abandoned on her desk. It had been harder to observe the experiments on Evan than she had expected. Her fingers curled on the dark glass. He was strong. She had known he would do well.

A chill shuddered under her fingers and she pushed off the dome, turned back to the file. Black leather curled around her as she leaned back in the chair. It was her favourite thing in this whole place. *Who needed a throne when you could rule the world from a soft chair that swivelled?*

The black monitor at the edge of her desk blinked redly, and she glared at it. It kept beeping. Leaning forward, she stabbed the intercom button.

"I said I was not to be disturbed."

"Doctor Jones is here. He says he has vital information about the merchild from the other day."

Her finger leaned into the button with force enough that the intercom shifted. "Show him in."

She took a moment to sit back, straighten her jacket, push her trembling hands under the desk. The greater good. All great things required sacrifice.

The doctor bowed himself in, losing his bustling pleasant demeanour as soon as the door closed behind him. Eagerness honed the sharp edges of his face, and his eyes burned with a light that brought her to the edge of her chair.

"Did you read the report?"

Her gaze flicked to the file, and she slid some of the photographs of Evan screaming on the lab bench back inside the manila covers.

Jones threw himself into the other chair, dragged it across to the desk, metal legs screeching. "No, not that one, the one I sent you last night."

She frowned. "Email? There were a lot of complex chemical justifications. but when I saw who you were talking about, I stopped reading. We don't test on children. There have to be some lines."

He raised a brow at her and she bristled.

"Lines are not weak, Doctor. We can get the information we need through adult subjects. There is no need to involve children."

He grunted. "Yes, I gathered that after you saw the footage of the mermaid and her child. It makes them a lot more amenable. You want good results; you do what it takes."

Anger sparked in her veins. "I'm not having this argument again."

He pushed his glasses up and grinned. "You don't have to. The tests have been done and they work."

She stared at him. He slid papers over to her.

"Take a look. The same dosage we gave to the adults. Completely different metabolization and adaptation."

Her nails pushed into the leather so hard she wouldn't have been surprised if they ripped it. Her voice required a lot of effort to not let it shake. "Am I to understand that you disregarded my explicit instructions and experimented on this child?"

He squirmed in the hard chair. Sweat beaded on his temples.

She tried to pull the rage back in.

"I know you didn't want me to do it, but the child was there and look, just read the report."

She snatched the papers from his thrusting hand and scanned them. He was right. The child had done better, much better, than every adult mer who had gone through the procedures.

Conflicting thoughts whirled in her head. "Do you think he will survive?"

"I'd be highly surprised at this point if he didn't." His mouth twisted as if he'd sucked a lemon. "Of course, now we aren't able to track his progress." The doctor leaned both forearms on the desk, his face coming closer to hers. "Ma'am. I know you don't like the idea of subjecting children to these things—no one does—but there are some real benefits. They don't fight back as hard so they suffer less damage being subdued; they are responsive to orders, and if they survive in greater numbers, then this is a benefit for the mer population. Less collateral damage."

The last two words swam through her mind, and her fingers tightened on the paper. Sacrifice. The greater good. Lines weren't weak, but maybe holding to a line when crossing it would bring the most benefit.

"Very well. Instruct them to bring in the children."

The doctor rubbed at his lip, and she raised her brows. "Is there a problem?"

"The children don't often come out with the adults. It will take longer to arrange."

She looked out at the dark waters. "Let me think on

that. I believe I can provide you the information you need."

Chapter Twenty-Eight

When Evan walked into the chow hall the next day, a hush fell, swiftly followed by a murmur. He walked past the stares, ignoring the pain shooting down his side. Breakfast didn't look appetizing today but he grabbed a tray and joined the line, keeping his gaze on the ladle and its slop of beans.

The guy ahead of him turned, then did a double take, his eyebrows raising. His mouth opened but Evan looked away, and he got the message. The bubble of silence followed him as he carried his laden tray over to a table in the middle of the room. *Let them stare. Make them wonder. Maybe they'd all stop pretending this was normal.*

He dumped the tray on the table with a clatter then sat and smiled. The muscles in his cheek pulled at the cuts on his face but he kept it on anyway. "Morning all. How's the chow today?"

Char laid down the dangling fork and raised a brow at him. "Same as usual."

"That bad, huh?"

He glanced to where Khalid sat, arms crossed, frowning down at his plate. "Clearly the slop doesn't meet Khalid's gourmet requirements today." His friend darted a gaze to meet his then stared back at his plate.

"Looks like they really did a number on you, Evan."

He shrugged, the lingering pain from the puncture wound tracking through his chest. "They tried their best."

Esther pulled up a chair next to his, her eyes shining with an intensity that drove him back to his eggs and beans.

"They're saying you were chosen for the lab. That you were there yesterday. How are you here?"

He picked up a soggy piece of toast. "Well, I walked out of my room"—he gestured with the bread—"down the hall—"

Char kicked him under the table, and he winced.

"Don't be a jerk."

He shoved the last bit of toast in his mouth and wiped crumbs off his hands. "Sorry," he mumbled around the food. He washed it down with a swig of tepid coffee. "Let's say they weren't too happy about me leaving, but I wasn't too happy about staying."

Esther gripped his arm. "Hudson. Was he there? Did you see him?"

Char drew in a sharp breath, and he pressed his lips together. Such a fine line. Esther deserved to know what happened to her buddy, but whether she could be trusted to not get herself in danger was another matter.

The mermaid flashed into his mind as she often did, her dying gaze forever behind his eyes. He pushed his plate away.

"Remember the experiment we assisted at?"

Esther's face sharpened into hard lines. "I can't forget."

He placed his hand on her shoulder. "They don't only test on the mers."

A frozen moment, then she jerked upward and he

pushed down on her shoulder. "Sit down. Don't make a scene. Trust me, they watch."

She trembled under his hand, anger burning through the tears.

He looked from her to Char and back. Maybe she didn't know what everyone knew. "What do you think they do with the mermaids, Esther?"

"Study them, like aliens, figure out how they work. Why would they need to do that on us?"

Char chimed in, "They don't. They want to make something in the middle, something with the strengths of both. I thought you knew."

Her skin paled. "I thought they took people away to train them with the mers. But changing their DNA? That's plain wrong. It's against God."

He removed his hand, satisfied she wouldn't make a fuss. "God or not, it's wrong."

Khalid gathered the empty trays, the clatter cutting through the quiet hum of the hall. "Wrong or not, there isn't a heck of a lot any of us can do about it. I'm getting seconds."

Evan raised his coffee cup in salute, conscious of the pull of skin around the puncture point. Esther's gaze went to the bruises, and he tried not to flinch at her sudden intake of breath.

"Is that what they did to you? Did they inject mer DNA in you?"

He met her fierce gaze. "To be honest, I don't know. I think they might have. It's pretty yuck."

Gray tinged eggs slid around on Char's plate as she stabbed her fork at it.

"Whoa, what did those eggs do to you?"

"Stop it. Just don't."

A twinge of guilt played in his gut but he went back to his coffee.

"She's right." Esther's voice wobbled but her fingernails dug into his skin as she grabbed his arm again, spilling his brew. "It won't simply go away and being flippant about it isn't helping."

His fingers tensed around the thin metal mug. "Sorry. I don't mean to be flippant or whatever. It's been a really long few days."

Char leaned her fists against her temples and her elbows on the table. "I get you. But we have to do something. How's the plan coming along?"

"Are we really going to do this here?"

"Why not?"

He gestured at the people around them. "For many obvious reasons, all of whom happen to be wearing uniform."

Esther's sharp gaze darted between them. "A plan? You've already been thinking about this? You should have told me."

"A secret plan isn't secret when everyone knows." He raised his brows at Char but she shrugged one shoulder and held a hand out palm up.

"Esther isn't everyone."

"So *now* you aren't picky."

Khalid returned, plunked a laden plate on the table and dragged a chair out. "You guys figured it out yet?"

He pushed back from the table, stretching out the pain as he stood. "I'm working on it."

Char stood too. "Mind if I walk with you?"

A smile spread even as his stomach dropped a little. "Sure."

Evan breathed out the tension in the quiet of the

corridor, a welcome hush after the buzz of the hall. He squeezed his eyes shut against the pounding in his head.

"You're an idiot."

His eyes flicked open. "What?"

"You should have stayed in bed. Were you trying to make a point?"

The hot disappointment at not seeing Ana in the canteen flashed through him. "No, just trying to get breakfast."

Her gaze ran over him, counting every bruise, tallying every hurt.

"I'm okay, Char. Really."

She shuddered and punched him on the arm. "Keep being okay, devil dog."

Chapter Twenty-Nine

Char hadn't wanted to leave him on his own but he'd promised to be on the alert for any warning signs of side effects. Evan stared out at the ocean. Not that he wanted to set a foot in the research center again if he could help it. His neck hurt and his vision kept blurring, but he'd had worse. Images of Hudson's staring eyes as he died floated in front of him. His hands clasped so tight his bones graunched. It wouldn't happen to him. If it did, he had the means to deal with it.

His watch beeped with the change of the hour. Ana hadn't been at breakfast, and she wasn't where her duty was posted. She disappeared a lot. Char's words echoed in his mind. *We only tell the people we trust beyond a doubt, and that's not Ana.*

Everything in his heart rebelled against that, but so much of his head agreed with her. He didn't really know Ana after all. Her background was shrouded in half-sentences and avoidances. He only knew the feel of her body, the shape of her smile, the gleam in her eye when she faced a challenge. His heart knew her. She'd burrowed into it so quickly after meeting him, but his brain still didn't trust her.

Quiet footsteps sounded on the walkway behind him. Ana's small shape reflected against the swirling depths beyond the glass.

"I've been looking for you," she said. "Char told

me you might be out here."

"You left early this morning."

Tight lines pulled around her brow. "I had to go. I didn't want to wake you."

He said nothing but stared at her as he held out his hand. After a moment's hesitation, she clasped it, and the vise in his chest eased a little.

She stepped closer. "Are you—how are you feeling?"

"Fine. Why? Do I look terrible?"

A light sparked in her eyes and she twined her fingers in his. "Awful. You look horrible."

"Nothing new then."

The little lift of her lips caught at his heart. He glanced around, then pulled her slowly toward him. She rested her hand on his chest and leaned back in his arm. "This isn't a good idea at this time."

"I know." He smiled, kissed her forehead and let her go. "Will you come by later?"

She crossed her arms, her smile a little tight. "Sure, if I can."

"Has your duty changed? Didn't see you earlier."

"Kind of. There are a few things I've been dragged in to help with."

"Oh?"

"Need to know basis."

"Gotcha."

She stood a mere foot away but the space between them stretched wide with unsaid words. He turned back to the ocean. Darkness stared back at him through the glass, and the ghost of Ana's reflection reached out a hand to him before curling it back. His back tightened. A month wasn't really enough time to fall in love with someone. But he'd done it anyway.

A blur of motion slipped past the glass outside, and his breath caught in his throat. He blinked and the blur slowed. A tail with drifting ribbon-like fins weaved through the inky water. He tried to catch sight of the mer's face. Ana came up to his shoulder, her warmth pressing into him.

"Did you see that?" he asked.

Silence sat like a muffler around her, and a hot tight feeling spread through his chest again. More lies. More distance.

She sighed. "Yes, I did."

The relief was twofold. He wasn't going crazy, and she hadn't dodged the question again.

"Do they often come up so close? I mean, given what happens here, I'm surprised they don't stay as far away as possible."

She stepped forward and laid a small hand on the glass. Her face was drawn, tight lines framed her mouth. Black circles shaded under her eyes. His arms ached with the need to hold her.

"Mer aren't easily scared. Dangers require patrolling, not avoiding."

"Do you think they know what happens here?" He regarded her closely, her face closing down.

"Who knows what they think?"

"Jones called them animals."

The scrape of her nails as her hand flexed against the glass set his teeth on edge.

"Do you agree with him?"

"No. I don't."

Her shoulders slumped as tension leached out. Fine blonde hair wisped out from her braid. She seemed smaller, more frail than before. He remembered the look on her face when he told her about the merchild, the anger burning in her tiny frame. Soft hair skiffed over his fingers as he tucked an errant strand behind her ear.

"You know the child I told you about? Khalid told me he heard the child had disappeared."

"Good for him."

"It got me wondering if there were more."

"More what?"

"Children."

She stilled then turned to face him, her eyes a shimmer of silver. "Have you heard something?"

He cupped her face, his thumb stroking over her pale cheek. "No. It wouldn't surprise me though. If there are, I hope they find the same help the boy found."

Her gaze slid from his but this time he didn't mind. A warm feeling spread through his chest. He'd wondered if she'd had something to do with it. Looks like he was right.

"It's okay. Ana, you don't have to say." Evan slid his arm around her, and she leaned into his chest with a sigh, her palms sliding against his shirt.

"Sometimes we have to do things we aren't comfortable with because it's the right thing to do. That's what our elders always taught us."

"Elders? Like in a church?"

"Kind of. My community was very tightly woven. The old people are very much in charge, they're the ones who tell the rest of us what to do."

A bitter tone laced her voice. He remembered some of the old men at the church he grew up in. They'd get up in everyone's business for sure.

"For what it's worth, I agree with them on that."

Her fingers hooked into his waist. "You do?"

"Yeah. Doing the right thing isn't always easy; usually you have to make sacrifices. It's worth it though, even if it makes us uncomfortable."

She cupped his cheek, and the warmth of her fingers spread from his face down his neck. "I'm happy you think so."

He bent his head and kissed her. She smiled into his kiss but disentangled herself.

"I do have to go now. I will try and see you later."

He wondered what it would take for them to trust each other.

Chapter Thirty

Klaxons sounded, the harsh low tones cutting through the silence of the platform. Evan lifted his head from his hands. The water outside the dome raged in a turmoil of darkness lit by white flashes. He rose to his feet, his hands curling into fists. A thunder of booted feet echoed down the metal gangway to his left. His gaze stayed fixed outward, on the flashes growing brighter, the white foam pounding against the glass.

"Hunter!"

He barely looked round before a dive suit hit him in the chest. He frowned at Khalid.

"Suit up, Evan. It's all hands on deck."

The neoprene squashed between his fingers as his grip tightened on the wetsuit. "What's going on?"

"Not sure, bro, they haven't said. Do they ever? But I have my thoughts."

He followed Khalid's gaze back to the roiling water. Something banged against the glass, and they both jumped. A trident lay across the plexiglass, sparks winding around the deadly looking prongs. His heart pounding as adrenaline surged, Evan stepped closer to the dome. A face appeared, shining white under curling horns from what may have been a helmet. The glow faded before it burst so bright his eyes shut instinctively. When he opened them, the mer was gone.

Khalid's olive skin paled, and the whites of his

eyes stood out. "Like I thought. The Dome is under attack."

Heaviness weighed down his stomach. This wasn't how it was supposed to go. He met Khalid's gaze, the other man waiting. Expectant. He looked down to where his hands clutched the suit, at his tattoo. The snarling helmeted dog chomping at a cigar stared back at him. *Semper Fi. I can't let them down.*

"We only have to drive them off, Evan. That's all. Protect the dome."

He inhaled sharply and jerked his head in acknowledgement. *That's all. Protect the base. I can do that.*

He stripped off his shirt as they raced toward the docking bay. For the first time he missed the light swing of the dog tag over his chest.

Blake stood at the entry to the sub. His lip curled as Evan and Khalid scrambled up. "Took your time, boys."

Evan didn't bother with an explanation but brushed past Blake, ducking his head to enter. Cramped quarters housed ten others. Char waved but Ana wasn't there. He pushed away the niggling disquiet at her absence. He wasn't a kid. Didn't matter if his crush wasn't on the same crew as him. She'd have a reason to be elsewhere.

The door hissed shut, and Blake pulled the lever, sealing the vacuum. Char stared silently at the opposite side of the sub. Her lips pressed tight together, and a bead of sweat slid down her face to the neck of the suit. He nudged her side, and a frown flashed over her brows.

"What?"

He ignored the tone and kept his own voice low. "You doing okay?"

"Yeah. Why? You not?"

"Nah I'm good."

Her glance flicked to the side, and he squashed a smile.

The submersible waited at the gantry. They would want to make sure the mers couldn't get in. As they shot out through the now closing door, bullets peppered the water in front of them. A tendon corded on his neck. Protection shouldn't come at such a cost. Blake stood at the front of the sub, one hand on his amphibious rifle the other holding a rung on the wall. The sneer that seemed to be a permanent feature intensified as he caught Evan's eye.

"It's like clearing the farm of predators, boys."

Char shifted next to him but when he turned, she was smiling at the excited young man next to her. *Jimmy? Mick? Something like that.*

White light flashed around the sub, and the engine stuttered. Evan braced a hand against the wall and scooped up Khalid's mouthpiece from where it rolled at his feet. Metal groaned and buckled under the force of the attack. A loud thump knocked the vessel sideways, and he flung out an arm to stop Char tumbling forward.

"What the hell was that?"

She pulled herself to her feet and checked her harness. "A mer. They use their tails to fight."

Another massive whack sent the submersible wheeling through the water, cracks appearing in the glass and metal bending. Blake stepped forward, priming his gun.

"Okay! Suit up! Out we go! Send these fish back to

where they came from!"

The door slid back and a cascade of water flooded in. He closed his mind to the memories of blood in the water. With a little stumble as the sub listed, he followed Khalid to the door, glancing back to check on Char. She was helping Jimmy. His harness had caught on one of the bars. Water rushed around their feet.

The young man's eyes showed more white than blue. Sputtering light carved grim lines into Char's face, but her voice surrounded the recruit with mellow tones. She pushed the younger soldier ahead of her and nodded brusquely at Evan. Tightening his mouthpiece, he shot a last glance at Char before pushing out of the vessel into the storm of the ocean.

A bolt of white energy shot past him and he threw himself back, spinning in a roll, fanning the water, avoiding ripped pieces of metal. Visibility was crap, too many bubbles and flashing lights and swirling currents.

He blinked through the goggles. Water seeped in, and he cursed inwardly at the rubbish gear. As the water covered his eyes, he squeezed his lids shut, then opened them to a different reality.

The flashing lights slowed, separating out into distinct beings. Tails and torsos shone pale luminescent amongst whips of kelp. Silver hair floated, braided and ornamented with spikes of shells. He reached up, fumbled at the straps on his temple. Tearing off the goggles, he glanced around, bubbles from his mouthpiece floating around his head, each one distinct in his new vision. *Holy crap, is this what the mer see all the time?*

His hand rested on his AAI, the bulky revolver with its flechettes dragging at his hip. But as he stared at the twisting beating tails, the bright shining beings, he found he couldn't draw his weapon.

His earpiece crackled and Blake's voice belted out orders. Nets. Spears. Flechettes shooting through the water. He shook his head, a slow wave in the water. This wasn't about driving them off. They weren't animals to be scared away by noise and firepower. The rookie swam up next to him, a bulky rifle clutched to his chest. A flash of white rose in front of them.

A mer darted through the water, her hair twisted up into points, her skin pulsing with a white glow. Jimmy raised the rifle, battling with the water resistance. Evan looked from him to the mer. Dark eyes stood out inhuman in the pale face. But lines etched their way around her mouth. She looked angry. And frightened. And not an animal to be put down.

He pushed himself around and shoved down on the barrel before Jimmy could fire it. The young man lost his grip on the weapon, and Evan scooped up the rifle. The mer reared back, long tail swishing in the water. He noticed for the first time that her tail wasn't only one shade. Bands of colour lit up along in the same pulses as the white glow on her torso: orange, blue, gold. Beautiful. His gaze met hers. She tilted her head to one side, like a bird, and he flinched at a buzzing in his ears. She stared a moment longer, then with a last glance at Jimmy, headed away.

Evan thrust the rifle at the young man and gestured back to the dome, trying to make him understand he needed to head to safety. If he wasn't careful, he'd get himself killed. Jimmy resisted and he shoved him. His eyes wide behind the goggles, Jimmy stared at the chaotic waves and the flashes of light and barbs flying.

He jerked his head in an abrupt nod and swam back to the dome.

Ignoring the shouts in his earpiece and the strange buzzing coming in flashes, Evan stroked his way through the water, part of his brain registering the ease with which he glided. Char was nowhere he could see, but he headed to the point of greatest turmoil.

Blood rippled from the chaos in a silky tendril. As he swam closer, two mers thrashed in a nylon net, their pulsing light growing weaker. One of the mers was much smaller than the rest they'd seen, a child or a youth. Sharp teeth flashed as its mouth opened in a soundless scream. The buzzing in his head intensified into a spike, and he winced.

Blake held his rifle up, aimed at the youth. His full helmet hid his eyes, but his voice held a familiar sneer. "Worse than animals, this lot. Dispatch at will."

The water turned to molasses as he lurched toward Blake. He couldn't reach him in time. High powered darts flashed from the rifle, slicing through scales and skin. The blood trail became a churning morass. The buzzing reached a painful pitch, and he wrenched out the earpiece. But the buzzing continued.

It's in my head. It's like they're screaming in my head.

His eyes watered, mixing with the salt, blurring the strange new vision. The net was unclasped, and the bodies of the mer were released. They drifted slowly downward, the arms of the larger one still wrapped in death around the youngling. Claustrophobia pressed down on him like lead. His lungs fought the oxygen filtering through the mouthpiece, telling his brain he needed to surface. Instead, he turned his gaze on Blake, his hand sliding to his revolver.

A hand grabbed his arm. Char. She shook her head slowly, the message in her eyes very clear. Not here. Not now.

His muscles strained against his common sense. The urge to shoot, to hurt, to strangle this murderous thug flamed through his bloodstream.

Blake squared up to him, his flippers a mockery of the mers he slaughtered. The other man's fingers moved from the rifle in a subtle but clear *bring it on* gesture. Evan's lips curled around the mouthpiece, nothing like the snarl he wanted to fling at him. He jerked his hand away from the revolver and headed back to the Dome.

Char swam alongside him, shaking her hand and gesturing back to where the dimming light of the merpeople showed their retreat, to where a second submersible was meeting them, to where more innocents waited to be slaughtered. He pushed her arm away, ducked, and swam lower.

The pressure built around him until the buzzing in his head stopped. His hand tightened on the strap of his holster but he didn't throw it away. Running wouldn't help. There was nowhere to run to. Not this time.

Dark rock spotted with young coral loomed ahead of him, ripped apart by great steel pylons rising out of the sea bed below. His first sight of the Dome had been overwhelming. The audacity and daring of human endeavour rang from every rivet and curved glass plate.

Now he saw it as a parasite. No better than landmines seeded through civilian fields. Whether he left or not, the dome would remain. Its generators sucking in water, turning it to oxygen, and spitting out waste. The oil pipeline was protected by nets and wire but the mer weren't fools. They wouldn't contaminate their own home. Humans were doing that for them.

Evan scanned the underside of the Dome. A faint light caught his gaze. Blinking through the salty water, he held his breath a moment. The light pulsed again. It stuttered and died. Faded kelp shifted limply in a light current. He parted the strands. Curled up, its tail tight to its chest, was a merchild. He thought at first that the shivers were the water flowing over its skin, but then the shudder of the scales became clear. The child shook in fear.

Inhuman eyes stared into his. All he saw were brown eyes gazing over the back of a pink cardigan as the bombs began to fall.

How did you tell a mer to leave? He reached out a hand. The child shrank back, baring its teeth, and a sharp spine of fins stood up along the back of its arms. *Okay. Not like that.* He drew his hand back, pushing himself away from the child. It closed its mouth, neck gills opening and closing rapidly, like the child in the lab.

He gestured away from the approaching sub and soldiers, faster movements when the child blinked at him. The buzzing returned, and he held his breath as words sounded underneath the hum for the first time.

"Where? How?"

No way did he hear that in his head.

But the child didn't break eye contact, those pale silvery eyes shone into his own, eyes that could now see through water as if it were air.

Fighting the urge to clench his fists, not wanting to frighten the child further, he thought as focused and as direct as he could. *"Anywhere but here. Go as fast as you can, now. Go."*

Kelp waved as the child's tail uncurled, translucent ribbons of fins gliding through the weed. A moment longer they stared into each other's eyes.

Then the mer arched its back, kicked its tail, and disappeared into the distance.

Chapter Thirty-One

Ana paused before going into the locker room, her hand gripping the metal edge of the doorframe. Evan stripped off his wet shirt. Lean muscles rippled. His hand touched the center of his chest before falling, as if he searched for his tags from habit. Char leaned back on a locker, her eyes closing. Her damp tank top clung to her stomach.

Evan closed his locker, leaning on the door before slamming his fist onto the metal. Char's eyes flicked open but she stared at the ceiling, not at Evan, not at Khalid who shoved past Ana to get out of the room.

Ana's skin pulled taut over her chest, her legs prickled. Her hand went to the amulet. Changing here would not be smart.

Char glanced at her. She bit her lip. Humans felt pain too. She forgot that sometimes. The other woman brushed at her eyes and glowered.

"Where were you, Ana?"

Evan stared at her for a moment before looking down at the dry shirt crumpled in his hand and pulling it on.

She fixed her gaze on Char. "I had duties here." The amulet glowed warm under her shirt. "I heard it was bad."

Evan tightened his belt, pausing to look up at her under his lashes. "You could say that."

Clearing her throat, she pushed out the words. "How many—"

"Did we slaughter?" he growled, his face like granite "Capture? I lost count."

Char scooped her shirt from the bench. "Don't think that way, Evan."

"Why not? Is truth something else we've sacrificed down here?"

Ana held her breath. Evan couldn't see the other woman's face but she could. She saw the tears threatening. The tightness around her mouth. Her gaze darted to Evan. His anger radiated like heat.

"Shut up, Evan," Char snapped. "You know why as well as I do."

Ana moved to the side as Char pushed past into the corridor. The regret that passed over Evan's face wiped clean as he glared at her. A sick feeling roiled in her stomach. Until she met them, she'd never thought humans could hold such strong emotions, could care so much.

She stepped closer to him. A tendon jumped in his jaw. For a moment all she saw was him. Not a human, not a soldier, not an enemy. Just Evan.

Her trembling hand stroked his stone-like cheek. He shuddered and she shifted closer. With a muffled sound, he scooped her in his arms and crushed her to his chest. His face was in her hair and she held him as he broke. She had never wished to cry before. But his pain tore at her, twisted in her blood, shredded her defences. All at once she wished nothing more than for him to see her as she was, as a mer.

She drew back, stepped away. "I need to tell you something." *Crazy. What am I doing?*

A shadow fell over his face, and his hand flew up as if to stop her.

"No, Evan, you need to listen."

His hand dropped, and he crossed his arms, looking down at the floor.

"I'm not who you think I am."

A heavy sigh escaped him and his shoulders sagged. "Are you a spy? You're never where you're supposed to be. You disappear at odd hours. You know a lot about things you shouldn't. I tried to deny it, pretend I didn't notice, but I'm not an idiot."

No, he wasn't. But he hadn't guessed the other, the deepest secret. Her hand stole up to the amulet, over her racing heart. She didn't need to tell him. But seeing his red-rimmed eyes, his pain, the thought of being herself in front of him, being Sariana instead of Ana, swept over her mind.

"Yes."

His eyes flashed and his hand covered them. She breathed in.

"It's complicated."

His lip curled. "It always is."

She pried his hand from his face. He didn't return her clasp, but he didn't pull away either. Summoning her courage, she slid her other hand up to the chain around her neck then pulled out the amulet.

His peered at it, the purple gem pulsing with a dim light in time with her pulse. "A spy for the mers, then." He appeared relieved.

"Yes, but that's not everything."

She stepped back, her blood rushing in her ears. Her arm trembled as she held it out, and she gritted her teeth. White light pulsed from her shoulder, winding down her arm. Spiny fins appeared on the back of her arms and webbing spread between her fingers in an opaque luminescence. Her vision changed as her eyes bled from blue to pale silver.

He snatched his hand out of hers, stumbling backward into the lockers. She moved forward, but he recoiled and she stopped. His face twisted and his eyes shuttered. The chill of the deeps flooded through her veins.

I should have known better. He feels sorry for us, but only as animals. Not as equals. Humans never can. She shuddered a breath and changed back.

His chest rose and fell rapidly, and he stared.

Lifting her chin, she dragged words out from the humiliation that tried to stop them in her throat. "Will you keep my secret?"

He pressed his lips close together and glanced around the room as if surprised to find himself still there. "How do I know you aren't dangerous?"

His words sliced through her armor, and she hung on to the amulet. Let it ground her. She was stronger than this.

"You don't. You'll have to trust me." She tucked her own hands tight against her so she wouldn't reach out again. "I promise I don't want to hurt you, Evan."

His reply came through clenched teeth. "I won't snitch. But if you do anything to endanger Char, Khalid, the others, I *will* stop you."

The knowledge settled into her bones. She'd hoped it would be different with him. It wasn't. She was mer and he human. They were predators.

The gong sounded for chow, cutting through the air with its prosaic whine.

He drew himself together, walked around her and out the door. It snicked shut.

She let her shaking knees crumple to the ground to sit, curled up and dry-eyed, until the lights turned off.

Chapter Thirty-Two

Boots scuffing the concrete floor, he strode down the corridor. The past few days had been hellish. Training sessions held an extra edge. Char noticed he avoided Ana, but she didn't say anything. Khalid had withdrawn into himself and didn't pull his punches. He wasn't meaning to hurt and Evan let him, it gave him an excuse to let loose a little as well. But that evening had been worse.

Blake was in charge of the roster. A smirk squatted on his mouth. That was Evan's first warning it wouldn't be great. Engineering needed assistance, he said, two people, working in the engine room. Evan stared at Blake. He refused to react as his name then Ana's were read out. He forced his shoulders to stay relaxed, refused to clench his fists. He stood back as she strode past him, her blonde ponytail swinging, and nodded at Blake. The slimebag winked, like it was all one big joke.

Char grimaced at him as he passed, sympathy in her face. He crossed his eyes at her, then smirked as she bit her lip. It was nice to see her smile. Even if she tried to hide it.

The walk to engineering was as awkward as he'd feared. Ana stalked off ahead, and he adjusted his gait so he wouldn't catch up to her shorter legs. She stopped at the next corner. He slowed, not sure if she wanted him to catch up or not. Her hands fisted at her waist, and she glanced back with a scowl. Taking care not to stand too close, he came up next to her.

"It's ridiculous, walking behind me like that. We're adults. Or can't you bear to even be next to someone like me?"

He'd been looking at the corridor ahead, anything to avoid her daggered stare, but at that he jerked his gaze to her face. "Excuse me? I'm trying to give you some space."

She snorted, and his heart squeezed at the sight of her scrunched-up face.

"Whatever you were doing, engineering is around there, and I don't fancy walking in with you lumbering in behind me for everyone to snigger at us."

"Fair enough."

Her chin rose, and his gaze landed on the strand of hair that always seemed to fall over her face. He rubbed his jaw.

"Well? Shall we?"

Blue eyes shimmered silver for a second, and he caught his breath.

"May as well get it over with," she said.

Walking at her side, he was conscious of every movement of her head, of the tightness in her shoulders. He kept his gaze straight ahead.

A bright blue door with a yellow sign opened onto a miasma of noise and steam and grease. The chief engineer smiled in relief when he saw them. He finished his instructions to the men with him, sent them off with a wave of his hand, and hurried over to them. His name tag declared him to be Mac. Copper hair sat in tight curls over skin that almost appeared gold with the number of freckles covering his face. Lines of fatigue framed pale blue eyes that passed over Ana with barely a glance but widened as he saw Evan. A blush crept up his neck, and Evan smiled as his irritation bled away.

"Thanks for the extra hands, guys. We've had a bit of overflow, and it's been tough to clear it and fix the circuits and machinery at the same time. We can certainly use the help."

These guys didn't have any truck with mermaids or laboratories. They simply made sure everyone survived.

"Not a problem, Mac. Happy to help. Where do you want us?"

The blush intensified. "I'm sorry; it won't be pleasant. We've managed to clear out the mess from all but the small auxiliary room. It's honestly just a lot of bailing."

Ana shrugged. "That's okay. I'm not afraid of a bit of water."

He nearly choked. She turned a bland gaze on him.

"What about you, Evan? Does water scare you?"

He ignored her and smiled at Mac. "Lead the way."

The room was smaller than he expected. What it lacked in size, it made up for in stench and dampness. A couple of buckets and a larger container on a trolley stood in the corridor.

He clapped Mac on the shoulder and cut off his apologies. "We'll take care of this. You guys have much more important things to worry about."

Mac hesitated a moment. "Thanks. You're the only ones who haven't been jerks about it. I know it isn't the excitement you signed up for."

Ana grabbed a bucket and flashed a cursory smile

at the engineer and stepped over the lintel into the room, a soft splash following her.

"Believe me, I think we've both had enough excitement to last several lifetimes. This is all good," Evan said.

Mac appeared sceptical but thanked him once again then rushed back to the main room and his broken circuits.

Ana stood in the middle of the room, her face dappled and distorted by the reflections of the neon light off the murky water. Her hand was white-knuckled around the handle of the bucket. He scooped up his own pail and ducked his head as he entered the tiny space.

"You okay?"

"I'm fine."

Lines of strain pulled at her cheeks, and her muscles corded tight. Maybe he should push the issue? *No, if she wanted to talk she could.* He rolled up his sleeves and started bailing.

The room was tiny. They kept knocking arms, her ponytail would fall forward onto his shoulder, and every accidental touch was bites of electricity on his skin.

She caught him glancing at her one too many times and stood, stretching out her back with a grimace. "Looking for gills?"

Blood rushed to his cheeks. "No, of course not."

She gave him a look but didn't say anything more, simply leaned against a cabinet and brushed her hair from a sweaty forehead. "You haven't told anyone."

It wasn't a question but he answered it like one.

"No. I said I wouldn't snitch, and I haven't."

She massaged her hands, glancing away. He nearly missed the mumbled thank you.

He lifted his bucket and grabbed hers, ignoring her protests. "You're welcome."

Filth and water cascaded from the buckets into the full container. They'd made a couple of trips to empty it in the nearest drainage chute. He glanced over at her. Exhaustion sang from every line of her face, and her normally strong arms shook.

"I'll take this."

She pushed to her feet. "It's my turn."

"Don't worry about it. I got it."

He turned away from her half-hearted protests and pushed the trolley to the chute, cursing once when the wheels juddered over an uneven part of the surface, and water sloshed over the side.

Here by himself he could admit it had been nice working with Ana again. Mermaid or not, she wasn't afraid to work hard. She hardly ever complained either.

He thought about her the whole way through getting rid of the water and heading back. Near the room, he slowed. Mac stood outside the door, bemused shock on his open face. He sped up, aiming the wheels at the juddery part of the hall, making as much noise as possible. The engineer turned to face him, a smile displacing the wariness taking over his expression.

"Hey! How's it going? You guys have done an awesome job."

"Yeah, I think we're almost done. It'll take a bit of cleaning after the water's gone though."

"I was coming to tell you not to worry about cleaning. Things have calmed down a bit on our end, and I've got a couple volunteers to finish it off after you've got rid of the water."

He grinned. "Not gonna lie. That's a relief."

Mac's cheeks flushed and his brows drew together. "Is she, I mean—" His mouth twisted.

Evan edged closer to the door, keeping Mac on him, not on whatever Ana had been doing. "Is she tired? Yeah, exhausted. But we'll finish up and get out of your way."

The engineer eyed him dubiously, clearly wanting to contradict him. Evan punched him lightly on the arm and winked.

"Thanks, Mac."

Blushing and grinning, the engineer gave a small wave and strode back to his station. Evan breathed out the tension from his shoulders and ducked his head under the lintel. Ana stood with her back to him. Dim light surrounded her outstretched hands, and water danced in beaded droplets on her skin. She moved her head at the snick of the latch, but the light didn't fade.

"You didn't tell him."

"Of course not."

Her gaze was fixed on her hand, the play of light and water. She didn't appear human, but in the dirty tank top and soaked cargos dragging low on her hips, she appeared small and fragile.

"I told him you were tired."

"I am. More than you can possibly understand."

He sighed and bent down to start sweeping water into the pail. "You don't have to keep doing this, Ana."

"I'm not talking about the cleaning up."

Water slick with grime and grease splashed up his arm, and he wiped it off. "Neither was I."

Silence answered him and he glanced up. The glow

around her arms had vanished, and a deep frown line creased her brow. "I don't give up on things because I'm tired."

He thought of the first time he'd seen her in the training room, hauling herself up the longest hanging rope, pushing on past when many of the men had fallen. "No. I guess you don't." He tossed her a pail. "Best we finish the job then."

She raised a brow and turned her back pointedly. The bristles of the small brush scattered water droplets, and he winced as they shone luminous and slow and perfect. He scowled up at Ana, but she worked in the far corner, back turned to him, seemingly unaware.

Glancing back to the water, he saw every swirl and ripple, exactly as he had out in the ocean. He shook his head, his pulse thundering in his ears. *Tired. That's all.*

****

Empty. Nothing but standard issue furniture and no window. Dim light. The small room seemed more barren than it had in a while. He grabbed a black hoodie, zipped it up, flipped the hood over his head, and headed back out. The door slammed shut behind him.

He dug his hands into his pockets and walked aimlessly, letting his feet take him where they would. Ana's face wouldn't leave his mind.

What would it be like, to live without guilt? To not fear your memories? Somewhere out of reach, covered by cloud, was a time when he'd been himself. He'd forgotten how to get there.

He ended up at the viewing platform, as part of him had known he would. No one came here but him, especially at night, when the glow of strip lighting

217

dimmed and the water lapping on the surface of the dome became inky black. He stood in the doorway as the depths rose above him. His shoulders hunched into the soft fleece of the hoodie.

Somehow they called to him, pulled like ropes of seaweed, dragging his mind to the water no matter how hard he tried to resist.

Every step toward the glass was a step away from what he knew, what he clung to. He traced the shifting green reflections until the black strip of studded lights on the edge of the glass warned him he had no farther to go. No more space to avoid.

He raised his head. A blurring glow spread over his eyes. He blinked. Crystal vision speared through the glass as if it were nothing. Dark water shimmered, pulling away from waving fronds of kelp. Brightly coloured fish swam in slow motion, every movement of their shining fins echoing through the currents in ripples that he felt under his skin. His knees weakened, and he flung out a hand to lean on the glass.

Suspecting and knowing were two completely different things.

Evan slid down, his knees thudded onto the platform. Chilled glass met his forehead. His hands curled into fists against the dome, and he fought to regulate his breathing. *This was the plan. It was supposed to work.* At least he wasn't a contorted bloody mess on a lab bench. Yet. The thought of what they might do if they found out it worked helped slow his racing pulse.

Disgust swam in his head, but it wasn't for what he was, what he was becoming. Ana's face streaked with tears filled his vision. He'd pushed her away, for being a mer, for lying. What was he other than a mutant who had been lying to everyone?

I don't trust her. But I think I love her.

In love with a mermaid. Like a happy ending waited at the end of that story.

He lifted his head, turning his gaze from the open depths. Happy ending or not, he owed her an apology. The dappled light on the floor slowly stopped pulsing and his vision returned to normal. His lungs expanded as he inhaled deeply. Every nerve, every muscle, stretched and hyper-aware, as if it was all so much more than before.

Settling the hood back over his ears, he paused as the shadows in the corner shifted, ever so slightly. He thought of the knife lying on the table in his room. Moments passed. He thought he heard a quiet snick, like a door closing, and the shadows lightened.

Nothing there.

Evan pressed his lips together and walked the other way. When the door slid open, he paused with his hand on the button. Nothing moved. Silence filled the platform. He stepped through and headed back to his room.

He'd talk to Ana tomorrow.

Chapter Thirty-Three

Reflections from the pool lit the ceiling with waving stripes of golden green. A technician nodded hello from under his towel as Evan walked past. Ana swam down the far lane, gliding through the water with barely a ripple. He sat on a bench, not caring about the water seeping into the fabric of his cargos. She swam three more laps. Each stroke, every sinuous turn filled with more than human grace, prodded him to wonder how he'd ever not realized the truth.

She surfaced, water beading on her pale face. A luminous glow seethed beneath her skin, waiting to be let out. His breath caught.

Inhuman. Alien. Beloved.

She tilted her head to squeeze water from her ponytail and saw him. She paused, head cocked like a startled deer. He smiled at the thought, then stopped as she frowned.

"What do you want, Evan?"

He leaned back on the wall, his hands resting on his knees, trying to ignore the throbbing in his temple. He'd faced war zones with more calm than this. "I wanted to talk."

"I thought we already had."

"Maybe. But I've been thinking, and I had a couple new things I wanted to say."

Droplets arced from her hand as she flung it up,

palm out. "Wait. I'm not talking to you like this. Not here. Throw me a towel."

She pointed to to a gray fluffy towel draped over a bag under the bench. Grabbing both items, he stood and walked to the ladder. He held out the towel, trying not to stare as she pulled herself out of the pool, water streaming from alabaster skin.

"Thanks," she muttered, draping the towel around her and snatching the bag. "Wait here."

He shoved his hands in his pockets and stared at the pool. A thought crossed his mind and, after a glance around, he tried to will his vision to change, to see the water here in the same way. Nothing happened. He bit his lip. Maybe it had been nothing. Maybe he shouldn't say anything to Ana about that. Stick to the apology.

She was out in only a few minutes, dressed in loose gray sweatpants and a fitted white t-shirt. Without a word, she stalked toward the exit, jerking her head for him to follow. They strode in silence until she turned left at the intersection, where the right turn led back to the mess hall.

"Where are you going?"

"You'll see. Are you coming or not?"

He shrugged and joined her.

The door she led him to was at the end of a short corridor. She jabbed in an access code, and he pressed his lips together. In all the turmoil of the mermaid stuff, he'd nearly forgotten the spy bit.

Salty air hit him as the door opened. The space beyond lay hidden in darkness. His pulse thudded, and he fought off the burst of adrenaline. If she'd wanted to remove him as a threat, she'd had ample opportunities already. She lifted her chin in a challenge, like she knew what he thought. He bowed her ahead of him and followed her in. Dampness settled on his skin, sparking a vibration from his fingers to his shoulders.

Ana tossed her bag to the side of the door, which closed behind them with an audible snick. Enclosing them in the dark. His muscles tautened. A glow pushed away the dark. It came from Ana, from her skin. His blood chilled and his chest constricted. She turned to him, her face an eerie opal in the gloom.

"Okay. Talk."

"What is this place?"

She raised an eyebrow. "You're leading with that? This is somewhere no one else comes to. It's a private dock. It's one of the ways I get in and out. I figure I want to be somewhere I can get away easy, if you've changed your mind about not snitching."

He tried to curtain the hurt, stop it showing in his face, but she flinched and turned her face away.

"You really think that's what I want to talk to you about?"

She shrugged, her skin moving like silk under the glow. "I don't see what else it could be."

He rubbed his chin. This was hard. "I wanted to apologise."

He risked a glance. Her eyes burned silver and he couldn't look away. She said nothing, stood silent and rigid.

"I still don't like the spying, but I understand why you're doing it." Her eyelids flickered and he pressed on. "Someone has to do something for the mers and you're doing what you can to help."

He stepped closer, his hand flexing against his side. "But I am sorry for pulling back, when you showed me what—who you are. I freaked out. But it was incredibly brave of you. And I wanted you to know *I* know how much courage that needed, and that I—" He breathed in. "I still think the world of you, Ana."

Darkness flooded her eyes for a second before she hooded them. Her voice came tight and harsh. "I thought you were disgusted. That you saw me as an animal."

He reached out a hand. "Never. Confused, freaked, shocked. Never disgusted."

She regarded his hand with ice blue eyes. An eternity passed before she stretched out a glowing limb and clasped it. His heart swelled so he thought it might burst, and a smile spread on his face.

"My beautiful lovely Ana. Will you forgive me?"

The darkness shuddered across her face again, and he wondered if this was how mermaids cried. Her voice whispered into the gloom.

"Yes."

Within a heartbeat, he pulled her into his arms, stroking back silvery hair from her ethereal face. She pressed against his chest, her body soft and strong, and he tightened his embrace. He bent his lips to hers, but hesitated before the tempting fullness—a silent question.

In answer, she leaned up on her toes, fastening her lips to his. With a groan he sank into the kiss. She might be a mermaid, but she had captured his heart and there was nothing in his head but her. His hands fisted in her t-shirt. He pulled her tight against him. Her hand slid up his chest, along his jaw, into his hair. Every touch of her skin sent a fire through his blood.

My Ana. His tongue played along her lips, seeking

entry. She opened to him and he thrust into her softness. She lifted her hips to his, and he slid his hands to the curves of her behind, holding her against the hardness of him. She murmured and he lifted his head. Her silver eyes were wide, and her mouth was bruised and red.

"Come into the water with me."

His hand slid to the waist of her sweatpants, his chest heaving with ragged breaths. "You know I can't breathe underwater." No matter what weird things were happening to his vision, surely it hadn't gone that far.

"I can breathe for you. Do you trust me?"

He stared into her face, his body hot for her and his hands slipping into her pants. "Do you have to ask?"

Silver eyes flashed and she fixed her mouth on his, hungry and demanding. He grabbed her behind, squeezing her against him. She stepped backward, pulling him with her. Cold water slipped around his ankles, and he shivered as goosebumps ran over his skin. Her hand slid under his t-shirt, tracing over his chest, his heart pounding a tattoo against his ribs. Gentle fingers tugged at his shirt, and he broke from her lips to rip it off and over his head, tossing it behind him onto the walkway.

Damp air wove around him in a caress. He kissed her again, pulling her lip between his teeth. His hands slid under her shirt, rising to cup her breasts. The soft swell of her flesh sent heat flooding through him, driving back the chill of the water as she drew him further into the pool. He pushed up the soft cotton of her shirt, and she raised her arms so he could slide it off. Balling it up, he twisted to throw it behind him.

This is crazy. I'm following a mermaid into the water.

She tugged him back around and beckoned him toward her with a grin.

I'm following my Ana into the water. He bit his lip and walked toward her, his cargos dragging as they became sodden. Her eyes clouded with desire as a flush spread on her cheeks. He leaned over her, his fingers stealing to her waistband.

"You're amazing, Ana. So strong and yet so fragile. I can't stop thinking about you." He tucked his fingers into the elastic and tugged her closer. "You've done something to me."

She trembled, her glance cutting to his, then she relaxed. "You've done something to me too. I hadn't thought I could feel this way, not about—"

"A human?" He paused with his hands pushing down the top of her pants. "Fair enough, I didn't think I'd feel this way about a mermaid."

Her hands slid down his chest, pausing at his pants button. His hips leaned toward her and he bent to bite her neck. Her lips were soft in his hair, against his ear.

"We are something new, something different."

Warmth spread through him. Yes. They were different but she was perfect.

Her fingers tugged at his button, slid down his zipper and he stopped thinking. She pushed down his cargos and he kicked off his boots. He stood naked before her, and she gazed at him wide-eyed with reddened lips. A thought hit him.

"Have you—I mean, human or mer, it's—well, I don't really know how this works either."

She smiled, her tongue sliding over her lip. "Let's find out together."

She wiggled out of her sweatpants, and he breathed

in sharply, a deep throbbing in his groin. Pleasure rushed through him.

His stomach tightened and he reached for her. She dived into the water, only the barest splash marking the way. Water kicked up as he strode forward, diving in when the floor dipped off rapidly.

Cool water slid over his heated body. She swam toward him, in her mermaid form. He stilled.

She floated in front of him, silver hair spreading in a fan, her breasts bare and a long tail swishing gently in the water. His gaze dragged up from the tail to her face. Her jaw was tight and fierce, but her eyes were pools of anxiety. He smiled. Her face changed, and she wrapped her hand around his cheek. He realised he was breathing.

Holy crow.

Small movements down his neck brought his hand up—gills. Panic set through him and he thrashed at the water. With a quick movement she caught him to her, holding him close. Her tail wrapped around him, the ribbon fins brushing over his legs. He held her close and buried his head in her hair, bubbles lifting the silvery strands.

She was right. They were something different. *He* was something different. Soft flesh gave way to scales under his exploring fingers. Not hard or rigid as he expected, but soft and smooth. His heart thundered. This was the most insane thing he'd ever done. He lifted his head, feeling bubbles floating around him from the air escaping his mouth. Ana traced his lips with her fingers, wonder in her eyes. He nipped at her finger, and she jerked in his arms before laughing, a stream of bubbles racing to the surface.

Bending his head he took her mouth in his, his tongue exploring, the sensation of the water sliding around him bringing him to full arousal again. Soft fingers closed around his shaft, and he groaned into her mouth, pushing closer. A soft shimmer of light, a sensation of movement, and her tail disappeared, replaced by slender legs wrapping around his waist. His hand slid along the silky skin of her thigh, close to the heated center of her. She trembled, her hips raising to his.

The urge to be inside her washed away all hesitation. He pushed down on her hips, thrusting upward. An incredible warmth wrapped around him, and he shuddered as she clenched, his fingers digging into the soft flesh of her behind. He stayed like that a moment, pulling back to stare into her eyes. She smiled and he melted.

Mine.

She was his and he was so far gone, he'd fallen for her and there was no way back. He thrust into her and she bucked, her teeth scraping over his shoulder. They became a whirl of water and heat and desire until at last she broke in climaxing waves, her nails digging into his back. He shuddered and buried himself deep within her, his own climax leaving him breathless and tingling. He wrapped his arms around her as if he could keep her there forever.

I love you. The thought escaped him, echoing in his ears and in his heart.

She trembled, and he kissed the top of her head.

They were something new. They would make it work.

Chapter Thirty-Four

The narrow bed creaked as he shifted, jarring in the dark quiet of his room. Ana lay curled into him, his arm around her. Her body was strong but so very soft. He kissed the petal-like skin on her shoulder, nibbled at her neck. He felt himself stir and smiled at her little intake of air. He held her closer, but the words that came out weren't soft.

"Ana, I have to ask you something."

Tension rippled through her stomach muscles under his hand, and her breath was warm on his arm. "What?"

"I know you go to lots of places in the Dome. But…the command center. Are you there a lot? I mean—"

"You mean am I spying?"

He screwed up his face against her nape, silken strands tickling his forehead. "Yeah. That's totally what I meant. Have you been spying like a super-secret agent?"

She rolled over to face him, shifting from under his leg. "You already know that I am, that I have been. What are you really asking?"

He propped himself up on one elbow. "There are a couple things I want to know more about, and I thought you might have some info."

Her eyes glinted in the dim light she'd asked him

to leave on. "I won't tell you anything that will hurt my mission."

He stroked down her ribs, settling his hand around her waist. "I wouldn't ask you to. This place, the Dome, how much is known about it from the outside?"

A moment passed as she worried at her plump lip with perfect teeth, and he tried not to do it for her. "I'm not sure. You have to understand—the Dome was set up some time ago. It's recently expanded but the mer have been dealing with it for many tides." She peered up at him, her hand curling against his chest. "I don't think many people on the outside know about it at all. They certainly wouldn't know everything."

His hand rose to cover hers, holding it close to his chest. "Sounds about right."

"Why do you want to know?"

Char's warning rang in his ears but Ana was warm in his arms and her heart beat against his. "There has to be someone out there who could stop this. I want to know if anyone's already searching."

Her hand tightened against his chest. "I would have heard of it if there were."

"Would you?"

She lifted her head to stare at him. "Evan, what were you doing in this part of the ocean?"

He moved his leg, draping it over hers. His foot hung off the small bed, and his back scratched on the wall but it was worth it.

"Like I said, helping a friend. Dan was carrying out some kind of research and wanted a hand. I had nothing better to do."

Her eyelids fluttered and she glanced away.

"That's another thing I hoped you could help with.

I want to know what's happened to Dan and the rest of the crew. I know they said there were a couple bodies, but I figure if a mermaid saved me, why not the others?"

Tension ran through her again, only for a second, but he was learning her body now, and he stroked a thumb over her back. "The mermaid who saved me said she wasn't supposed to do it. Are you not supposed to talk to humans?"

"For many tides, we have not encouraged it. It's more complicated now because of this." She gestured at the room around them.

"I get that. What about this? Us? Will you be in trouble?"

"The only one who might know is my sister."

"If she's anything like mine, you should be safe until she gets over-excited and says more than she means to."

Silence followed his words and he bit his lip. "I didn't mean—I'm sure she wouldn't say anything."

Her breath brushed warm against his skin. "Are you close to your sister?"

"Very close." He tried not to imagine Kelly mourning him, thinking he was dead. "She's a lot younger than me. I remember the day she was born. For the first time in my life I didn't feel alone. I did a lot of the parenting when we were kids, and she's always had my back."

"In the histories we are taught, humans do not value family. This is different from what I expected."

"In the histories I read at school, you belong in fairy tales, so…"

A sigh shuddered through her and she nestled into

him. He wrapped his arms around her, holding her close, trying to take her into himself. Evan began to drift off, warm and cocooned and, for this moment, content with the world. Ana's voice against his breastbone brought him alert.

"The enclave might have a better answer about your friend, but they won't tell me, I've asked. They might tell you though."

Every nerve stood on end.

"Are you suggesting what I think you are?"

"Come with me to the enclave. Talk to the council. Ask them to give you the information."

"Didn't we, like only a moment ago, establish you aren't supposed to talk to humans?"

"Didn't we establish that I'm a spy? Talking to humans is my job."

His thoughts whiplashed inside his head. "I guess, as long as they don't know you do more than talk, it will be okay."

The blush he loved crept up her neck. "They will not be happy, but these are different times now."

He leaned up on an elbow, tucking her under him on the narrow mattress. "Different and crazy. But not all bad."

Her eyes softened, turning to liquid sapphire. "Not all bad at all."

He smiled and bent his head to her lips.

Chapter Thirty-Five

Ana flipped her tail and spiralled downward through tall fronds of luminous green. Evan swam next to her, lean arms cutting through the water. Water flowed over his body, his breath dancing in bubbles from his lips. She pulled up, fins spreading and her tail waving through the current. The muscles in his shoulders rippled and he smiled, a crooked grin. Her gills twitched and a strange ache spread in her chest.

Pushing her hair from where it floated in front of her face, she moved closer to him. A glint lit his warm brown eyes, so different from her own. He reached for her, and she let him catch her around the waist, pull her close. Heart pounding in her chest, she traced her fingers over his lips. He grinned and an answering smile spread on her face, sparkling into her blood.

Sand from the sea bed rose in a glittery burst as her tail caught the ground. She quirked a brow at Evan, pressed a kiss to his full lips, and pulled out from his tightening embrace.

"Come catch me."

His eyes widened and excitement rippled under her skin.

"Did you hear me?"

A frown of concentration settled on his brow, and a faint voice echoed in her mind. *"I heard you. Can you hear me?"*

Her tail twitched. The experiments had been far more effective on him than she had guessed. Anticipation floated through her like the wake following a boat. *Yes! You can speak like a mer but can you swim like one?* She wheeled around in a somersault, beckoning him to follow.

Sunlight filtered through the shallows in streaks of pale green. Ana sped through the water, dancing through the beams of light, her fingertips grazing the feathery weeds. Her tail moved steadily but slowly, allowing him time to catch up. A disturbance in the current warned her he closed in, and she darted a glance back at him. Each kick of his legs held so much power and grace. She'd admired him on the training floor but seeing him here, in her element, did things to her heart she wasn't sure she was ready for.

He reached out a hand to close on her tail, a smug smile on his face. With a buck of her tail she pushed the water at him, and he tumbled. She laughed a stream of bubbles and waved her fins at him.

"When I am in a human body, the world is dull and solid." She swam in a somersault and came up in front of his face, her hair floating in a fan of silver in the water. *"Except for you. You shine, Evan."*

The chase led them close to the edge of mer territory. Bringing him here held no harm. He wouldn't be able to find his way around the ocean without her, no matter how well he swam. His watchful gaze scanning the seabed was curious. That was all.

Gliding next to Evan, she held his hand. He glanced up from the seabed. Such an easy smile he had. Her own came more slowly, but the sparkle in his eyes lit a lava stream inside her and her ribbon fins fluttered.

He pulled her close to him, dipping his head to hers. Her hand clutched at his chest as his lips sent a hum of pleasure through her.

This is dangerous.

The realization chilled her despite the sunlight warming the water. She pressed closer to him, desperately seeking the warmth that her fears had sapped. Her tail curled around him, and his muscles clenched. Only for an instant, but his shoulders were tense under her hands and her lip trembled.

She touched her amulet. Shining light beamed from her skin, and her scales shifted and moved in a swirl of purple energy. Wrapping her now human legs around his waist, she moved higher against him, her foot rubbing the back of his thigh. His hands gripped her waist and his heartbeat under her hands thundered against his ribs. They rose in a slow whirl of a dance, his skin silky under her hands, her legs tightening around him. His lips moved down to her neck, and she tilted her head to give him better access. Her gaze drifted to the reef. They were so close to the boundary. She hadn't been out here in a long time.

She stilled. Shoving against his chest, she pulled away. He let go and she spiralled downward, her legs turning to tail again.

A wasteland of coral lay before them, bleached, dry, dead. Anger waved through her. She pulled her fins in close, the spikes on her tail standing up.

The coral had survived hundreds of years of human exploration and longer than that of mermaid occupation. The prickling on her skin, the rash covering the tails of those mer who lived out this way, all signs of humanity's arrogance.

"What happened here?"

She snapped her teeth at Evan and he frowned. Closing her eyes, she concentrated on letting the water fill her mind. The anger ebbed, but the tide threatened still.

"Acidic seas, warming oceans. That's what happened."

He treaded water next to her, his gaze fixed on the coral graveyard. *"I'm sorry."*

She shook her head, her hair floating in front of her, curtaining the anger she couldn't keep from leaking out her eyes. *"Come, we shouldn't linger here. The same poisons killing the coral are toxic to my kind."*

The water chopped around her, no longer smooth but hitting her with every grain of sand that floated. Her brother's earnest entreaties to the council had done him no good, his attempt to work with the humans had brought him only death. He hadn't figured out the best way to solve the problems.

Now I have, everything is falling into place.

Evan swam alongside her, his face grave.

I simply need to not be distracted.

Chapter Thirty-Six

The cavern loomed above him, darkness edging into green light. He pushed wet hair from his face and scanned the platform. The rock was heavily chiselled and covered in ornate carvings by the water's edge. Ana pulled herself up, her tail sweeping over the edge in a surprisingly graceful movement. She touched the carvings and smiled at him, a softness in her eyes.

"For grip. Lichen can be a bit slippery sometimes."

A booming echo sounded through the open space, followed by a rush of whispers. Waves. He'd been so long under them without hearing them.

Water rushed off his body and from his clothes as he hauled himself onto the platform. Chilled air mobbed him and turned his skin to ice.

"Does this place get any warmer?"

Her laugh was startling, a bell-like sound he'd not heard before. A smile spread on his face even as his teeth chattered. The swell in his heart leaked out into a grin he couldn't stop. If someone had told him even a week ago he'd fall in love with a mermaid, he'd have had them committed. A shimmering light pulsed into a fully human and naked Ana. The same joy reflected in her eyes. Then a clanging boom very unlike the rushing echo of the waves resounded through the cavern.

"Oh, son of a whale!" she said.

He tried not to laugh at her consternation. "I guess

that means no time to play?"

She twisted her lips to hide a smile. "Oh, shut up."

Ana strode toward a stone bench. Her skin glistened in the faint light, and he looked away resolutely, trying to get himself under control. A pair of sweatpants hit him in the side of the head, and he grabbed them. She had pulled on her own pair and dragged a large t-shirt over her head. His smile grew at the sight of her small frame in the large sweats. He shuffled into the pants and stood at the same time as footsteps sounded at the end of the platform.

The young man approaching them was unlike anyone Evan had ever seen, but with the carriage and bearing of a village elder. The assumption of authority, the confidence of leadership emanating from him brought Evan to a wary attention. His hair hung in black dreadlocks tied back with a cord clattering with the crisp shells threaded through it. He wore trousers with dark whorls of kelp woven through the material, but his chest was bare. Where Ana's skin shone with luminous silver, this mer's skin was a deep dark tinged with green. Purple eyes fierce as a hawk stared at him then Ana.

"So, Sariana, you have returned."

"Greetings, Myrndir."

Although both were in their human forms, their outstretched hands glowed and webbing appeared between their fingers, which they touched together in what seemed to be a formal greeting.

The merman's gaze flicked over him once more. "We were not expecting you back so soon. Why did you bring this human with you?"

"He has valuable information for you. And you

have information for him in return."

"Ana, no. That information is not for us to share."

"I think you will change your mind once you hear him out."

"We need nothing this human has to offer."

Evan stepped forward, stopping short of waving his hand in the mer's face. "Yeah, this human has a name, Evan Hunter. Nice to meet you."

Myrndir's brows shot up, the ends of them long and pointed. "Evan Hunter?"

The burning anger floating through him turned to a chill wariness. "Yeah. That's what I said."

A moment of silence hung between them like stone.

"There is someone who will want to see you. She wonders often what has become of you."

"Amatheia? Is that her name?"

"Yes, it is she."

"I would like to see her." He thought to the last time he'd seen her, outside a corridor metres away from the broken bodies of his comrades, only days before he held down a mermaid whose DNA was extracted before leaving her to die. "I don't know that I should be here, to be honest."

The merman regarded him, his head cocked to one side. Dark eddies in his purple eyes set Evan off balance.

"We know about Shodica. But we also heard about her youngling. How you and others of the humans visited him, sought to comfort him. The boy is grateful for it."

Relief swept through him, even as his mind grabbed onto the mermaid's name. *Shodica.* He would remember. "The kid is here?"

"Ana brought him to us."

Evan glanced at her as his heart swelled. She stared down at the floor, her shoulders rigid. He placed his hand on the small of her back, his fingers curling into the baggy shirt, seeking warm skin.

"I wondered if she had."

Myrndir's gaze narrowed and slid to Ana's face. He pressed his lips together and walked away, clearly expecting them to follow.

Ana stepped away from his hand.

"Will it matter, that he saw me touch you?"

She shook her head. "He is my sister's mate. He would not lose her another sibling. One was enough."

"Did something happen to your other sister?"

"Brother." Her mouth twisted. "It's a sad tale with only one thing to be learned; those in charge don't always know what they're doing."

He risked a quick kiss on the top of her head. "I'm sorry for your loss. I know about those in charge making bad calls. It sucks and there's never anything you can do to make it better."

"I'm doing something. I'm following through on his mission. He won't have died for nothing."

Guess that was as good a reason as any for the spying.

Evan followed them toward the back of the cavern. Large slabs hewn from a dark rock framed an entrance set into the back wall of the cavern. Beyond lay a darkness illuminated by luminous specks that on closer inspection appeared to be a form of lichen. He ducked his head and thrust up a hand. The ceiling of the passageway was a bare few inches from the top of his scalp. He stayed slightly hunched, tracking the soft swaying of the glowing hair of Ana and the merman.

A chill air nipped at his bare torso, and he rubbed his arms, trying to warm up. The merman didn't seem to mind the cold. His feet were bare like Evan's but he trod down the uneven rocky tunnel with none of the wincing.

Light filled the end of the corridor and unexpected relief flooded through him. The dark tunnel was too much of a reminder that they were under the water. He stumbled over a rock and caught at Ana's shoulder for balance. She flashed a tight smile but moved from out of his grip before stepping into the light.

The cavern they entered was even larger than the one before. His heart hitched, and all other thoughts fled his mind. High rock walls rose around them, lit by incandescent clusters of some kind of bio-luminescent plant. A melodic hum filled the air, seeming to come from dripping crystal needles hanging from the roof of the cavern. They passed pools of water lit by glowing green plants with narrow waving fronds. Mers filled the space, some in human form, most lounging in the pools or darting along the channels cut through the rock platform, tails cutting cleanly through the water.

It was like a movie set. Barely real. His mind struggled to accept that the beings moving so swiftly around him, darting glances from inhuman eyes, were more than extras on a fantasy film.

Mermaids. I'm hanging out with mermaids. He flexed his fingers and fought to keep his jaw from hanging open.

As his brain grew accustomed to the sights and smells, he noticed a few of the mer they passed had a different expression when they stared at Ana. His chest tightened, and he found himself peering closer at those they met. Most spared only a glance for Myrndir and Ana, focusing with wary curiosity on the strange human in their midst. But there were some whose eyes darkened, the glints deep within almost a hidden message.

Ana strode on, seemingly oblivious, but her fingers curled and her shoulders hunched under the baggy shirt.

He was right back to where he was before. He didn't trust her, but his heart didn't care. He walked as close to her as he dared, knowing she didn't want him to touch her here in front of her people. Both of them were in over their heads in more ways than one.

They skirted a channel around where some mermaids plucked shells from baskets and wove them into a braided skein of some kind of cord. Farther on, some younger mer scraped kelp and weed into long fibres, hanging them on racks to dry.

Ana cast him a glance, and murmured quietly. "This is our crafting place for those things best created outside of the water."

The thumps in the distance were stonemasons. Strong arms lifted hunks of rock as if they were pumice.

They approached an area sheltered by waving fronds of multicoloured dried seaweed, the patterns of shells telling a story he didn't have time to decipher before Myrndir parted the curtain and waved them on.

Beyond the curtain was a large chamber half submerged in water. A great throne-like chair rose from the dark pool, and on it perched an older mermaid, silvery hair gray in the green-tinged light, her skin unwrinkled but faded around the nose and mouth, eyes a dull sheen. She held up a hand, and the humming chatter of the other mers died down.

The urge to fidget pressed at his skin. He was not the only one with a bare torso, but he felt naked and vulnerable in the center of that focus. Milky eyes bored. Evan's tongue cleaved to the roof of his mouth.

"Myrndir, Sariana, why you have brought a human to the enclave?"

He darted a glance at Ana. The old mermaid didn't sound pleased, and Ana's jaw tightened. Her chin raised, and she glared at the other mer.

"Humans have not been allowed here since the dark times. You know our laws; you know our reasons. Explain yourselves."

He scanned the room for Amatheia. The faces of the enclave ranged from forbidding to curious. Every mer appeared different. Some had pointed ears, some had bony frills poking out behind where their ears hid beneath matted hair. Others had wound shells through their hair or used braids and cords. Even the tails were different on those in mer form. Starting at the waist, they coiled down in scales of light to dark green, some with striped bands of deeper colours. The ribbon fins he'd found so enticing on Ana were different on these mer, translucent and pale.

Myrndir stepped forward, holding out a trident. "Mighty Meliandra, I beg pardon for this transgression. Believe me I would not do it without great cause. There are those among you who have argued Sariana's mission has gone too slowly, that the information she has managed to find has brought us no reward and much pain. But today she brings us news, and a human, who may change that."

Wariness ran like electricity in his veins. "I don't remember being a part of this discussion," he murmured.

Ana ignored him and stepped forward too, her hand gesturing slightly at him to stay back. She sank to a knee and bowed her head.

"I seek pardon, mighty one. I would not have brought Evan Hunter here without great need."

Butterflies swooped in his stomach. He couldn't help noticing the large altar-like stone in the alcove behind what he thought of as the throne. Humans bound mers to tables and bled them; who's to say mers wouldn't do the same to a human given half a chance?

Silence had fallen once more, the only sound the distant surf at the cavern entrance. Myrndir and Ana moved to the side, leaving him a clear walkway to the throne. Wiping sweaty palms on his trousers, he wished more than ever that he had a shirt—maybe a Kevlar vest—hell, maybe even a gun. He approached the old mer, fighting the urge to avoid her milky stare.

"Uh, hello. I'm Evan. It's nice to meet you. Thanks for having me here."

"I will not bid you welcome yet, Evan Hunter, but in the light of the two mer who vouch for you, I will extend to you our bond that you shall not be harmed, at least not whilst you remain in their keeping."

A smile tugged at the corner of his mouth. Something about this mer reminded him of his grandmother.

"Fair enough, thanks for the warning, your mightiness."

Ana's elbow dug sharply in his side, and he

scowled.

"What? You all called her mighty. I thought that was her title!"

Her eyes blazed but the older mer said, "Do not be angry, Sariana. I see he meant no harm."

He risked a glance up at her and although her mouth still lay in two narrow lines, her milky eyes had warmed. He smiled and she inclined her head.

"Greetings then to you, Evan Hunter."

"I apologize if I offended you. This is all a bit new to me."

An angry voice echoed from one of the submerged seats, a husky mer with what may have been a seaweed cloak. "I would imagine it must be. You seem more used to cutting up merfolk than talking to us."

His gaze slid away from the mer's flashing silver eyes to stare blindly at the ornate floor carvings, seeing them run red with blood. His arms remembered the feel of the dying mermaid, his mind flashed images of dead civilians under rubble.

"It is for that reason he has come," Myrndir said. "He has information to share."

I do?

"And a boon to ask."

A what?

The angry mer backed down in the face of Myrndir's authority. Evan raised his head, guilt dragging at his chest. Hopefully, one of them would tell him what information he was supposed to be carrying.

Ana turned to him, her face narrow and intent. "Tell them about the experiments, your part in it, what's happened to you, to Hudson."

"I'm not a spy."

"No. I am. You knew that and you came here with me. Don't pretend you didn't think something like this would happen."

He gazed around the colourful enclave and the glowing vines. "I don't think I could have imagined this in my wildest dreams."

"You know what I mean. I can tell them, I have told them, but they don't understand. They need to see, to know."

"But what will they do with the knowledge?"

A shadow darkened her eyes. "That is up to them."

"We are waiting."

He gripped her shoulder and stared down into her shuttered face. "You promised you wouldn't hurt Char or Khalid, or the others. If something happens to them because you brought me here, I won't forgive you."

Soft lips twisted in an unhappy frown. "And still you doubt me."

He wanted to stroke her hair from her face, fold her into his arms, whisper that none of it mattered because his treacherous heart was at her feet, and he couldn't get it back even if he wanted to. Instead, he gripped her shoulder tighter. "I doubt you because you avoid answering. Will you promise me you won't endanger them?"

She winced under his grip and some of the mer mumbled. Not many though. He was not the only one who knew how tough she was.

"I would never intentionally hurt them. I can't promise more than that."

He inhaled deeply and forced his fingers to let go.

"I guess that'll have to do."

Inhuman eyes gazed back at him as he scanned the

assembled mer. "The experiments aren't only on the merfolk. They experiment on us too. Not all of us feel like we have a choice. We signed a contract. Our families are in danger."

Ana moved a little, and he glanced at her from the corner of his eyes. Maybe it wasn't only his family in danger.

"The procedures on both our species don't always go well or as planned. I've seen some of the end results. It isn't great."

A soft splash sounded from behind the leader's chair, and Amatheia pulled herself onto the platform in front of it, her gaze burning into his. "You signed a contract?"

Heaviness settled on his shoulders. "Yes. Turns out that wasn't smart."

"They never are. Tell us, please, what they're hoping to achieve?"

The vice squeezing his chest loosened. He raised his arm, his pulse thundering in his ears. "On some of us, the procedures work."

He concentrated. His arm began to glow, and small fins darted from his skin up the back of his arm.

The leaden silence that fell was worse than the cacophony he'd expected. Amatheia's eyes widened and she stared from him to Ana.

Ana reached out a trembling hand and touched his arm. "I didn't realise it had gone so far."

He kept his voice low, for her alone. "You aren't the only one with secrets."

She flinched.

"We will speak of this and of what we mean to do at a later time. What is it you would have from us, Evan

Hunter?" said the mighty old lady.

"Four weeks ago my friend Dan and I were on a boat that capsized. The ocean destroyed it. I survived." He avoided glancing at Amatheia, not sure how much she'd told the rest of them. "I hoped to hear if you had seen or heard anything about what had happened to the rest of the crew, to my friends."

Murmurs broke the silence and he scanned the faces. Amatheia wouldn't meet his gaze and dread coiled in his stomach.

"I am sorry not to have better news for you, especially given the significance of what you have shown us today. But we found no bodies. I am sorry."

Hope leached out of him, leaving leaden darkness in its wake. Rocky walls closed in on him and he dragged in a deep breath, wishing intensely for blue sky and sunshine and grass. Ana's shoulder bumped his arm, and she frowned at her sister.

"The council is dismissed." The leader slipped from her chair, into the channel of clear water. "Sariana, I would have a word with you before you go. A private word."

Chapter Thirty-Seven

Everyone else either marched, swam off, or loitered with purpose. Evan shivered as a chill drifted across his torso. He was used to being the tallest person in most rooms, but most rooms didn't have everyone else swimming at ground level.

He scanned the cavern for Amatheia. He'd never thanked her properly for saving his life, and now it turned out she was Ana's sister.

He caught a glimpse of silver hair shot with purple slipping away through a kind of screen. He hesitated for a moment then followed, leaping over one of the channels streaming through the floor. A bitter smell wafted from the dehydrating seaweed, and the rocks here had a crumbly bone-dry appearance. He stopped outside the room Amatheia had disappeared into, behind a curtain of bright shells. Myrndir's voice floated out and Evan hesitated, his hand a mere inch away from parting the shells.

"You can't give Sariana the information."

"Do you not trust her?"

"Do you?"

Silence.

Evan fought off the sick feeling of dread creeping through him.

"No, I don't. She's my sister though."

"Her emotions are too strong. Ever since Baruthial

disappeared, she has been bent on revenge."

"Can you blame her?"

The voices sank, as if the two of them had moved closer together. "Theia, my love, the sorrow of his death lies heavy on us both, yet we are not driven by revenge. Security and peace are what we seek. Not vengeance."

"I think Sariana wants it all."

Evan shifted, and his elbow knocked the ropes of shell. A chattering melody cut through the silence as they bounced off each other. For a second he hesitated, then barged through the curtain. Brazening it out would be better than pretending he hadn't been there at all.

He acted as if he didn't see Myrndir's trident held at an attack angle, or the way the merman shifted to stand in front of his mate. Grinning, he stood in the entrance, untangling shells from his arms.

"Amatheia! I'm glad I tracked you down. I wanted to thank you for saving my life."

The frown between her brows cleared, and she smiled, pushing Myrndir's arm away. "Did you not thank me before?"

His smile relaxed. "I honestly can't remember. Someone hit me on the head shortly afterward."

She grimaced and he laughed.

"I don't blame you, and I really did want to thank you, especially now I understand so much more about how much you were putting yourself at risk."

She held out her hand, and he held his own up, palm to palm with hers. A shock ran through him as her webbing appeared, and tingles spread over his arm.

"I have never been comfortable with leaving people to drown, no matter how much damage they do to us."

Myrndir strode around the back of her, stopping short of circling them. Evan stared at the trident and the fierce expression on the merman's face.

His fingers curled back and his arm dropped. "I have no way to say how sorry I am about the Dome, about the whole thing."

"It was here before you came and will no doubt be here when you are gone."

"You sound certain I'll be gone."

"I don't believe you are one to let a contract bind you, no matter how damning the terms."

"I don't think that's a big secret. I want out of here. But I also want it shut down."

Myrndir snorted. "And how would you do that?"

He rubbed his jaw, salt and sand clinging to his skin.

Amatheia's hand went to the mess of shells and netting around her neck. "What of Sariana?"

A hot ache spread through his chest. Could he leave her? She couldn't—wouldn't come with him.

"You care for her?"

His hands went to dig themselves into nonexistent pockets, and his ears burned. "Very much."

She darted a glance at the looming merman, who shook his head once sharply."Your friend, the one you asked me about the first time we met—"

"Daniel?"

"Yes. You care for him?"

The hollow feeling spread through his chest once more. "Yeah. We've been buddies since we were young. He's always been there for me. *Was*. He was always there for me." *Grief never got better, it just got duller.*

"Theia, " Myrndir's voice rumbled a warning.

She turned her shoulder on her partner, her eyes intense silver. "I know where he is."

The world rocked. Around him the stone walls decorated with carvings, and arrangements of dried seaweed faded into a fuzzy blur .

"Alive?"

"Yes. I am sorry we deceived you. We had reasons, but I know we should have told you the truth at the beginning."

He uncurled his fists, pushing away the rising burn of anger. "Where is he?"

Myrndir stepped forward, his amulet gleaming in the low light. "This we cannot tell you. Theia, you must not; the council have expressed their decision very clearly."

He straightened to his full height, glaring down at the merman, the rage banked but steaming. "If she wants to tell me, she should. In fact, you should all let me know now where my friend is. If you've imprisoned him, I will fight to free him."

The mer's lip curled. "You wouldn't last long."

Theia laid a hand on her partner's shoulder, and he stepped back, a fierce stare holding Evan's.

"We have not imprisoned Daniel Kim. He is safe, and continuing his work." She smiled gently. "He has spoken of you often."

His teeth ground in a tightening jaw. *Bet they'd lied to Dan too.* "Dan's work?"

"I think it's best if he fills you in on it himself. But be assured, he is working toward the same end as you."

He frowned, unease threading through him. "You

seem to know more about what he's been doing than I do."

She turned to Myrndir and held out a hand. Her mate stared at her as if they were having some silent battle. With a huff, he pulled out a decorated stone from a pouch at his waist. She took it from him with a smile and the gruff merman smiled ruefully back.

The stone fit in her palm, and inlaid shells reflected the dim light of the room as she stretched it toward him. "This will guide you to your friend. I will key it to you. You must hold out your hand, and you must trust me."

A clatter of shells sounded behind him, and Amatheia drew the stone back, staring at Ana coming through the doorway.

"What are you doing, sister?"

Ana's voice rang like steel, and he flashed a glance at her from the corner of his eyes.

"Your Evan wishes to find his friend. I am setting a guide stone for him."

Her face set in rigid lines. "Why not for me?"

"It will work better for him."

"You would send him into danger?"

Amatheia's face shone with a cold light. "The only danger to him will be what he takes with him." She grasped his hand. "Do you trust me?"

He inhaled, trying to still his racing thoughts. "You saved my life. I will always trust you."

Even if you lie to me about my friend.

Chapter Thirty-Eight

Ana swam away from the enclave. *Theia had known all this time and no word, no sign! So much for sisterly loyalty.*

Her tail whipped the water, and she pushed farther on, back to the Dome. Evan kept pace with her for the most part, except for when she burned the edge off her churning emotions by darting through the kelp forest. She shot out of the waving fronds in a spin, her hair flicking through the current. Her fins dragged behind her, and she scanned the water for Evan. He swam toward her, strong arms cutting the water.

"What the hell is going on, Ana?"

"A lot of things."

"Have I pissed you off somehow?"

"What? No!"

"Then stop pushing me away."

Her fins curled around her arms, waving from her tail toward him. She stroked the hair from her face. *"I'm not trying to. I'm mad at Theia."*

"Do I look like Theia?"

That brought her up. It wasn't his fault.

"No. Not yet anyway. Why didn't you tell me?"

He hunched his shoulders, his arms moving in the water. *"There didn't seem to be a good time."*

"Really? Because I seem to remember showing you I was a mermaid. Seemed like a good time then, or

when we swam in the water? That would have been a good time to show me. Or when we made love?"

The anger burned away to a darker, more painful sensation in her chest. He still didn't trust her. Thoughts shoved at the shield in her mind, and she ignored them. Anger was easier than guilt and a lot easier than hurt. She stoked the fire again.

Theia had given the locator rock to Evan, keyed it to him. She said because Dan was his friend, the magic would work more strongly if he was the one to wield it. But she knew Theia as well as she knew herself. Theia didn't trust her either.

The anger surged, this time riding a cresting wave of fear. She didn't want Evan to be hurt. That had never been part of her plan.

He backed away from her now, darting a glance at her tail. She glanced down, at the darkness pulsing in jagged stripes through the scales. She whipped her tail behind her, focused, and light shimmered down through her fins.

Evan bit his lip. *"Maybe I should have told you earlier. But you know now. Does it make a difference?"*

"It does make difference, but in a good way. Think of it, Evan. You are breathing underwater, speaking to my mind, able to create light. Imagine all the other things you will learn to do!" She undulated closer to him. *"The two of us together—it seems more a possibility than ever."*

He frowned. *"True. But at what cost? The guilt eats at me, Ana. Every time I feel joy in the water sliding over our bodies, I remember why it is possible."*

Icy cold slid through her veins. So much sacrifice. She blinked and grasped his hand. *"Feeling joy is not a bad thing, Evan. It's not something I've had a lot of before, and I admit I'm relishing each moment, each bubble of happiness.*

He pressed a kiss on her palm, folded her fingers over it.

A fierce determination settled in her bones. This would be different.

She would make it so.

****

A bead of water dripped down the back of Evan's neck, and he wiped his ear on his shoulder. He laced his boots and glanced up at Ana. "I've got duty at ten. It'll be noticed if I don't go. I'll meet you back at my room about one, and we can talk to Char then. Start things rolling."

"We don't need Char."

He frowned. Neither Char nor Ana trusted each other, even though they seemed to get on well.

"We need her. She's trained, and I trust her at my back."

"And you don't trust me."

"What makes you say that?"

Her mouth turned down. "It doesn't matter. If you think we need her, then we better take her. I didn't want her to get hurt."

"Why would she get hurt?"

"Why do you think we need an extra person?"

He raised his brows in acknowledgement. "Fair call."

He stood and stepped toward her, folded her into his arms. "Try not to worry, sweetheart. We'll do this, then we will bring the whole place down."

She leaned her forehead to his chest, her voice

muffled. "You really want to destroy it, don't you?"

"Yes. I've seen what it does to people. I might have benefited but others, so many others, died."

Her breath sighed out warm against his shirt. "I guess they think a few sacrifices are worth it for the benefits."

His arms tightened around her. "People justify all sorts of atrocities. I've seen it before. But I promise you, Ana, I won't let them destroy your people."

She trembled in his arms, a long shudder that melted his heart. He leaned back and tucked a finger under her chin to tilt up her face. Her eyes stared wide and silver, and her mouth drew into a tight line. He rubbed his thumb over her lips.

"Oh, sweetheart. I'm so sorry. I wish I could make it all better."

Her voice came out in a harsh whisper. "I don't know that anything can."

He bent his head to hers and placed a kiss on her lips. "When I was drowning, you gave me some of your air. I want to give you some of my hope, and any strength I have is yours."

Her mouth twisted, and she wound her hands in his shirt. "You are too good to me, Evan. This is like an unreal dream, and I don't see a happy ending."

"You're talking like we're in a storybook. I believe we make our own destinies. Who's to say we can't be happy?"

"Would you want that? To be happy with me?"

"More than anything."

A smile like sunshine spread on her face. "Then let's do this."

Chapter Thirty-Nine

The room closed in with the three of them in it. Char fidgeted with a fake rose from the vase on the table. Her brows lowered, and her gaze kept darting to and sliding away from Ana.

"Let me get this straight. You're a mermaid. You've been some kind of double agent and now you're helping Evan find his friend? What for? Love?"

Ana had been scowling back at Char, but at the word *love* a blush cascaded down her cheeks to her neck.

Evan squirmed and Char shot him a glare. "Yeah, you should feel guilty, devil dog. You knew this and didn't say a word. I'm mad at you too."

Ana crossed her arms, her lips pressing tight together.

Evan sighed and leaned forward on the table. "Yeah. Ana's a spy. But she's on our side. That is, if you still want to bring this place down?"

"I'm not saying I'm mad about the spy thing. If I was a mer, I'm sure I'd be spying for them too. It's the lying-to-your-friends thing I'm not happy about."

"You consider me a friend?" Ana said quietly into the awkward silence.

"Sure. I mean, don't you think of me as a friend? Or is it different for mer?"

He reached out to hold of one of Ana's hands,

twisting in the hem of her sweater. Her pulse fluttered under his fingers.

"It isn't different. We have friends. I value you highly, Char."

"So we're all buddies. Means I don't think we have a problem here except for how we get to Dan and what we'll do with him when we find him." Char rolled her eyes and waved the rose in a salute. "Fine. Tell me your plan. What d'you need me to do?"

He cleared his throat. "Ana's sister gave me a...a magic rock."

Her eyebrows nearly hit her hairline, and he shrugged, heat flaring on his cheekbones.

"I know, it's all bizarre. Ana, a little help here?"

Ana leaned back in the chair, drawing her hand away from his and crossing her arms. "It's a map."

Char stared. "The rock is a map. Does it sing, too?"

He snorted and Ana stared in bemusement. "The stone Theia gave Evan is keyed to him, so he will have to lead us. It will point the way to Daniel Kim."

His hand went to the hidden rock in his pocket. "Will it work in a sub or do we have to swim?"

Char sat forward, her lips pursing. "It would be easier in a sub, unless your pal is a certified diver?"

"Dan? Not that I know of. Although it turns out there's a lot I never knew about him."

"Yeah," Char said. "It sucks when your friends keep secrets from you."

He gave her a look. "Short story—we have to get a sub bug, follow the rock map to wherever Dan is, and find out what he was doing here and whether he can help us get out." *Then I can see him again. Make sure he's really alive and well.*

"We don't know what we will find there. It could be dangerous." Ana shot a glance up at Char. "I wouldn't like for you to be hurt. There is no obligation to come."

She tugged at her lip, assessing Ana. "Nah, we good. Going into danger to protect people is kinda why I signed up in the first place. I'm happy to be back up." She leaned forward. "I like to take care of my friends. Sometimes you have to sacrifice for a higher cause."

Ana let her breath out slowly. "Yes. That is true. Some causes are important enough that sacrifices must be made."

Uneasiness prickled down his spine. "All this talk of sacrifice is making me edgy. Seriously, all we're doing is finding Dan holed up in some cavern getting sick of eating fish, and we'll bring him here where he can hole up in a room and get sick of eating fish."

The two women shared a look and Evan suspected he'd missed a whole stratum of the conversation. He pushed out of his chair.

"First things first, stealing a sub bug."

They walked to the dock with purpose and with smiles. Char kept up a patter of banter and he'd waved at a couple of people.

Nefarious deeds feel stranger in the daytime.

People bustled on the dock the same as always, crews in and out, maintenance workers, and guards, at all hours.

Evan steepled his hands against his lips. "Wish me luck."

Ana caught his arm as he stepped forward. "I'll go."

"Why?"

She flinched. He hadn't meant to sound so interrogatory.

"This won't be the first time I've done this. Wait here."

She walked up to the two men on the desk, pulled a piece of paper from her pocket, slid it over and gestured at the two of them. The first man nodded and handed the paper back before pulling up a screen and tapping at it. Within a minute they were directed to a sub bug, told they had an hour, and to make sure they didn't run it aground.

"How the hell did you do that, Ana?" he demanded.

"Forged signature. Works every time."

He pressed his lips closed on questions. Espionage might be necessary but it always made him uncomfortable. *Give me a wrench any day.*

The sub bug was cramped but Evan was used to it now. He shifted next to Ana in the driver's seat and fished out the rock. He rested it gingerly on the dash board and stared at it.

"Does this actually work?"

"Yes."

"How do I turn it on?"

Char snorted behind him, and he flipped her the bird.

"Wait until we are out in the ocean and I'll show you. It takes concentration and the touch of your hands, that's all."

Char snickered. "That's what she said."

His ears warmed, and he stared fixedly out of the window. The metal doors slid open. A part of him still waited to be summoned back, but the signature and whatever Ana had said seemed to have worked wonders. They slipped out with no trouble.

Bubbles from the engine rose around them and he sighed, remembering the feel of skittering water and air over his skin and the intoxicating feel of breathing underwater.

The stone reflected the light filtering through the water in a way it hadn't when they sat under the fluorescent lights. Small inlays of shell shimmered with a gentle glow, and he touched it with a hesitant finger. It was warm to touch, and his fingers curled back against his palm.

Ana steered the sub bug a good distance away from the Dome and about midway to the enclave lands. She brought it to a hovering halt.

"Pick up the stone, hold it in both hands, and think of your friend."

"That's all?"

"That's all."

"No magic words?"

"Evan—"

"Okay, sorry." He huffed a breath out and picked up the stone. It seemed so small nestled between his two hands. The warm weight of it spread through his palms and up his arms. He closed his eyes and pictured Dan.

"Holy shit." Char's startled voice brought his eyes flashing open and the light beaming from the rock flickered out.

Ana huffed an exasperated sound. "You have to concentrate. You don't have to shut your eyes but you do have to keep thinking about him."

He curled his hands around the stone's smooth

edges, thinking of Dan and how crazy he'd find this. A beam of light spread from the stone, out through the sub bug window, and around to the left.

Ana smiled. "Left it is."

Chapter Forty

The deeper they got into mer territory, the more the small roof of the sub bug pressed down on him. They puttered through valleys in the sea floor, exposed and vulnerable. The mer had shown how formidable an enemy they could be, and he didn't relish the thought of one of those energy blasts hitting this bubble of a vehicle. He might have been given this key but it seemed damned clear he wasn't supposed to have it. Evan shifted in his seat and tore his gaze from the sun-streaked water in front of him, down to the rock pointing the way.

The shimmering beam of light spreading in a path before them sent shivers down his spine. Part of him knew the mers must have magic but seeing it like this set his teeth on edge. The pale glow bounced off a rocky cavern to their right. Ana brought the sub bug close to the rising stone wall. The light floated over the rock and settled on a narrow dark chasm leading into the rock face.

Ana frowned, and her hands clenched white-knuckled on the steering stick. Monitors binged and pipped.

"I'll set it down here. We'll need to swim the rest of the way." She pointed to the screen. "That trench narrows pretty quickly and this won't fit."

"Right," he said. "Suit up, Char."

"Do you think she should stay here? Guard the sub?"

Char snorted and stood. "Like that will happen. If there's any danger, it's in there, not out here. We didn't see one mer on our way in. I figure they've been told about us."

It's what he'd thought too.

Char pulled on a tank and hose, spitting on the mouthpiece before sliding it into her mouth. Goggles sat ready on her forehead. She waggled her brows at him, and he smiled through the racing adrenaline.

Evan glanced down at his t-shirt and cargos. It jarred him, not buckling into harnesses and straps and tanks before leaving the vehicle. Ana passed him a pistol. He checked the safety and tucked it in his belt. She hefted one in her hand and passed it slowly to Char, who slid it into the holster attached to the tank harness. He hoisted a waterproof rucksack of new clothes onto his shoulder and slipped out of the sub.

The water soaked his clothes and he inhaled, the slits on the side of his neck opening and closing with a steady beat he found reassuring.

The current slipped around him, his fingers weaving a pattern through the water. Char's eyes widened through the goggles. Hearing about it and seeing it were two different things. He concentrated and a luminous glow flared down his arm. She jerked back, ripples and bubbles wending toward him.

"You're scaring her."

He turned to Ana. *"No. She's freaked out and I get why. But she isn't scared."*

Ana ducked down and twisted in a coil of tail and fins and streaming hair that wound its way into his heart, leaving him breathless.

"Come, this way. We're wasting time."

He cut through the water, following her into the trench between rock walls. His breath caught in his chest, and he fought against the enclosing feel of the rock looming above him. At points the trench narrowed, but there was always space between his shoulders and the walls. After a few minutes, his pulse returned to normal as his body caught up with the rational brain.

He glanced over his shoulder at Char swimming behind him, bubbles rising from her regulator.

They got through the channel and surfaced in a large cavern. Not the one he'd washed up in, but pretty damn similar. Evan frowned. He and Dan had been closer than he thought when Amatheia left him on that rock. Metal doors rose beyond a large slab of stone protruding out into the water. He narrowed his gaze. Char lifted her goggles on her head and removed her mouthpiece, also fixed on the door. Ana's hair spread over the surface of the water in a sheaf of silver as she floated next to him.

Ana's voice sounded tight and grating. "I knew the operation gave the mer equipment at the beginning when we tried to work with them, but I had thought it all lost in the conflict that followed."

"More secrets?"

"Yes."

He glided over to the platform, hauled himself up, water streaming from his clothes. He slipped off the rucksack and unzipped the waterproof inner. The sweatpants and top inside were damp but not wet. He held them out and Ana touched the amulet, concentrating. Her tail blurred and shimmered in a ripple of scales, leaving legs behind. He passed her the clothes and turned his back, catching Char trying not to watch. He didn't blame her. He was nearly used to it by now, but it still creeped him out that his own skin could change.

The APV pistol was bulky, and he shifted it from where it pushed his waistband down. He hadn't thought they'd need the weapons, but the metal doors gave him pause.

Evan strode forward, leaving wet footprints on the rock. Ana, small and incongruous in her sweats and pistol, walked close beside him, and Char squelched along behind, her gun out at the ready.

The doors were locked, but the rock grew heavy and warm in his pocket. Gingerly, he drew it out. The swirls of shells glowed in a pattern different from the one before.

Char stepped closer and pointed at the rock wall beside the door. "Look! There's the same pattern!"

She was right. He glanced at her, her face in the same expression he figured he must be wearing. *Magic was kinda cool, but fully creepy as well.* "Ana? Do I hold the stone up to it or what?"

Silence came from his right side. He turned to her. She stared at the floor, a deep frown between her eyes.

"Ana?"

She glanced up and a sigh that seemed to come from her toes escaped her lips. "Yes. You hold the stone up to the pattern and keep it there until the door unlocks."

Slivers of ice slid through his bloodstream. Something wasn't right. His fingers played over the stone, and he stared at her. She smiled, her mouth tight.

266

"Don't you want to get your friend?"

Char nudged him. "Come on, Evan. Let's find Dan and get the hell out of here. This place gives me the creeps."

Something deep in his gut told him not to but he overrode it and placed the stone, shells facing out, onto the pattern by the door. After a second, a clunky snick sounded and the door shifted. He peeled the stone off the wall and grasped the door handle. "Ready?"

Ana nodded. "Always, devil dog," Char said, cocking her pistol.

He pushed the door open, his gun ready in his other hand. A short corridor hewn from rock laid out in front of them, wide-open doors on either side of the tunnel.

They padded down the corridor. Ancient-looking lights strung along the roof of the corridor, dim but lit. He wondered where the power source was. What it was.

He peered into the open doors as they passed them. They led into rooms full of what appeared to be salvaged equipment and boxes. Pieces of metal from submarines and boats. His brows contracted.

The last door was closed. He tried the handle and was surprised when it turned. A man sat at a chair in front of a small computer array. The murky glow of the monitor lit up his face, scarred but familiar.

Joy and relief fizzed through him. "Dan!"

Dan spun in his chair, an amazed grin splitting his face at Evan filling the doorway. He pushed himself from the black leather chair, limping toward Evan. Dan stopped as he approached, his eyes widening in shock as he stared at Char. She glanced between him and Evan and flicked a small wave at him.

"She's a soldier." Dan's voice grated, as if from

disuse.

He shook off the unease. "And I'm a marine. Although technically neither of us are. It's complicated. But you're alive!"

Dan gripped his arm and flashed a smile but his fingers tightened on Evan's forearm. "Do you know what they are doing down here? What they've done?"

Char stiffened and Evan shifted uncomfortably.

"Yes, I do. I guess I'm one of them. But we're here, all of us, to see if we can help you. Amatheia said you were working on bringing down the Dome?"

The other man, more pale than usual, his eyes a little wide, nodded. "I've been scanning the seabed for months. Tracking the variations, the changes. I knew there was something going on down here." He moved back to the monitors. "I've been communicating with the CIA. The mer told me and showed me what was going on. I've been collating the data. They got me these old computers, I think they're from a sub, but I've managed to get it all here. I don't have the bandwidth yet to send it. But I can copy it, give it to you to send."

Ana walked over to the computer. "You say it's all in here? All the data?"

"Yes, they salvaged the computer from my boat—that had most of it—but when it died, I transferred it to here."

"But it must be somewhere else?"

Laughing, he pointed at his head. "Well, it's all in here. Eidetic memory. I don't forget anything."

"That's such a shame," Ana said.

Something in her tone rang a warning bell in Evan's mind. He stood frozen as she raised her gun and shot the computer. Bullets ripped through the hard drive, destroying the data.

Evan jumped. "What the hell?"

The woman before him changed almost imperceptibly, her face drawn in harsher lines. She cocked her head, and her hand slid to the pendant around her neck. The motion tugged at a memory of a woman shrouded in darkness, threatening his family. He staggered back.

No. This couldn't be Ana. "Who are you?"

Dan's voice cut through the painful maelstrom in his mind. "She's the Siren. The one behind all of it."

How he'd not managed to identify her as Ana was beyond him. *Perhaps I didn't want to.*

The ground rocked beneath his shaking legs and he fought to breathe as knife-sharp emotions tore a jagged path through his heart.

"No. She can't be." He stared at her. "You can't be."

Sariana met his gaze, her eyes shining luminous in the dim chamber. She raised her arm and fired. He spun but wasn't fast enough. Time slowed to a crawl.

A dull *thwack* sounded, and Dan fell, a bullet through his forehead, blood seeping out of the hole, staining the dirt floor.

His body wouldn't move. He wanted to pick Dan up, pretend he would be okay. He wanted to strangle Ana. He wanted to hold her. Evan stood, shaking as his world fell apart. Char stumbled to Dan's side, her face slipping into combat mode, eyes wide but fierce.

Ice burned its way through his veins. "But why?"

"Can't you figure it out?" Did her voice tremble when she answered? Or was it hopeful thinking?

"Tell me." The hollowness in his chest filled with a

screaming he refused to let out.

"For a higher cause. I never pretended to be fighting for anything else, but the cause is more than you think. Once I killed the commanding officer, it was ridiculously easy to bring the others under my sway. With the combined power of human and mer, we can take back the mainland, force the humans to respect us, protect and safeguard the waters. Why should they have so much when we have so little, a little that they poison continually?"

"But you used your own people. You used children!"

Her lip trembled. "That was a last resort. I did it to save more lives. You of all people should understand."

He flung up a hand, blocking her out. "No. No I can never understand that."

"But you've said it before. Sacrifice, for the greater good."

He recoiled. "Jesus, Ana, I meant we sacrifice ourselves! Not others!"

Dan's blood pooled at his feet. Evan's fingers strayed to his gun and she tracked the movement.

"Did you ever trust me?" Pain laced her voice.

"No." The words tore out of him. "But I loved you."

Her face crumpled and she stared down at the gun in her hand.

Tears threatened. "Was any of it ever real?"

She stepped back, knuckling her chest as if it pained her. "More real than I ever wanted it to be."

Char rose from where she'd knelt by Dan's body. She stood shoulder to shoulder with him and faced the Siren.

"Pretty words Ana, if that's even your name, but falling in love with Evan doesn't excuse what you've done."

He searched for the truth in her face. Had she loved him at all? Char raised her gun.

The Siren shook her hair back over her shoulder, her own gun rising to aim at Char. "I wish you hadn't come, Char. I never wanted you to get hurt."

Adrenaline buzzed through his chest. "Both of you need to lower your weapons. This is ridiculous."

"She killed your friend."

Blood reached his boots.

"I am sorry he was your friend. He would have ruined everything I have fought for." Ana stared down the barrel at Char. "Would you really fire it?"

"Would you?"

"Yes."

The bullet sped from the gun.

Evan yanked Char from its path. Stone chips flew behind them as the bullet hit the cave wall. Char pulled the trigger, but the gun didn't fire.

He fired his own into the ground. Nothing happened. She'd given them duds.

"I'm so very sorry. Some things are too important." Ana raised the gun again. "I'm so sorry, Char."

Evan leaped in front of Char a moment before Ana fired. She jerked. The bullet missed him.

But Char collapsed with a cry.

He whirled. She lay on the ground, blood pouring from her leg, her hands trying to staunch the flow. He tore off his shirt and pressed the fabric down onto the life spilling from her. She blinked twice. He swallowed, and inclined his head a fraction, then turned back to

271

face Ana, keeping his body in front of Char. Shadows danced in Ana's eyes.

"This is a line you don't want to cross, Ana."

A sad smile tugged at her face. "I'm already so far over the line I can't remember where it is. You think hurting my friend will hurt me? I've watched them cut open mer I've known since I was a youngling. Humans destroy more than they pretend to save."

Another hot aching wave spread through his chest. "I am human."

Her eyes lit up with a disturbing intensity. "But different! This time it can be different. It worked on you, Evan. You are more than human now."

He raised his arm, sensing the spiked fins ready to slide up. Pale light pulsed through his skin.

"This is another uniform, another person trying to bend me to their will, to fight their fight for them." He closed the distance between them, conscious always of the pistol in her hand. "But I don't fight for what I don't believe in. And I will always be human."

The gun shook in her grasp. "You could stay here with me, help me build a new world."

"No, I can't."

"Killing you would destroy me, but I can't let you stop this."

"And I can't let you do it."

She cut a glance over his shoulder, to Char. "She needs medical attention or she will die. You are a man of your word. Swear you will join me, that you won't leave me. Choose me and I will let her live."

He cupped her cheek. Satin-soft skin slid under his fingers as she leaned in and he stroked down her throat.

Then ripped off her amulet.

Chapter Forty-One

The chain bit into Ana's neck. Shock froze her. He stood there, wide-eyed, fingers clutching the jewel she had not needed for some time. *He doesn't know that.*

As he wrenched her pistol from her hand and shakily raised it, the shards of her heart tore further into her chest.

He tried to kill me.

Darkness clouded her vision. His voice came through a muffled fog of pain.

"Looks like I'm not the only one who changed."

Her hands twisted by her side, and the chill of the deeps slid through her. "I was one of the first, after my brother failed. The only success so far, apart from the children. Apart from you."

The mention of the children flicked a shutter down over his expression.

"I'm taking Char back to the base, out of here."

She swallowed, trying to get moisture into a bone-dry mouth. "Where do you think you can run to?"

"Away. Doesn't matter where. Someplace where I can tell Dan's wife he's never coming home."

The stark stone in his voice cut into her soul.

"I didn't want to kill him."

"But you did. He's dead because of you."

Only the width of an anchor lay between them but he was an ocean away. His bare chest heaved. She stepped back so she wouldn't throw herself on him, beg for forgiveness, for his arms to wrap around her, shut out the world.

He'd chosen. And he didn't choose her.

Now he never would.

She raised her hands, palm out. "Go, then. You won't get far."

"You forget, I have a key. You don't."

The shells winked at her reproachfully in the weak light. "You would leave me here to rot?"

His lip curled. "Your sister once did as much to me. Did she know about this? Are you all in on this plan?"

Theia. Shreds of her heart fluttered around her like the ribbons of her fins. "No, she doesn't."

Char shifted, knelt on her good leg, and pulled herself up as Evan backed toward her. A sodden tourniquet stemmed the blood flow, the once white t-shirt now bright red. Ana watched his pistol hand and remained against the wall.

His hand slid under Char's elbow, helping her stand, before his arm went around her back. There was no room for jealousy. He'd chosen the human, chosen a different path. She'd thought he would be the one to understand, to make things different.

I was wrong.

The door slid shut behind them and she frowned. He clearly thought she wouldn't follow. Daniel Kim's body lay shattered on the floor. Char had tried to straighten his limbs, close his eyelids. But blood congealed around his torn skull and turned the floor into a sticky puddle. She knelt next to him, paused, and slid her hand into his pocket. Nothing in his trouser pockets. She really hoped it wasn't underneath him, being this close to the blood turned her stomach. Much harder to avoid the reality of what she'd done.

For the mission. For a higher purpose.

Evan was so close to him. Her chest constricted. *Don't think of it.*

She patted the pocket of his shirt and her fingers closed over an oval shape. Feeling his cooled skin through the thin fabric, she drew out a stone key and a bent piece of paper.

She unfolded it and froze. The man in the picture looked younger than Daniel Kim had appeared. *Before I blasted a hole in his head.* Her fingers tightened on the paper. He wore a red shirt and Christmas antlers and had his arms around a beaming woman. His wife. It must be. Not sure why she did it, she tucked the photo in the waterproof case she carried, next to a shell from Shodica's boy's amulet.

The stone clutched tight in her fist, Ana stood, and after a final glance at the devastation in the small room, opened the door and left.

She didn't run. She knew where they were going. Once back at the Dome, she had a whole force under her command. Shells from the stone glistened in the dark, fitting into the lock on the side of the door. The metal doors slid open, and she breathed in the salty tang of the ocean.

Sand floated up as she scuffed her foot over the bloody drops on the stone. She hoped they made it back in time for Char to get proper help.

The sweats slid against her skin. She shed them. Cast away the painful thoughts and moments to the side.

With a blink she changed into her mer form, the last flick of scales forming over her legs as she dove into the water.

Chapter Forty-Two

The sub bug moved through the water, churning a white wake of bubbles behind it. Evan curbed his impatience. Desperately needing it to go faster didn't make it any speedier. He glanced at Char in the seat beside him. Her head leaned back on the chair, tight lines ringing her closed eyes. He'd done his best with the first aid kit under the dashboard, but she needed better bandages and a crutch and stronger pain meds.

Brown eyes flicked open, as if she could feel his concern. "Don't worry. I've had worse. I'll make it."

He slowed the vehicle as they neared the Dome. Biting his lip, he glanced at Char. Blood was everywhere.

"What's the plan?"

"Well, you aren't exactly inconspicuous and we're one crew member short." He thrust away the crushing weight of betrayal. "I figure we won't be able to brazen it out quite as well as before. Do you think you can swim a bit longer?"

"Break in one of Ana's secret spy ways you mean?"

A hot ache spread in his chest. "Yeah. Think you can make it?"

Her jaw tightened and she gave him the thumbs up. "Sure."

The sub bug hovered and he set it to autopilot. He

helped Char into a harness and checked the tank. With it on, he couldn't support her under her arms so he slipped his hand under her elbow, and she rested her weight on him. In the water with it supporting her weight would almost be better.

Cold water bubbled over them as they opened the outside door of the sub. He held Char under one arm and cut through the water with all the power he could. No one was on the alert. Made sense. Ana was either back at the cavern or swimming back. They'd be faster than her.

Steel and glass rose in front of them. He wound his way to the dark and kelp-covered place Ana had taken him through. Thoughts of her ambushed him so he swam harder, swiping away the kelp with vicious cuts of his hand.

The hatch was sealed tight. He pulled Char's sagging form closer to his side, the fingers on his other hand gripping tight to the metal ridges around the seal, holding them up. No obvious lever or switch or anything remotely helpful. Char's weight dragged at his arm. She was fading and needed care. Ana would get out, and she knew where they were going. A shaky finger waved in front of his face and pointed up.

Above the hatch was a small shield, the faded strip of yellow warning tape mostly pulled off. He kicked his feet and reached higher, wincing as Char bounced on the metal. The shield flipped up, and there was the lever he'd been searching for. It wasn't what Ana had used, but a satisfying whirr rumbled through the metal after he pulled it.

Impatience seethed through him as he waited for the antechamber to fill with water. He raised his brows at Char and she nodded, letting go of him and reaching for the lip of the opening hatch. A small boost and she was through. He scrambled after, turning as soon as he was in and pressed the button to shut the hatch.

Char was already on the surface, pulling herself onto the ledge and into the metallic air of the small space. Muscles straining, he swung his legs over onto the chain like walkway. Water streamed from his clothes. Char shivered and her leg spasmed.

"Come on, let's get you out of here."

He clasped her raised forearm. Her skin was clammy and cold under his wrinkled fingertips. Pain shot over her face as she stood. Maybe he should carry her? She flicked him a glance as if she'd heard his thoughts and straightened.

Crisp, diesel-tainted air greeted him as he opened the door into an empty corridor. He helped Char over the step and slid the door closed again. Drips of salty water pooled at their feet. His mind spun possibilities. There was a small room down the corridor, a change room for the engineers. Could be clothes he could grab. Too public for them to hide though.

Char leaned on his shoulder. He bent in front of her and pulled her onto his back. She murmured a protest against his neck but her body relaxed on his, tension leaching out of her. Quick strides took him toward a door halfway down the corridor, a small label declaring it was a supply closet. The handle turned, and he sent up a quick prayer of thanks.

Narrow shelves leaned in on them in a tunnel like entry but opened into a small square lined with metal shelves and racks. He knelt, letting Char's feet touch gently before swivelling to help her lie down. As soon as she was safe on the floor, he shot to his feet and scanned the shelves. Somewhere in here there must be something to keep her warm. Ratty sticker labels with scrawled handwriting were no help at all. Finally he found a small stack of plastic-wrapped thin blankets labelled for emergency use only.

After ripping the plastic off and discarding it, he laid one blanket on the floor and helped Char shuffle on to it. He passed her the other blanket. "I'll be back as fast as I can. I'll lock the door. Take this."

He passed her the revolver, and she gripped it in a shaking hand. Shock was definitely setting in. He tucked the blanket closer around her. She breathed out, her cheeks puffing out and pain drawing tight lines on her face.

"Don't be too long. Take care out there."

"Don't worry, I will."

Chapter Forty-Three

Ana strode into the command center, hair in a tight bun, wearing the black suit of the Siren like another costume, another disguise.

"Ma'am, we received your signal and sounded the alarm. What are we searching for?"

"Fugitives are at large. They killed two civilians and attempted to murder a superior officer. Track them down and contain them." Her fingers went to the spot on her breast bone where the amulet used to lie, heart cold and heavy in her chest. "Do *not* shoot to kill. Is that understood? Containment only."

"Yes, ma'am."

The junior officer scurried off and she stalked to the viewing console. They couldn't be allowed to escape, to spread word. She would keep them here. Her fingers trembled, and she tightened her grip on the back of the leather chair. The man's forehead exploding circled on repeat in her mind. The twisting recognition of betrayal marking Char's face as she shot her.

Scalding pricks like jellyfish stings ran under her skin, sinking into her heart. She raised her chin. Were she human, she would curl up and weep, but she was a mer and the harsh life of the ocean formed her, ran in her veins. The right way was always the hard way. If Evan couldn't see that, then she couldn't let him stop her.

She jerked forward as one of the flashing monitors showed shoulders she recognized. "Stop. Go back to that camera."

The technician toggled backward, and Evan's back filled the screen. He turned and stared right up at the camera. She held her breath. His head cocked, and he drew a gun, aiming it at the screen. It went black.

"Camera down in sector 4, corridor 110-A."

The words washed over her, and she gestured to the side. An aide gave commands to seal off the corridor, send some of the special guard.

She had to cough to get her voice to work properly. "Where does corridor 110-A lead?"

"It's by engineering."

Her fingers tapped a frustrated rhythm on the chair back. They would have come in the way she'd shown him. He wouldn't stay, not once he realized the cameras tracked him.

"Keep searching. He will go off grid as much as possible." An idea struck her. "Can you recall that image, before he shoots out the camera?"

The tech toggled and punched keys and Evan appeared again, turning to the camera, his gaze boring into hers.

"Stop there." She peered at his hands, at the bundle of white he held. "Bandages. His accomplice is hurt. Search for blood trails and in rooms off that corridor. He won't want to move her unless he has to."

The technician turned away to pass on her instructions into a microphone, leaving up the image of Evan. Ice spread through her, and she resisted the urge to rub her arms. This was a cold nothing could help. She tried to summon a fiery rage to burn it away, thinking of how he'd tried to hurt her. But the pain in his eyes overshadowed everything and the chill turned to a darkness threatening to consume her.

"Why did you do this?" she murmured.

The tech's eyebrows rose in a question, and she pressed her lips together. She didn't even know if she spoke to Evan or herself. Dragging her gaze from the screen, she strode to a narrow door by the end of the consoles and swiped her card.

Her office was normally a quiet haven, but today she saw only the gloom of isolation. Ignoring the stack of files on her desk, she trailed her fingers over the dome, leaning her forehead against the glass. The ocean called to her, as it always did. For the first time since starting her mission, she wondered if she could ever go back. Evan would tell Theia, then they would either kill him or, if they believed him, they would never rest until she was destroyed. Either way she would lose. Ana pushed off the glass, staring at her reflection.

She could not lose. The mission was too important. No one understood, but they would.

A few casualties now for a greater win in the future was a sacrifice they had to make. She nodded at her reflection, then turned back to her desk.

What about Evan? Will I sacrifice him?

She stumbled to a halt, as if caught in a tangle of ropey weed. The loss of him was a bleeding hole in her chest. Never should have lost focus. Never should have fallen for a human. Evan was right. This had been a dream.

The heart wants what it wants.

A keening noise escaped her lips, and she clapped a hand over her mouth.

The intercom buzzed, and she stared at it for a moment. When it buzzed a second time, she pushed the button and straightened her jacket.

"Yes?"

"We think we've located the fugitives. You asked to be notified."

Her spine hardened. "I did. Send through the images of their location. Tell Roberts to get a strike team ready, and meet me outside my office in the corridor in five minutes."

"You don't want me to notify Blake?"

Her lip curled. "No, I don't. He has his own duties to see to." No need to give Blake another opportunity to target Evan.

Ana switched off the intercom and frowned at the desk. She had to go. Make sure no one got trigger-happy. Seeing Evan had nothing to do with it.

She strode to her closet, slid open the door, and surveyed the options. Her fingers closed on a hanger with a black combat outfit.

Chapter Forty-Four

Char winced and inhaled sharply.

"Sorry." Evan focussed on the task at hand. His shredded heart bled out as the last few hours played again and again in his mind.

"What will we do?"

"We can't wait for plan A. You saw what she did to Dan. What she tried to do to you. We have to get out of here now."

"How could she do this to her own people?"

He pinned the bandage and stayed on one knee, staring anywhere but at her face. "I don't know. It's like she's two different Anas."

He didn't only see Dan's head jerking back as the bullet sprayed blood; he saw Ana's expression as he ripped off the amulet. It sat heavy in his pocket. He'd tried to kill her to protect Char.

The line she'd drawn in the sand was a jagged line ripping him in two.

Char's hand closed around his wrist. "Hey. Evan. You did the right thing. That's why it hurts so much. And you saved me. Even if you suck at bandaging."

His lip lifted less at the joke and more at her attempt to cheer him up. "I know I'm not supposed to feel bad now that she's the bad guy, but I do."

She pulled on his wrist to get herself into a sitting position. "It's a heck of a thing. Ana was my friend too."

"You never trusted her."

"Did you?"

Sirens sounded somewhere in the distance. He'd figured it would only be a matter of time. He hauled her up gently.

"Are you able to do this?"

"You know me, ready and able. But I still don't know what the plan is." Pain laced her voice but she grinned.

He regarded the steel girders, the strengthened glass, the iron floors. "It all has to go."

"What do you mean?"

"All of it. We blow it up."

"You did *not* just say that."

"Think about it, Char. We get out of here, fine. What happens to the mers? To the rest of the crew?"

"In this plan, it sounds like you're blowing *them* up."

He huffed, tension running through muscles like fire. "Of course not. We evacuate first."

She stared at him, the insanity of his plan reflected in her face. "We'll never get everyone out."

"We can. It will take time, but think about it. The big sub can take a couple hundred? Then there are all the smaller ones. It will be tight, but I think we can do it."

"You're talking about blowing up a massive structure. There's no room for *I think* in this plan."

"We target the labs first, the engine structure. It can be done."

She worried at her lip, and he waited, his need to be doing something roiling in his blood. "We'll need a vehicle for us, I can pilot maybe but…"

"Khalid can pilot."

"They might need him on the evac sub."

"I know you can do it. I need you to run the evac, get everyone clear. Threaten them if you have to. Get them to move. Get Khalid and Esther to help. I'll take care of the explosives."

"Which you'll get from where?"

"Armory."

Her hands were on her hips and her eyes flashed but fatigue cut deep lines down her face. "Under Cody Blake's jurisdiction. By yourself. Nope. Not happening."

"Trust me, I can deal with Blake."

"This isn't the time for pointless heroics."

"It's exactly the time for it. You're wounded and a liability to me in a fight anyway. Right?"

She scowled but didn't disagree.

"We're running out of time. Here." He passed her a radio and held up the matching pair. "Channel three."

She held out her hand and he clasped it. "I'll wait for your signal then."

"And Char, you promise me you don't stay too long to wait for it. If you need to get clear, then you get clear."

"You marines aren't the only ones who won't leave anyone behind."

He gripped her hand tighter. "Not this time. You promise me."

"I'll wait 'til the very last second."

He pulled her into a hug. His pulse raced in a counterpoint to the blaring sirens. "Be careful."

She drew back, moving stiffly on her injured leg. "You too, Evan."

Chapter Forty-Five

Alarms blared, and booted feet boomed down the hall. Evan wrenched open the handle of the nearest door, then spun and locked it. He leaned against the metal and listened.

"Evan? What's going on? Is everything okay?"

He spun, his hand on the grip of his Glock. Mac stumbled back, eyes wide, hands flying up.

Evan raised his finger to his lips and slid his hand away from the gun, palm toward Mac. The engineer nodded slowly and ran his hands through his mussy hair.

His mind raced. Char should be fine. If they were down this end, they'd be searching for him. He scanned the room, but there were no obvious exits from the small office.

Mac sat down on the edge of his chair. "I take it the sirens are for you?"

He raised his brows in acknowledgement and turned back to the door.

"Should I be worried?"

He cast a tight smile over his shoulder. "Not yet. And not because of me. Well, not totally. But you should get ready to evacuate."

"Is it the mer?"

He leaned his back on the door and regarded Mac. "What would you think if it was?"

The engineer's chin went up. "I'd say good on them."

"I would too. But it isn't them. Things are changing here. Listen for the signal and get out."

Mac pushed his chair back and strode toward him, eyes burning fiercely. "Let me help."

"No. I don't need that on my conscience."

"It isn't on your conscience if I'm the one who makes the choice. I'm not a soldier, but I know what I'm doing."

"Okay. Two things you can help me with, then you get the hell out. Find Char and get gone. Deal?"

"Deal."

"First thing. How many explosives to bring this place down? Where should I place them?"

Red suffused Mac's face. "You're kidding!"

"No, I'm not. I figured I'd place them inside but is that best?"

The engineer fidgeted with his belt, a frown of concentration on his face. "You want to place them on the outside. Where the supports meet the base. Probably about fifteen would do it. On a timer?"

"Remote detonation. I don't want to run the risk of people still needing to evacuate. Once we get the all clear, I press detonate."

"Okay. And the s-second thing?"

"Can you draw them away so I can get to the armory?" He jerked his head to the hallway. "Maybe tell them you saw some suspicious people heading to Sector D."

Mac jerked his head in a nod, and Evan gripped the engineer's shoulder.

"Thank you. You don't need to help and it means a

lot that you are. Don't do anything to put yourself in danger."

A grin flashed on Mac's face. "I won't. You be careful, Evan."

Mac slipped out of the door. Evan closed it carefully behind him as light footsteps raced down the hall toward the search party. Voices filtered through the wall. Then the sound of many running people clattered past.

He counted to one hundred and cracked open the door. No one moved. He slunk out and kept to the wall as he raced toward the armory.

The door to the armory was locked by a key pad and monitored by cameras. Evan drew his Glock and thumbed the safety. With more time, he'd have set up some kind of loop to play on the cameras, but rough and ready would have to suffice now. He grinned. *Might even get two birds with one stone.*

He stood out of the line of sight of the cameras and aimed. Two quick shots and the corridor filled with sparks and shards of glass. He ran to the door. As it cracked open, he shoved it further, smacking Blake in the face and knocking the gun from his hand. Evan kicked the other man's pistol away and aimed his at Blake's head.

"You wouldn't shoot me; not like this, you're too much of a Boy Scout."

"You really want to test that?"

Blake rolled and grabbed under a bench, drawing out a pistol. Evan fired but the shot missed Blake, and he dodged to avoid the bullet coming his way.

"Hey, Blake! Shooting up a room full of explosives isn't the smartest thing we can do. How about we settle this man to man?"

"Nice try." A bullet grazed the shelf he sheltered behind.

"Scared, Blake?"

The other man laughed. "Getting desperate there, Hunter. Why would I be scared of *you*?"

"Prove it." All he wanted was to not blow up this room before they'd got everything sorted.

"And how do I know you'll put your gun away, and face me hand to hand?"

He tossed it on the floor. "There."

"You really are a Boy Scout."

"At least I don't act like the loser bad guy."

Blake swore then placed his gun on a bench and squared up to Evan. He didn't wait, there wasn't time for this bullshit. He aimed a punch right at Blake's temple. The other man blocked it, but Evan's fist went straight through, glancing off Blake's head as he dodged. Evan swallowed surprise; they'd been evenly matched when they first sparred. *But I wasn't full of mer juice then.*

His focus narrowed, thinking of each move, each hit, rolling with the impact. Every snide comment, every nasty thing Blake had done, became a symbol of everything he most hated. It was people like this who treated the mer like nothing. Ana's face flashed into his mind, superimposed over his loathing for the Siren.

He smacked his fist into Blake's jaw, holding back nothing, letting the rage take over his muscles. The other man stumbled back, shaking his head. He kicked at his kneecap, dropping him to the floor. Remembered to pull back the full force. He didn't want to cripple him.

He wiped blood from the corner of his mouth, his tongue pushing at a loose tooth. Blake groaned. He picked up his gun, hefting it in his hand. If he knocked Blake out, he'd have more time to gather the explosives. But if he was knocked out, he wouldn't be able to evacuate. He slid his gun into the holster. The guy was a jerk but didn't deserve to die.

He stripped off his t-shirt, wincing as his bruised ribs stretched. Grabbing a carabiner, he fastened the shirt around him. Mines followed, stuffed into the holsters. At least he wouldn't need an oxygen tank. A detonator and switch was the last thing, and he zipped it into one of the pockets on his trousers. He strode past Blake who slowly pushed himself to his feet, clutching his head.

"You're insane, Hunter."

"For the first time since I got here, I feel completely sane. Better get going, Blake."

He raced down the hall toward one of the hatches he'd taken note of ever since the first time Ana had taken him out of one.

The harness of the carabiner cut into the bare skin on his shoulders. He punched Ana's code into the lockpad by the hatch. Metal clanged down the corridor. He wrenched the hatch open and struggled inside without knocking the mines. He pulled the hatch closed, shutting out the light.

Chills ran over his bare skin. Here in the dark it all became more real. The explosives pulled at his shoulders, and his eyes adjusted, the gloom fading in a shimmer of light until every rivet stood out.

Evan slammed a hand on the button to open the water lock. Doors groaned below and water began to flood in. He kicked off his boots, placed them high up. He drew the strings of his trousers around his ankles, not that it would do much. Flinched as a burst of air rushed around the gills opening on his neck. Dark water swirled around his feet.

He stepped through the opening, out into the inky depths.

Chapter Forty-Six

The currents dragged at his cargos, pulling at the charges strapped around his bare chest. They weighed no more than air tanks but the heavy fabric pulled at his waist and slowed his movements.

Still better than swimming in boxers. He could handle a bare torso but bare legs were way too vulnerable. He pulled himself up on the strut of the Dome and reached into a pocket for a cable tie. Evan unhooked a charge from the carabiner and placed it on the underside of the dome. The charge suctioned itself to the metal. A few key strokes and it was set. He shoved the remote back in his pocket, zipping it tight.

Three more and done.

Doubt ate at his mind. There was no other option he could see. Dan's data was gone. There were files he could download from the Dome, but no guarantee anyone on the outside would listen. He didn't have Dan's contacts. This was the only way he could see to get rid of the evil.

The charges sat heavy on his chest. He swam toward the next post. A churning wake pulled at him, and the kelp fronds below flattened. He spun around, his arms stroking through the water. A horde of merfolk filled the ocean, armed with blazing tridents and curling stone knives. Ice seeped into his veins, and adrenaline anchored him in place.

A buzzing in his head turned to a rising tide of angry voices. An assault force. They were attacking the Dome.

The remote for the bombs weighed heavily in his pocket. Maybe he wouldn't have to blow it up.

The faces of the mer were silver pulses of light, blinding in their fury. In his head, the raging green depths turned into an abattoir of blood. They would all die.

Unless he could turn them back.

He swam toward them. A great cry went up, and he threw back his head as the voices battered at his mind. Four large warriors encircled him, tridents threatening jolts of energy and powerful tails thrashing the water, keeping him off balance.

Evan held up his arms, palms outward, calling in his head for Myrndir, for Amatheia. A tail smacked into his ribs, compressing his lung. He fought against the winding sensation, felt openings on his neck rise, move in the water. He keeled over and displayed his neck, like he'd seen dogs do.

The immediate cessation of movement shook him. He began to sink and slowly moved his legs to tread water. Dark ribbon fins spread from the mermen, their heavily muscled torsos ornamented in coloured ink and shells.

"You hear us?"

"Yes."

The merman glanced at his brothers. *"He is the one they spoke of, the human Sariana brought to the enclave."* He shot forward with a boost of his tail. His hand wrapped around Evan's neck. *"Tell us, human-who-is-mer, what have they done with Sariana. Is she with the children?"*

His thoughts split open again with the pain of hearing her name, but the last word brought him up short. *"What children?"*

The hand tightened and he fought to stay still, to not thrash or rip at the iron hands cutting off his air and his pulse.

"The children your people stole from us."

"I have only seen one child."

"They came in the night, snatched our children from their beds, stole them away."

A deep dread filled him. Only one person knew where the enclave was.

"You have betrayed us, human-who-is-mer."

He fought then, to get his face close to the merman, to show the truth of his words. *"I didn't betray you. It's the one you sent. She betrayed us all."*

The fingers grew slack around his throat. He pulled back, rubbing at his neck, tears mingling with the salt water, blurring his vision.

"Sariana. She would not—"

"She did. She has."

"But she brought us the child, eight tides ago. Why would she do that, then steal more?"

Defeat was a leaden weight dragging him down. *"I don't know."*

A high-pitched buzz speared through his mind as the mermen glared at each other. He treaded water, trying to pick out words from the hum. Tails whipped the water around him into a churning mess and energy leached from his muscles.

"Lying—"

"But what if—"

"—the children—"

"This ends now!"

As one they swam on toward the Dome. He grabbed at the closest one's arm, unable to stop the merman and dragging along with him.

"You can't do this. You'll die."

The mer's face was carved out of stone. *"You underestimate us."*

The detonator sat so close to his hand. *"I can stop this, blow the whole thing up."*

Rage twisted the mer's expression. *"You would murder our children?"*

He recoiled. *"Of course not! I would make sure they're safe first."*

The merman clasped his shoulder, staring into his eyes. *"I believe you would."* He gestured behind him at the others, swimming in formation to the Dome. *"But they will not believe or care. Sometimes folk have to do things themselves."*

He grabbed at the mer but his fingers closed on water.

In a chaotic whirl of waves and bright light, the mer attacked the gate. Blasts from their tridents spattered across it. Their great tails smashed at the metal.

Bubbles swirled and obscured the mer, they blurred, as they had done in the first fight. He blinked and peered again. Faces fierce with rage came into focus. Myrndir was nowhere to be seen but he must be here.

The doors buckled and gave way beneath the combined efforts of the smashing tails and the energy blasts. A wave pushed him back. *Any time. They could have done this at any time.*

Ana's double agent role made more sense now. She'd kept them off the Dome by convincing them she undermined it from within. She would have persuaded them more mer would die in the attack, but now that their children were gone they didn't care.

Grief stabbed at his chest. She was the only one in the Dome who knew where the enclave was. The only one who could have given the kidnappers directions. How could she have betrayed her people?

Divers wielding ADS rifles swam out from the shattered door, firing rounds into the mer. Fins ripped, leaving shredded ribbons dangling uselessly. Blood trails oozed bright in the dark water. A burst of energy from a trident caught the top of a diver's oxygen tank, disconnecting it. Bubbles streamed to the surface.

Evan treaded water, frozen with indecision. He didn't know who to help, which side to take. Tingles sparked down his arm. Pulsing white energy rippled down his skin, pushing water forward in a wave of cascading power. *Crap.* He shook his arm, trying to stop it. But the currents swirled around him in a maelstrom.

He flexed his fingers, the water flowing with his movements. Curling his hands to fists, he stared under his brows at the melee. None of them would listen to reason, maybe they would listen to this.

Ribbons of blood floated around him as he swam into the chaos. Dark-finned shapes circled at the edges. The carnage must be tantalizing. He blinked, his eyes adjusting to a blinding light from his torso. Water buffeted him on either side. His arms cut through the roiling waves and he pushed himself in front of a diver from the Dome. The woman's eyes widened through scratched goggles.

He recognised her from the first fight against the mer. Ashley. The knife in her hand twisted around to face him, jagged edges glinting against reflected luminescence. Sharp fins lifted from the back of his forearms and he spread his arms wide, letting the glow surround them. A pool of silence rippled out from where he floated. He mouthed at the woman, "I am not the enemy." Wide hazel eyes darted a glance from him to the mer behind him. The knife wavered. He turned his back on her, facing the mer.

"This won't end well."

"You cannot stop this now."

"I can try."

He focused on the sensation of water surrounding his body, the energy streaming through him. White light beamed from him and he brought his hands together, shaping it, rolling it. A buzz tingled through his palms up into his shoulders. The mer backed up, tridents lowering to point at him.

"So, human-who-is-mer, you have chosen a side."

"I choose the side of stopping all the bullshit and killing the fewest people." A small kick of his legs brought him to a position where one shoulder faced each side. *"This needs to end now."*

He thrust an arm out to each group and jerked as waves of energy raced from his chest through his fingers. Mer and humans tumbled through the water.

The humans retreated, diving back toward the gate. A second, safety gate, slowly sliding closed behind the wrecked door, divers pulling at the debris blocking the new door from closing.

Gills sucked at the water as he tried to catch his breath. He flexed shaking fingers. He'd not even known if it would work.

When the gate shut on the last human, Evan confronted the mer. They floated, a line of warriors, every one with a trident glowing and pointed at him.

The merman's head cocked and his hand shot up in a gesture mimicking quiet, as if he were listening to something. A buzz sounded in Evan's head and he tried to connect the words.

"We will leave. Our task is done."

In a mess of tails and fins and rippling shells the mer behind the leader swam away.

His head reeled. Too easy. Where was Myrndir?

"This was a diversion?"

The leader swam closer to him. *"Yes. We will get our children back and destroy the traitor."*

His pulse raced.

Ana!

Chapter Forty-Seven

The trident rested sharp points against Evan's skin. *"You have great power, human-who-is-mer. I would rid us of you now, but that Amatheia spoke highly of you."* The trident lifted and his tail swished as he backed away. *"Wield the power carefully. Do not be tempted onto the wrong path."*

The ocean emptied of all other forms. He lingered, holding his hands palm up, staring at them as if he could see the power still tracing over his skin.

The detonator dragged in his pocket, a reminder that he still had a job to do.

He swam around the edge of the Dome, following his instincts. A broken piece of metal floated slowly toward the sea bed. Rounding the last pylon, he saw the hatch ripped open, blast marks on the steel around it. He slid his pistol from the holster. The door was still open a crack in the small access room, water seeping around the edges. Sirens echoed through the water, muffled until his head breached the surface. His hand grabbed the once-dry ledge and found nothing.

A sodden white shirt floated in the water. He fished it out, contemplated pulling it on but tossed it back on the ledge.

Once through the door he leaned on it, pushing it closed against the force of the water. There were blast marks on the locks. He raced toward the end of the corridor, passing strewn debris from the supply closet, glad that Char was out of there, wondering about Mac and the other engineers. Aware of the detonator in the other, he fished the radio out of his pocket. "Char, come in."

"Evan, where the hell are you! The mer are in the Dome!"

"I know. They came in the hatch. The front was a diversion."

"Shit!"

"Where are you?"

"Herding evac. I don't know what happened out there but most people are pretty happy to leave now."

"There are more children."

The radio went silent.

He glanced down, making sure the green light still flashed. "Char?"

"Jesus, Evan. Do you know where?"

His fist curled. "No." *But I'll find them. No matter what it takes.* He pushed away thoughts of Ana and the constant leaden betrayal weighing him down. "Listen, I need to get the detonators to you. How far away are you from engineering?"

"We're close to medical. We evacced the staff. I got more pain stuff."

He wheeled about and sprinted down a side corridor, noting the blood spatters and blast marks. "I'm a couple minutes away. I'll meet you there."

He thumbed off the radio over her crackled affirmative. If she was in medical and there were staff to evacuate, then it sounded like the mer hadn't reached there. Maybe they didn't know the way, or maybe they were hunting Ana.

He raced through doors hanging off their hinges and skidded to a halt as Char spun, her weapon raised. She smiled and lowered the gun.

"You weren't kidding. I figured you'd take longer."

"Are the children in here?"

"No. We searched every room." Her face shuttered but her eyes flashed. "A lot of evil, but no children."

"Where did the mer go?"

"I don't know, but I think a lot of them were killed."

He stared at her, not sure what to think. She took a breath and the words tumbled out.

"I saw Ana."

His world turned into a whirl of images. Broken metal doors. Blood-spattered cavern walls. Pain-drenched eyes. He gritted his teeth and focused on the woman in front of him.

"Where?"

"She was with a unit. She left when the mers came. I don't know where she went. It got kinda busy after that."

"I tried to warn them, but maybe I could still have stopped it—"

"Hey, it's not your fault the mer came. It isn't your fault they died."

She was right in a way, but he knew it was one more tally on the guilt counter.

"If the children aren't here, I don't know where they would be. But the mer were definite they'd been stolen."

"That slimy doctor would know."

"Jones?" Hope curled in his gut. "Yeah, he would."

He shoved the detonators into Char's hand. "Take these. I'll find Jones and I'll make him tell me where the children are. I'll get them. But you have to stick to the timing. Stagger them. Once they're gone, they're gone. But promise me you'll get out before it all blows."

She flipped him a small salute and smiled through trembling lips. "I promise. You promise you get them out."

He gripped her shoulder. "No child gets missed on my watch."

He didn't want to leave. Khalid shouted from the other door and he pushed her toward the exit.

"Go. I'll get Doctor Jones."

"Happy hunting."

****

Closer to the command center, debris crowded the scorch-marked halls, broken pieces of wiring dangling from ripped metal. They had definitely come after Ana.

The sirens faded into the background. He scrambled over tumbled tables and through blasted doors, trying not to peer too closely at the bodies scattering the floor. No blonde ponytail spread over the tiles. His footsteps pounded as he sprinted toward the command center. The doctor was too high up in the Siren—in *Ana's* work not to be holed up safely with everyone in charge.

He concentrated on the feel of his muscles working, ignored the emotions emotions inside him. *Breathe in. Breathe out.*

A soldier lurched to her feet, gun aimed at him. He turned his run into a flying kick, knocked the weapon out of her hand, spun and hauled the woman up.

"Get out. It's over. You need to leave."

She cradled her arm, eyes flashing. Then spit at him from a bloody mouth and stumbled away.

Heavy doors sat ajar. He stepped over the commander's body—pale face in a torn rictus of fear—and into the dark, silent room beyond. Blast shields had been lowered over the Dome and not one monitor glowed with information.

Evan paused in the doorway, his pulse thundering in his ears. He slid his hand into a pouch on his belt, drew out a flashlight. Ten seconds passed. Thirty. At sixty he flicked the flashlight on. He scanned the outskirts of the room first: shot-out monitors, bodies slumped over keyboards, blood dripping to the floor. No movement caught his eyes.

The flashlight's beam narrowed with a flick of his thumb. He focused it on the bodies, starting with the ones in front of him. Mer and human lay strewn in the ungainly poses of the dead. His stomach twisted but he shone the light into each face, telling himself he only looked for the doctor. But when he found him halfway through the room, he had to quash an urge to check every face for blonde hair and smiling blue eyes.

Jones definitely appeared dead, but he held fingers to the man's throat in case.

Shit. No Jones, no computers. I'll have to search every room.

He patted down the man's pockets and fished out a pen, a notebook written in some kind of shorthand gibberish, and a key card.

Evan stared at the card. The medical staff all had one with a red and white stripe. He shone the flashlight onto the man's chest. A lanyard and medical key card.

This one had no stripe. He checked the necks of the nearest command center crew. A purple stripe.

He flicked the card in his fingers, freezing as he noticed shadowed ridges on the card. Angling it, he saw a string of letters and numbers. C41-ZH12.

This had to be it. If he could figure out what area the card was for, he'd find them.

Ana may have taken over operations but when the Dome was built, it was built by human contractors. Human operations required maps and evacuation procedures in every room. The flashlight's beam picked out a metal map riveted to the wall by the side of the door. Surely zones would be labelled.

Yet he didn't move. His fingers tightened on the flashlight. Finally he turned, scanning the rest of the bodies. Only one shock of blonde hair caught the light. He lunged toward it before realizing the body was too big to be Ana.

A wedding band glinted and Evan turned away, rejecting the reminders that these were real people with lives and loves. He couldn't deal with that now. Later the nightmares would come, and the guilt.

But right now he had children to save.

Chapter Forty-Eight

His feet pounded down the corridor and the broken radio hummed uselessly in his pocket.

One turning, two. He swung around the corner. Door after door lined the hall. Handles refused to budge. He eyed his revolver. Bullets used here meant fewer in case someone turned up.

As if I could actually shoot Ana anyway.

He flipped the gun, using the handle as a blunt instrument, and bashed at the lock. It wouldn't move. He slammed his shoulder into the hard metal. *Fuck!* Shielding his eyes, he raised the weapon and shot the lock. The door opened and he rushed inside.

Huddled in the far corner were three merchildren. They were in human form, but their hair still showed the twists and colours of the sea. One, a girl by the looks of it, stood in front of the two smaller children, her outstretched hands trembling, Transposed over her still figure was the girl in Kabul who shepherded the snaking line of children from the school. Same expression in their very different eyes.

He tucked the gun in his waistband, wishing for a holster. *"It's okay, I'm here to get you out."*

Her eyelid twitched and relief flooded him. She could hear.

"Your families have come, but there is danger. The building will blow up. How many more of you are

there?"

She cocked her head and her hands moved, like she stroked water.

One of the younglings behind her said, *"There are twelve of us."*

So many.

"Do you know the way out?"

Three faces stared at him.

"I'll take that as a no. Wait outside the door. I will be as quick as I can."

A far off boom filled the air, and the building shook. First charges gone then. Char had followed through. Alarms blared.

He rushed to the next room, aware as he blew off the next lock that the girl had come with him. He let her go in to get the four merchildren, then waited at the next door. Two in this room. Some stumbling on their human legs, the children ran down to huddle with the others.

The final room and one more bullet in his gun. Evan shot the lock and ditched the revolver. He swung the door open and three children rushed him, their hands and feet flailing, small fists having little impact but the ferocity in their faces breaking his heart.

He tried to push them back gently. He threw an appeal over his shoulder at the older merchild, but she only walked slowly toward them, her gaze on his. Eventually she hissed at the three younglings. Panting, they stopped, their gaze darting from her to him. She held the hand of the smallest and stared up at Evan.

"They need to know they can fight back."

"I get that, but we all need to leave. Now."

He shepherded them out in front of him. The group

reached the end of the corridor, small legs stumbling and wide eyes staring at the unfamiliar surroundings. They rounded the corner, then jerked to a halt.

Ana stood there, clothed in black, hair tumbled around her shoulders. She didn't look like Ana, and she didn't look like the Siren.

He pulled the children close, and they scrambled in behind him. All other thoughts fled his brain. She was here, where the children were. To help them or to take care of them in another way he no longer knew.

"How could you do this?" The words ripped through the swelling pain of betrayal in his throat. He wanted to think that the shadow crossing her face was shame.

"It was the best way forward for the mission."

His lungs seemed to fall in on themselves, so small he couldn't get enough air. "Listen to yourself, Ana! What happened to you, that you could ever think this was okay?"

Her hands stretched out to him, her face intent, pleading. "This way there would be less death. They do better in the procedures than the adults; they will be strong, unstoppable. I was trying to reduce collateral damage, like you wanted."

He recoiled, staring at her. She believed it. "If you ever considered what I wanted, you would have stopped it. All of it. It's wrong, Ana. So wrong."

Her hands dropped. "There's a greater good to come from this. You can't see it yet, but you will."

Speechless, he shook his head.

Her face closed down and she raised her chin. "You understand the decisions one has to make. You made yours when you ripped off my amulet, when you chose Char over me. When you left me to die. Don't pretend you have no death on your conscience."

Anger rose in a tide, and he stepped toward her before the little hand tugging at his shirt reminded him of where he was.

A squeal of static sounded from Ana's waistband. Char's voice crackled over the radio.

"Evan? Evan, if you can hear me, you need to get out of there!"

He yanked the radio from her hip and shoved her backward.

"Char, I have the children. I'm heading out now."

"You need to hurry, the timer's running out."

"I will."

Ana stretched out a hand. "Wait—"

"No, not for you. Not anymore. These children need to get to safety."

"I know a faster way."

He glared at her. "In what world do you think I would ever trust you again?"

"I never wanted them hurt and I wouldn't leave them to die."

Evan hesitated, but she knew this place like the back of her hand. He wanted to believe she would never hurt a child.

She returned the boy. She stole the others.

He moved toward her but stumbled as the building shook. The blast ripped through the floor, shattering windows, twisting metal. A jagged tear appeared in the floor, accompanied by screeches of steel torn asunder. Small flames flickered as electrical wiring shorted in the broken flooring.

He pushed himself off the wall where he'd landed

next to Ana. Out of instinct he reached for her before snatching his hand away and checking on the children.

A wail echoed from the opposite edge of the tear, where a small hand clung, white-knuckled, to the snarled teeth of torn concrete and steel. A boy clung to the side of the concrete as explosions rocked the dome, glass panels and steel shrieking as they fell around them.

He stared at the yawning chasm. Smoke filled the corridor. The boy slipped, grabbing tighter to the edge.

Without another thought, he stepped back to get a better run-up. The older girl tugged at his arm.

Ana raced past him and leaped over the gap. Her foot caught on the edge, and time stopped. She rolled forward then scrambled to the edge and hauled the boy up.

Evan strode to the edge. There was no way out. She nodded at him and he readied himself. She whispered in the boy's ear, then tossed him. Evan caught the boy, setting him down as a burst of flame and a shuddering tilt of the floor set them off balance. The Dome collapsed around her. He held out a hand.

"Jump!"

The radio squealed. "Evan! We're running out of time! If we don't take the sub away soon, we risk being caught in the destruction."

He ignored it, his hand stretching further. "Ana. Jump."

The girl pulled on his arm and he dragged his gaze away from Ana's pale face. The children huddled, the youngest doing a face shudder that he now recognized as crying.

"Go! Evan, take them and go!"

"Not without you!"

The tugging on his arm increased.

"Please," the girl whispered.

"Go, please. I'll be okay."

"I can't leave you." His heart tore in two.

She smiled shakily. "You have to."

He wheeled around, picked up the girl and raced back to the others. He wouldn't glance at her, wouldn't say goodbye. If he didn't say it, it wouldn't be true. They rounded the corner as the roof finally collapsed. Water seeped in and a part of him hoped that she found her way out into the depths of the ocean.

Small fingers traced the tears falling down his face. "What are these?"

He tried to smile through the pain. "Tears. They come when we're sad."

"Are you sad for Sariana?"

"Yes, I am."

The girl examined the wetness on her finger before tasting it. "I am sad too." She gazed at the small group of children in front of them then behind, where echoing groans of bending metal cut through the air. "She used to be kind."

His knees weakened and he nearly stumbled as the floor buckled. He pushed the children ahead.

She killed Dan. I should hate her but I can't.

They sprinted to the nearest airlock. He used Ana's key. The second door shuddered against the impact and he wrenched it open, letting in the sea. The children chirped and changed, diving in and disappearing in a swirl of tails and bubbles.

He shot one last glance at the Dome, then followed them.

Chapter Forty-Nine

Evan stepped away from the glass, sinking into a seat. Char peered at him but kept her mouth closed. He couldn't stop Ana's face filling his mind, or the memory of her smile smashing his heart. Her face in the water, her soft hair floating around like a halo.

Khalid's voice broke into the turmoil in his head. "Where are we headed? Other than far away from this hellhole."

He clenched his jaw, his hands squeezing into fists. Char touched his back. The warmth of her hand chased away some of the chill.

"Evan? We don't need an end game right now. But we do need a first port of call. The fuel in this isn't made for long distance."

They needed him to make a decision. He'd set himself up as leader. He couldn't complain. Evan breathed out, stood and stooped. The cockpit was an even tighter fit. He pointed at the monitors.

"Can you pull up the surrounding locations?"

The maps showed a worrying distance between their location and the nearest landfall. Char came up to his shoulder.

"There's a life raft."

He rubbed his jaw. "Paddles?"

"I don't know, don't think there would be."

Khalid spoke up. "We'd drift, maybe come back on

our tracks. It's gotta be a last resort."

"Agreed. Closest point on the map, what is it?"

Esther spoke over his shoulder, her voice heavy with loss, burn marks down her face. "Adamstown, part of the Pitcairn Islands."

"Think there'd be a boat we could commandeer?"

"You mean steal?"

He peered back at Char. "Yes. What else do you suggest? Hi, we're escaping an angry mermaid horde?" He patted the USB stick in his pocket. "I got a few files from the one undamaged computer I found but the mer attack damaged pretty much all of it. We have very little to back up our claims and I don't think the local authorities in Pitcairn will be happy to hear it."

"I know; I get it. I don't like being a thief."

He hugged her shoulders. "None of us do. But I'd like a military prison cell less."

"Once we get the boat, then what?"

He regarded the map. "South America, for starters. We need to lie low until we figure out whether we're on a Most Wanted poster or not."

The atmosphere was heavy. None of them had signed up to be traitors, just to serve their country, and regardless of active service, they still were. Part of him wanted to apologize, but then he remembered the faces of the children as they swam back to their home.

It was worth it.

****

The stolen boat puttered into a small dock on the edges of Sao Grande. Several times in the trip, he thought he'd caught sight of a large tail flashing through the water beside the boat, but had managed to convince himself it was a dolphin.

They unloaded, taking weapons, clothes, first aid kits, and the small amount of cash found in a battered tin box in the galley of the boat. Char pursed her lips and Evan grimaced. He tore the sailor's ID off the screen by the wheel, promising himself to somehow track down and repay the man.

Walking onto the shore and leaving behind the smell of the sea hit him in the gut in a way he hadn't expected. He breathed deep of the earth, diesel, and hot concrete, spicy food, and the fragrance of flowers. All one overwhelming assault on his senses. He tugged the baseball cap farther down over his brow.

The cheapest hotel was a dingy dive of a place, surrounded by dodgy bars and the kind of people you'd not want to meet out alone. The woman on the desk tapped her pen against her teeth and paused as she saw them, scanning them up and down.

"*Que paso?*"

Char shot him a glance and stepped forward, speaking to the woman in Spanish.

"I've got us a room for one night. She says we're not supposed to, but if we don't mind double bunking, she'll let us have the one room. It will cut costs. She also said there's a guest computer with an internet connection. It costs though. I don't think we have enough."

He glanced around the room, at the door falling off the hinges, and the out of order sign on the coffee machine. "Ask her if we can earn some time if we fix things up for her."

The woman beamed.

****

The only names on the news were Char and

Evan's. They'd been the ones targeted by the Siren on their return to the Dome and it was likely their names had been transmitted then.

He turned to Khalid and Esther. "Seems you guys are free to return to the States."

"Listen, Evan," Khalid said, "I'll check on your mom and your sister. Want me to send them down here?"

The Siren had already placed surveillance on Kelly, and he didn't know if those orders had been cancelled with the loss of the Dome.

"If she can make it down to the border, she might get through. Char, what about your mom?"

Char tugged at her lip. "I hadn't thought about what might happen to her. Do you really think they might take action?"

Ana filled his mind, the expression on her face as the Dome crumpled around her.

"I don't think Ana would. But I also don't think the Siren is in charge anymore."

"Hard to be in charge when you're at the bottom of the ocean." Esther punched Khalid on the arm. "What? Like I'm supposed to not be happy that she got her comeuppance? She's the bad guy. That's what happens to bad guys."

He closed his mind to eyes brimming with pain and sorrow. "Regardless, I don't know who's running things now and better safe than sorry. Char, if your mom can make it, she should probably come. Any other family?"

"No. Just me and Momma."

He tuned out the discussions for how Khalid and Esther would get back, how they'd wire money down.

His fingers went to the amulet in his pocket, thoughts centered on the tail that tracked them from Pitcairn to Sao Grande, on a mermaid he hoped with every fiber of his being had escaped.

Chapter Fifty

Three months later

The sun sank into the ocean and Evan lifted his beer in a silent salute. Sand shifted under his legs, still warm from the late afternoon sun. Char sighed at him when he lingered by the ocean, but every evening he came out and watched the waves.

When Ana walked out of the sea, long dress pulling against the waves, the lifting starlight shining on her silver hair, he let out a long-held breath. Alive and vibrant, she glided across the sand and his pulse accelerated.

He wanted to look away but couldn't help but soak her in. She stopped a little way from him, her assurance seeming to fall away from her. In his mind she'd become taller, harsher. But now she was his little Ana.

He swigged again, his eyes burning. *My Ana no more.*

"Hello, Evan."

Her voice snagged his heart and he closed his eyes. "How did you find me?"

"The ocean tells me many things."

Yeah, right. More likely she'd tracked them when they left.

"Why are you here?" His ears caught her little intake of breath, and he pushed down the urge to reach out to her.

"I wanted to see you."

The tremulous note in her voice opened his eyes. She stood barefooted, hand twisted in the folds of her light green dress. Her hair shifted in the breeze. More beautiful than ever.

"Why?"

She closed the gap between them and sat down next to him, her legs tucked up under her. "I needed to ask you to forgive me."

The words stuck in his throat but he pushed them out. "I can't forgive you, Sariana."

He refused to glance at her, but she reached out a finger, touching the chain hanging around his neck.

"If you really mean that, you wouldn't wear this."

He pulled away from her. "It's a reminder. Nothing more."

"Of something good or something bad?"

He slugged back a mouthful of beer, ignoring the ache spiking in his chest every time she spoke. "A reminder of something."

She heaved a sigh and leaned back on her hands, stretching her legs out, wiggling her toes in the sand. "I miss it, you know. Walking around, the training, the spicy food. I miss *you*, Evan."

He frowned at the bottle to avoid her face. "How did you survive?"

A soft sigh floated through the salty air. "Theia. The dome collapsed around me but in the midst of shattering steel and glass she found me and broke me free." She laughed, a short bitter sound. "Then she banished me."

"Can you blame her?"

"All I wanted was for us to be safe. For the humans to fear us. For us to never have to submit. Everything I did, I did for my people."

His eyes burned. She believed it. That almost made it worse. "You shouldn't have come here, Ana."

"You left behind a sea bed littered with steel and glass, pollution from broken tanks. My people would kill me if I stayed, but there was nothing for me to stay for."

He closed his eyes again. Maybe if he shut her out she would leave, let him heal. Maybe it would be another dream.

Her breath warmed his cheek and his fingers tightened on the bottle.

"Come with me, into the deeps. You don't have to be alone."

His eyes opened. Moonlight glowed in her face, her skin shining like the stars. From the shack behind him music wafted from the open window, carried on the air with the scent of chili and beans.

He touched her then, cupping her cheek in his hand. She smiled and his heart broke at the delight he saw there.

"I'm not alone, Ana. It's you who are alone. I wish you weren't. But I also wish you hadn't betrayed me. Wishes are for children. There's no happy ending for us."

Shadows covered the moonlight in her eyes. Her shoulders sagged. She drew her fingers through the sand, letting the grains flow down.

"I don't believe that. Someone once told me that we make our own destiny. I thought he was wrong, at the time. Now I agree with him."

He covered his face with his hand. "Too much has happened, Ana. I see you and I see Dan's death. Char still limps when she's tired."

"And you tried to kill me."

The amulet lay heavy against his chest. A reminder.

A whisper of air played around his head. The smell of the ocean still calmed him. She rose to her feet, lithe and graceful. Sand clung to her dress. He forced himself to not glance away.

"I will go. But this isn't goodbye. One day you may change your mind. If you want me, all you need to do is tell the ocean. I will come."

He bit his lip to stop the words from spilling out of his mouth. To say he hated her. To tell her to leave and never come back. That his heart might be torn but his mind wasn't.

To ask her to stay.

She smiled, the shadows hanging around her now, then walked back into the ocean. He watched, his fingers clutching the amulet so tight the ridged edges cut into his skin.

The surf caught at her dress. It began to glow and shift until swirling fabric turned to translucent fins, and with a leap, a dive, and a splash of her tail, she was gone.

****

He sat for some time under the empty sky, letting the sound of the waves settle in the hole in his chest. Guilt for missing her would come later. It always did. He rose and dusted the sand off his jeans. Each step away from the ocean and toward the shack tore another strip off his heart.

Warm light spilled out as he opened the door. Smiles and mirth filled the small space. Kelly and Char got on like a house on fire, and Mrs. Lewis raised a brow at him as he forced a smile back.

She passed him a plate loaded with chili and tacos. Kelly turned up the radio and hummed tunelessly to the local station. Every day she pretended they were on vacation, and every day he let her. Char glanced from him to outside, shrugged, and went back to her dinner.

Evan relaxed into the chair. He'd spoken only the truth to Ana. He wasn't alone. Here in this tiny shack in the middle of nowhere, he was more at home than he'd been in a long time.

Home is what you make it and this is mine.

The amulet hung heavy over his heart and his gaze went to the window. From outside the shack, a keening melody rose above the waves.

A song of farewell, and of promise.

A word about the author...

Clementine Fraser lives in the City of Sails in the land of the hobbits with two boisterous sons. In her day job, she teaches teenagers to love history. Fantasy fiction in all its magical variations captures her imagination and makes it sing. When she is not writing or working, you might find her curled up in an armchair with a good book or trying not to kill the flowers in her garden.

Her core story is about vulnerability, and loyalty, and facing who you are and where you are with strength and dignity. Whatever the setting, whatever the genre, this filters through into her stories.

~*~

http://clementinefraser.com

~*~

If you enjoyed this story, leaving a review at your favorite book retailer or reader website would be much appreciated. Thank you!